A Fine &
Private Place

A Fine & Private Place

PETER S. BEAGLE

A ROC BOOK

ROC
Published by the Penguin Group
Penguin Books USA Inc., 375 Hudson Street,
New York, New York 10014, U.S.A.
Penguin Books Ltd, 27 Wrights Lane,
London W8 5TZ, England
Penguin Books Australia Ltd, Ringwood,
Victoria, Australia
Penguin Books Canada Ltd, 10 Alcorn Avenue,
Toronto, Ontario, Canada M4V 3B2
Penguin Books (N.Z.) Ltd, 182-190 Wairau Road,
Auckland 10, New Zealand

Penguin Books Ltd, Registered Offices:
Harmondsworth, Middlesex, England

Published by Roc, an imprint of New American Library, a division of Penguin
Books USA Inc. Previously appeared in a Viking edition.

First Roc Printing, May, 1992
10 9 8 7 6 5 4 3 2 1

Library of Congress Cataloging-in-Publication Data

Beagle, Peter S.
    A fine and private place / Peter S. Beagle.
      p.   cm.
    ISBN 0-451-45096-5
    I. Title.
    PS3552.E13F56   1992
    813'.54—dc20   91-48054
                                                                  CIP

 REGISTERED TRADEMARK—MARCA REGISTRATA

Printed in the United States of America

Set in Bembo
Design by Leonard Telesca

This first one
for my parents, Simon and Rebecca,
and for my brother Daniel,
and, as it must be,
Edwin Peterson

The grave's a fine and private place,
But none, I think, do there embrace.
—ANDREW MARVELL
"To His Coy Mistress"

A Fine &
Private Place

1

The baloney weighed the raven down, and the shopkeeper almost caught him as he whisked out the delicatessen door. Frantically he beat his wings to gain altitude, looking like a small black electric fan. An updraft caught him and threw him into the sky. He circled twice, to get his bearings, and began to fly north.

Below, the shopkeeper stood with his hands on his hips, looking up at the diminishing cinder in the sky. Presently he shrugged and went back into his delicatessen. He was not without philosophy, this shopkeeper, and he knew that if a raven comes into your delicatessen and steals a whole baloney it is either an act of God or it isn't, and in either case there isn't very much you can do about it.

The raven flew lazily over New York, letting the early sun warm his feathers. A water truck waddled along Jerome Avenue, leaving the street dark and glittering behind it. A few taxicabs cruised around Fordham like well-fed sharks. Two couples came out of the subway and walked slowly, the girls leaning against the men. The raven flew on.

It had been a hot night, and the raven saw people waking

on the roofs of the city. The gray rats that come out just before dawn were all back in their cellars because the cats were out, stepping along the curbs. The morning pigeons had scattered to the rooftops and window ledges when the cats came, which the raven thought was a pity. He could have done with a few less pigeons.

The usual early fog was over Yorkchester, and the raven dropped under it. Yorkchester had been built largely by an insurance company, and it looked like one pink brick building reflected in a hundred mirrors. The houses of Yorkchester were all fourteen stories tall, and they all had stucco sailors playing accordions over the front entrances. The rear entrances all had sailors playing mandolins. The sailors were all left-handed, and they had stucco pom-poms on their hats. There was a shopping center, and there were three movie theaters, and there was a small square park.

There was also a cemetery, and it was over this that the raven swooped. It was a very large cemetery, about half the size of Central Park, and thick with trees. It was laid out carefully, with winding streets named Fairview Avenue, and Central Avenue, and Oakland Avenue, and Larch Street, and Chestnut Street, and Elm Street. One street led to the Italian section of the cemetery, another to the German section, a third to the Polish, and so on, for the Yorkchester Cemetery was nonsectarian but nervous.

The raven had come in the back way, and so he flew down Central Avenue, holding the baloney in his claws. The stretch of more or less simple headstones gradually began to give way to Old Rugged Crosses; the crosses in turn gave way to angels, the angels to weeping angels, and these finally to mausoleums. They reared like icy watchdogs over the family plots and said, "Look! Something of importance has left the world," to one another. They were aggressively Greek, with white marble pillars and domed roofs. They might not have looked Greek to a Greek, but they looked Greek to Yorkchester.

One mausoleum was set away from the others by a short

path. It was an old building, not as big as some of the others, nor as white. Its pillars were cracked and chipped at their bases, and the glass was gone from one of the barred grates over the front door. But the two heavy door-rings were held in the mouths of two lions, and if you looked through the window in front you could see the stained-glass angel on the back wall.

The front door itself was open, and on the steps there sat a small man in slippers. He waved at the raven as the bird swept down, and said, "Good morning, good morning," as he landed in front of him. The raven dropped the baloney, and the small man reached forward eagerly and picked it up. "A whole baloney!" he said. "Thank you very much."

The raven was puffing for breath a little and he looked at the small man rather bitterly. "Corn flakes weren't good enough," he said hoarsely. "Bernard Baruch eats corn flakes, but you have to have baloney."

"Did you have trouble bringing it?" asked the small man, whose name was Jonathan Rebeck.

"Damn near ruptured myself." The raven grunted.

"Birds don't get ruptured," said Mr. Rebeck a little uncertainly.

"Hell of an ornithologist *you'd* make."

Mr. Rebeck began to eat the baloney. "Delicious," he said presently. "Very tender. Won't you have some?"

"Don't mind," said the raven. He accepted a piece of baloney from Mr. Rebeck's fingers.

"Is it nice out?" Mr. Rebeck asked after a moment.

"Nice," the raven said. "Blue sky, shining sun. The world stinks with summer."

Mr. Rebeck smiled a little. "Don't you like summer?"

The raven lifted his wings slightly. "Why should I? It's all right."

"I like summer," Mr. Rebeck said. He took a bite of his baloney and said with his mouth full, "It's the only season you can taste when you breathe."

"Jesus," the raven said. "Not so early in the morning. Incidentally, you better get rid of all those old paper bags. I can see them from outside."

"I'll drop them in the wastebasket in the men's room," Mr. Rebeck said.

"No you won't. I'll fly them out. People start wondering, you know. They see paper bags in a cemetery, they don't think the Girl Scouts are having a picnic. Besides, you hang around there too much. They're going to start remembering you."

"I like it," Mr. Rebeck said. "I'm very fond of that lavatory. I wash my clothes there." He locked his hands around his knees. "You know, people say the world is run by materialists and machines. It isn't, though. New York isn't, anyway. A city that would put a men's room in a cemetery is a city of poets." He liked the phrase. "A city of poets," he said again.

"It's for the children," the raven said. "The mothers bring the kids to see the graves of their great-uncles. The mothers cry and put flowers on the grave. The kids gotta go. Sooner or later. So they put in a big can. What else could they do?"

Mr. Rebeck laughed. "You never change," he said to the raven.

"How can I? You've changed, though. Nineteen years ago you'd have been sloppily thankful for a pretzel. Now you want me to bring you steaks. Give me another hunk of baloney."

Mr. Rebeck gave him one. "I still think you could do it. A small steak doesn't weigh so much."

"It does," said the raven, "when there's a cop hanging on one end of it. I damn near didn't get off the ground today. Besides, all the butchers on this last frontier of civilization know me now. I'm going to have to start raiding Washington Heights pretty soon. Another twenty years, if we live that long, I'll have to ferry it across from Jersey."

"You don't have to bring me food, you know," Mr.

Rebeck said. He felt a little hurt, and oddly guilty. It was such a small raven, after all. "I can manage myself."

"Balls," said the raven. "You'd panic as soon as you got outside the gate. And the city's changed a lot in nineteen years."

"Pretty much?"

"Very damn much."

"Oh," said Mr. Rebeck. He put the rest of the baloney aside, wrapping it carefully. "Do you mind," he said hesitantly, "bringing me food? I mean, is it inconvenient?" He felt silly asking, but he did want to know.

The raven stared at him out of eyes like frozen gold. "Once a year," he said hoarsely. "Once a year you get worried. You start wondering how come the airborne Gristede's. You ask yourself, What's he getting out of it? You say, 'Nothing for nothing. Nobody does anybody any favors.'"

"That isn't so," Mr. Rebeck said. "That isn't so at all."

"Ha," said the raven. "All right. Your conscience starts to bother you. Your cold cuts don't taste right." He looked straight at Mr. Rebeck. "Of course it's a trouble. Of course it's inconvenient. You're damn right it's out of my way. Feel better? Any other questions?"

"Yes," said Mr. Rebeck. "Why do you do it, then?"

The raven made a dive at a hurrying caterpillar and missed. He spoke slowly, without looking at Mr. Rebeck. "There are people," he said, "who give, and there are people who take. There are people who create, people who destroy, and people who don't do anything and drive the other two kinds crazy. It's born in you, whether you give or take, and that's the way you are. Ravens bring things to people. We're like that. It's our nature. We don't like it. We'd much rather be eagles, or swans, or even one of those moronic robins, but we're ravens and there you are. Ravens don't feel right without somebody to bring things to, and when we do find somebody we realize what a silly business it was in the first place." He made a sound between a chuckle and a cough. "Ravens are pretty neurotic birds. We're closer to people than any other bird, and we're bound to them all our lives, but we don't have to like them. You think we brought Elijah food because we liked him? He was an old man with a dirty beard."

He fell silent, scratching aimlessly in the dust with his beak. Mr. Rebeck said nothing. Presently he reached out a tentative hand to smooth the raven's plumage.

"Don't do that," said the bird.

"I'm sorry."

"It makes me nervous."

"I'm sorry," Mr. Rebeck said again. He stared out over the neat family plots with their mossy headstones. "I hope some more people come soon," he said. "It gets lonesome in the summer."

"You wanted company," the bird said, "you should have joined the Y."

"I do have company, most of the time," Mr. Rebeck said. "But they forget so soon, and so easily. It's best when they've just arrived." He got up and leaned against a pillar. "Sometimes I think I'm dead," he said. The raven made a sputtering sound of derision. "I do. I forget things too. The sun shines in my eyes sometimes and I don't even notice it. Once I sat with an old man, and we tried to remember how pistachio nuts tasted, and neither of us could."

"I'll bring you some," the raven said. "There's a candy store near Tremont that sells them. It's a bookie joint too."

"That would be nice," Mr. Rebeck said. He turned to look at the stained-glass angel.

"They accept me more easily now," he said with his back to the raven. "They used to be dreadfully frightened. Now we sit and talk and play games, and I think, Maybe now, maybe this time, maybe really. Then I ask them, and they say no."

"They'd know," the raven said.

"Yes," Mr. Rebeck said, turning back, "but if life is the

only distinction between the living and the dead—I don't think I'm alive. Not really."

"You're alive," the raven said. "You hide behind gravestones, but it follows you. You ran away from it nineteen years ago, and it follows you like a skip-tracer." He cackled softly. "Life must love you very much."

"I don't want to be loved," Mr. Rebeck cried. "It's a burden on me."

"Well, that's your affair," the raven said. "I got my own problems." His black wings beat in a small thunder. "I gotta get moving. Let's have the bags and stuff."

Mr. Rebeck went into the mausoleum and came out a few moments later with five empty paper bags and an empty milk container. The raven took the bags in his claws and waved aside the container. "I'll pick that up later. Carry it now and I'll have to walk home." He sprang into the air and flapped slowly away over Central Avenue.

"Good-by," Mr. Rebeck called after him.

"See you," the raven croaked and disappeared behind a huge elm. Mr. Rebeck stretched himself, sat down again on the steps, and watched the sun climb. He felt a bit disconcerted. Usually, the raven brought him food twice a day, they exchanged some backchat, and that was that. Sometimes they didn't even talk. I don't know that bird at all, he thought, and it's been all these years. I know ghosts better than I know that small bird. He drew his knees up to his chin and thought about that. It was a new thought, and Mr. Rebeck treasured new thoughts. He hadn't had too many lately, and he knew it was his fault. The cemetery wasn't conducive to new thoughts; the environment wasn't right. It was a place for counting over the old, stored thoughts, stroking them lovingly and carefully, as if they were fine glassware, wondering if they could be thought any other way, and knowing deeply and securely that this way was the best. So he examined the new thought closely but gingerly, stood close to it to get the details and then away from it for perspective; he stretched it, thinned it, patted it into different shapes, gradually molding it to fit the contours of his mind.

A rush of wings made him look up. The raven was circling ten or fifteen feet above him, calling to him. "Forget something?" Mr. Rebeck called up to him.

"Saw something on the way out," the bird said. "There's a funeral procession coming in the front gate—not a very big one, but it's coming this way. You better either hide in a hurry or change your pants, either one. They may think you're a reception committee."

"Oh, my goodness!" Mr. Rebeck exclaimed. He sprang to his feet. "Thank you, thank you very much. Can't afford to get careless. Thank you for telling me."

"Don't I always?" the raven said wearily. He flew away again with easy, powerful wing strokes. And Mr. Rebeck hurried inside the mausoleum, closed the door, and lay down on the floor, listening to his heart beat in the sudden darkness.

It was a rather small funeral procession, but it had dignity.
A priest walked in front, with two young boys at his right
and left. The coffin came next, carried by five pallbearers.
Four of them were each carrying a corner of the coffin, and
the fifth was looking slightly embarrassed. Behind them,
dressed in somber and oddly graceful black, came Sandra
Morgan, who had been the wife of Michael Morgan. Bringing up the rear came three variously sad people. One of
them had roomed with Michael Morgan in college. Another
had taught history with him at Ingersoll University. The
third had drunk and played cards with him and rather liked
him.

Michael would have liked his own funeral if he could
have seen it. It was small and quiet, and really not at all
pompous, as Michael had feared it might be. "The dead,"
he had said once, "need nothing from the living, and the
living can give nothing to the dead." At twenty-two, it had
sounded precocious; at thirty-four, it sounded mature, and
this pleased Michael very much. He had liked being mature
and reasonable. He disliked ritual and pomposity, routine

and false emotion, rhetoric and sweeping gestures. Crowds made him nervous. Pageantry offended him. Essentially a romantic, he had put away the trappings of romance, although he had loved them deeply and never known.

The procession wound its quiet way through Yorkchester Cemetery, and the priest mused upon the transience of the world, and Sandra Morgan wept for her husband and looked hauntingly lovely, and the friends made the little necessary readjustments in their lives, and the boys' feet hurt. And in the coffin, Michael Morgan beat on the lid and howled.

Michael had died rather suddenly and very definitely, and when consciousness came back to him he knew where he was. The coffin swayed and tilted on four shoulders, and his body banged against the narrow walls. He lay quietly at first, because there was always the possibility that he might be dreaming. But he heard the priest chanting close by and the gravel slipping under the feet of the pallbearers, and a tinkling sound that must have been Sandra weeping, and he knew better.

Either he really was dead, he thought, or he had been pronounced so by mistake. That had happened to other people, he knew, and it was entirely possible—not to say fitting—that it had happened to Michael Morgan. Then a great fear of the choking earth seized him, and he pounded on the coffin lid with his fists and screamed. But no sound came from his lips, and the lid was silent under his hammering.

Frantically he called his wife's name and cursed her when she continued her ivory weeping. The priest intoned his liturgy and looked warningly at the boys when they dragged their feet; the pallbearers shifted the coffin on their shoulders; and Michael Morgan wept silently for his silence.

And then suddenly he was calm. Frenzy spent, he lay quietly in his coffin and knew himself dead.

So there you are, Morgan, he said to himself. Thirty-four years of one thing and another, and here is where it ends. Back to the earth—or back to the sea, he added, because he could never remember where it was that all protoplasm eventually wound up. His consciousness did not startle him too much. He had always been willing to concede the faint possibility of an afterlife, and this, he supposed, was the first stage. Lie back, Morgan, he thought, and take it easy. Sing a spiritual or something. He wondered again if there might not have been some mistake, but he didn't really believe it.

A pallbearer slipped and nearly dropped his end of the coffin, but Michael did not feel the jolt. "I don't *feel* particularly dead," he said to the coffin lid, "but I'm just a layman. My opinion would be valueless in any court in the land. Don't butt in, Morgan. It was a perfectly nice funeral till you started causing trouble." He closed his eyes and lay still, wondering absently about rigor mortis.

The procession stopped suddenly, and the priest's voice became louder and firmer. He was chanting in Latin, and Michael listened appreciatively. He had always detested funerals and avoided them as much as possible. But it's different, he thought, when it's your own funeral. You feel it's one of those occasions that shouldn't be missed.

He knew no Latin, but he clung to the falling words of the chant, knowing them to be the last human words he would ever hear. "Ashes to ashes," I suppose it means, he thought, "and dust to dust." That's all you are now, Morgan—a cup of dust scattered to the wolves of night. He considered the phrase and rejected it reluctantly. What, after all, would wolves want with dust?

The first clods fell on the coffin lid, sounding for all the world like a knock on the door. Michael laughed inside his head. Come in, he thought, come right in. The house is in a bit of a mess right now, but I'm always glad of company. Walk right in, friend. This is Open House.

Sandra was crying loudly and quite thoroughly now, but her sobs were beginning to sound like yawns. Poor Sandy, Michael thought. They probably got you up early for this, too. I'm sorry, lass. Just a minute or so—then you can go home and go back to sleep.

The earth-sounds became fainter. Presently they stopped.

Well, here we are, said Michael Morgan to himself. He realized the absurdity of the words and defiantly thought them again. Here we are. Here we are. Here we are. Here we all are. Here we go around the prickly pear. Prickly pear. Here we are, prickly pear. Over here. He stopped that finally, and thought about Heaven and Hell and Sandra.

He had never believed in either of the first two during his life, and he saw no reason to start now. I'm in this worm Automat for the duration, he thought, and in a few minutes I will turn over and draw eternity up around my neck and go to sleep. If he was wrong, one of two Old Gentlemen would be around to see him shortly, and a number of things might finally become clear. In the meantime, he decided to think about Sandra.

He had loved Sandra. Thinking about it in a detached fashion, he dared anybody not to love Sandra. She was all the world's loved objects in one, and she showed them off slowly and lazily, like a revolving dish of diamonds in a jeweler's window. Besides, she looked needing, and she had a sad mouth.

They had met at the small reception that had been given for him when he joined the Ingersoll faculty. She had come with her uncle, who taught geology. Their glances had crossed, and he had put down his drink and gone to her. Within fifteen minutes he had been quoting Rimbaud for her, and Dowson, and Swinburne, and his own secret songs. And she had heard and understood: Michael wanted to go to bed with her. So they were mature and civilized, and she took him into her huge, warm bed, in which she managed to look quite affectingly lost.

Michael loved that lost quality of hers. It made him feel necessary and useful. He discovered a strong protective streak in himself, and was in turn irritated by it, amused by it, and vastly delighted with it. He was all the more captured by her moments of cool brilliance and lazy wit; it made her three-dimensional. And Michael had ridden in search of the third dimension for a long time.

So they were married, and Michael received what the president called "a bit of a raise." It was just that, but it enabled Michael and Sandra Morgan to move into an apartment in Yorkchester and Sandra to quit her art-gallery job. They had been married for four years, and much of it had been happy.

And now he was dead, Michael thought. Dead and buried, humus for the hungry earth. And he would never see Sandra again. The thought hurt him, even through the numbness that had stroked him with its witch-fingers. His body was nothing to him now, but a deal of his soul seemed to have been left where Sandra was, and dead, he felt naked and somehow incomplete.

He prayed for sleep, and when it did not come he invented ways of passing the time. He broke down his life into periods marked Youth, Harvard, Europe, Korea, Ingersoll, and Sandra, and examined them carefully and objectively. First he decided that his life had not been wasted, and shortly after, he decided that it had. He thought of all the tiny factors that had gone to make up the mortal existence of Michael Morgan, enumerated them, weighed them, and decided that they had individual meaning but no collective significance; and then he thought it might be the other way round. With death, he had discovered, there came the power of disinterested scrutiny of the way he had come. Along with it, however, came a peculiar lack of interest in much of what had once been a very important world. Only Sandra seemed real now—Sandra and perhaps the good New York springs and finding the one student in his class who understood the lonely steel mill that was Bismarck and the ice emperor Bonaparte.

After that he tried to recall all the great music he had ever heard, and quickly discovered that his education had not been nearly so complete, his interest so great, and his memory so retentive as he had hoped. Only the Chopin Preludes that he had learned as a boy stayed with him, along with some Rimsky-Korsakov, a few passages from the Ninth, and a plaintive, wandering strain he decided was Weill. The rest was gone, or he was gone from it, and he was sorry because it would have been nice to have music.

You have to be very deep to be dead, he thought, and I'm not. He began to have some concept of forever, and his mind shivered as his body had when he had wakened in the cold nights and thrust his hands between his thighs to keep warm. It will be a long night, he thought.

Suddenly he remembered an early morning with Sandra before they had been married. They had sat at her little kitchen table, eating bread-and-jelly sandwiches. She had gone to the icebox for a bottle of milk, and he had sat and watched her move. Her feet made a very small, among-friends sound on the linoleum. As he thought of it now, the pain seemed to snap him like an icicle. He cried out, hearing it as a great animal yawp of terror—and then he was standing beside his own grave, calling, "Sandy! Sandy!"

She did not come, and he knew she would not, and still he called, thinking, I will close my eyes and count a hundred, and when I look up she will be there—the way he did when he was waiting for a bus. But he could not close his eyes, and the numbers rattled in his head like dice. Finally he forced himself to stop calling, and after a while he sat down in the grass.

It took him a while to realize that he had left his grave, and when he did it didn't seem very important. I'm out, he said to himself, and I can talk again and move around, and I'm no better off than I was. Alive, he could at least have kept up the pretense of having somewhere important to go; but now apparently he could just sit by the roadside for the next few million years, if he felt like it. And he did feel like it. He wanted only to sit in the grass and watch the ants running and not think about anything. I want my mind to be white and clean and unmarked, he thought, like my bones. That was the answer to everything, and he hadn't seen it. "You can have my skull," he said politely to the ants. "I won't be needing it." But they kept running in the grass, and he became angry with them. "All right," he said. "And the hell with you too." And he got up and went over to look at his grave.

There was no stone yet, only a small metal marker. It said: "Michael Morgan, March 7, 1924–June 10, 1958," and he felt very pleased with its conciseness. Like a *Times* headline, he thought, and he looked at it for a long time.

My body is there, he thought. All my chicken dinners and head-scratching and sneezing and fornication and hot baths and sunburns and beer and shaving—all buried and forgotten. All the little pettinesses washed away. I feel clean and light and pure. He thought about book-hunting on Fourth Avenue and decided that he felt like a smashed light bulb.

"Good-by," he said to his body and walked away down the paved road. He wanted to whistle and felt cheated when he found he could not.

Michael Morgan walked through the graveyard and his feet made no sound. The sun shone hot on him and he did not feel it, nor did he feel the tiny winds that chuckled between the stones. He saw a ring of Greek pillars that held up nothing, and near it a concrete birdbath. He saw fountains and flowers and a wheelbarrow half full of earth. Once a car rushed past him as he walked along the side of the road, but nobody in it looked at him.

He saw family plots, with the little headstones bunched together like frightened cattle; and he saw a great mausoleum four stories high, with an angel on marble guard. He saw a clump of cherry trees, and their boughs were thick and swollen with the red fruit. Spaced at regular intervals, twenty-foot spires pointed the way to Heaven, for the benefit, Michael decided, of lost souls and tourists.

He felt as if he were walking in a slightly leaky vacuum. He could see the sun, and he assumed it was still burning, but he personally felt neither hot nor cold. He knew there was a breeze, for he saw leaves wander across his path, but he felt no air on his skin. Faintly but clearly, he heard birds singing and water flowing, but the sounds meant nothing to him, and he never even thought of trying to pick a cherry. It wasn't that he didn't give a damn—Michael had been trying very hard not to give a damn for most of his life—but that giving or not giving damns never entered the question. "I feel mediocre," he experimented. "Luke-warm"—but the words were meaningless.

He walked for a long time. The black paved road became dirt, and then gravel, and then pavement again, and other roads ran away from it; sometimes it was broad, and other times as narrow as the cold bed of Barbara Allen; but it did not end, and Michael walked on and never grew tired.

Maybe there is no end, he thought. Maybe I just go on walking—and felt nothing but a whispery amusement at the prospect.

Then he came over a low hill and saw the mausoleum and the small man sitting in front of it. The man had his knees drawn up and his chin on his folded forearms and was looking at nothing.

Sensation seemed to return to Michael: curiosity, interest, a little fear, pleasure, and a spoonful of hope came slowly back, saying to one another, What is this? How is this? Is the house not empty yet? And Michael Morgan called gladly, "Hello!"

The small man blinked, looked around, and smiled at Michael. "Hello," he called back. "Come on down."

Michael came slowly down the hill, and the man got up to meet him. He looked to be in his early fifties, for his shoulders were a little rounded and his hair was gray-white. But the smile he gave Michael was warm and youthful, and his eyes were the color of the earth. "How do you do?" he asked. "My name is Jonathan Rebeck."

"Michael Morgan," said Michael, and suddenly he was so happy to see this small man, and so happy to realize he was happy, that he grabbed for Mr. Rebeck's brown hand—and watched in dull horror as it went completely through his own.

Then he remembered, and for the first time he saw life as the dead see it. He backed off from Mr. Rebeck, and would have turned to run if the small man's eyes had not been full of brown sadness. So he sat down on the steps that led up to the mausoleum and tried to cry; but he didn't know where to begin.

"All right," he said finally, "I'm dead."

"I know," said Mr. Rebeck gently. He paused and then added, "I saw your funeral procession."

"Did you?" Michael looked up. "How did it look from the outside?"

"Very nice," said Mr. Rebeck. "Very quiet and tasteful."

"That's good," Michael said. "Man comes into the world with a maximum of fuss, as it is. Let him—"

Mr. Rebeck began to laugh. "A maximum of fuss." He chuckled softly. "Very true. Very funny and very true."

"Could I finish?" Michael asked coldly.

"What? Oh, certainly. I'm awfully sorry. I thought you were through."

"Let him leave with the minimum," Michael finished, but he trailed off disgustedly at the end. Mr. Rebeck laughed politely, and Michael scowled at him. In the middle of the scowl he began to laugh, hiccuping, machine-gun laughs, and when he stopped he knuckled at his eyes. But there were no tears to wipe away, and he looked soberly at Mr. Rebeck.

"I don't feel dead," he said slowly. "Would I still be making those lousy epigrams if I were dead? I feel as alive as anyone. As alive as you."

"I'm not a very good standard," Mr. Rebeck said softly.

"I don't feel dead," Michael said firmly. "I feel my body on me like an anchor." The simile pleased him. "An anchor. A nice, comforting anchor holding me to earth. If I'm dead, how come I don't just go billowing off into the

beyond like a sheet blown off a clothesline?" He felt a vague
regret that Mooney, head of the Classics Department,
couldn't hear him now. They had stayed up late together,
Mooney and he.

"I know a good metaphor," Mr. Rebeck said thoughtfully. "Don't people who have had their arms or legs ampu-
tated always say they can feel them still? They say they itch
at night."

Michael was silent for a long time.

"I know a better one," he said finally. "It's an old super-
stition. Some people believe that if you kill a snake in the
daytime its tail won't stop wiggling till sundown." He
looked at Mr. Rebeck. "All right. I'm dead. How long till
sundown?"

"A while yet," Mr. Rebeck said. He sat down beside
Michael. "You see, Michael, nobody dies just like that. The
body dies quickly, but the soul hangs on to life as long as
it can because living is all it knows."

"Soul?" Michael felt faintly worried. "I do have a soul,
then?"

"I don't know if that's the right word. Memory might
be better. Living is a big thing, and it's pretty hard to
forget. To the dead, everything connected with life becomes
important—striking a match, clipping your toenails. Not
only does your own life pass before you; everybody else's
does. You find yourself becoming greedy of people; whenever they come to visit here you watch every movement
they make, trying to remember the way you used to do
that. And when they leave you follow them all the way to
the entrance, and you stop there because you can't go any
farther." He paused. "They had it all backwards, you see,
those old ghost stories about the dead haunting the living.
It's not that way at all."

Michael smiled faintly. "You know more about death
than I do."

"I've lived here a long time," Mr. Rebeck said. "Death

is something that has to be learned. Just like life, only you
don't have to learn so fast because you've got more time."

"Will it be like this—forever? I mean, so far it's just like
being alive, only less rushed."

Mr. Rebeck didn't laugh. "It's different," he said, "but I
can't really tell you how. I could if I were dead, I think—
only then I wouldn't want to." He saw Michael blink puz-
zledly and went on. "This much I can tell you: you forget
things. A week from now you'll have forgotten a few
things—what music you liked, what games you used to
play, little things. In two weeks a few bigger things may
go—where you worked, where you studied—in three weeks
you won't remember that you ever loved or hated anybody.
In four weeks—I can't exactly put it into words. You just
forget things."

"I forget everything?" Mr. Rebeck could barely hear
Michael's voice. He nodded.

"Everything? Talking—thinking?"

"They become unnecessary," Mr. Rebeck said, "like
breathing. You don't really forget them, you just don't have
any use for them or any need. They atrophy, like the appendix. You aren't really talking right now. How can you?
You haven't got a larynx, you haven't got vocal cords, you
haven't got a diaphragm. But you're so used to talking and
you want to talk so badly that I hear you as clearly as if
you could make sounds. Nothing's going to stop you from
talking as long as you want to. You just won't want to
after a while."

"It is Hell, then," Michael said slowly. "It really is Hell."

"Funny you should say that," Mr. Rebeck said. "I always
thought of it as a little like being an angel. You can't be
touched any more, or jarred, or hurt. All the little hypocri-
ses that hold life together drop away from you. You
become a sort of closed circle with no end and no beginning. I think it's the purest state of existence."

"Like an amoeba," Michael said. "They don't get trau-
mas either."

"Not like an amoeba. I'll show you. Look up, Michael. Look at the sun."

Michael raised his eyes and saw the sun. It was red and swollen in the late afternoon, and its heat had become vengeful and vindictive. Mr. Rebeck blinked rapidly as he looked at it and turned his head quickly away. But Michael stared hard at it and saw only a shriveled orange hanging in a crumpled tree. He felt a great pity in him, and a corner-of-the-mouth scorn.

"You see?" Mr. Rebeck asked when Michael finally turned undazzled eyes on him.

"God," said Michael.

"That may be," said Mr. Rebeck. "If I had looked at the sun that long I'd be blind now. You can look at it all day. You can watch it move, if you care to. Nobody can blind you now, Michael. You will see more clearly than you ever saw in life. Nobody can lie to you now, because three-fourths of a lie is wanting to believe it, and believing makes no difference to you any more. I envy you a great deal, Michael."

He sighed and juggled two small pebbles in the palm of his hand. "Whenever I get to thinking I'm dead too," he said softly, "I look at the sun."

Michael wanted to look at the sun again, but he looked at Mr. Rebeck instead and said, "Who are you?"

"I live here," Mr. Rebeck said.

"Why? What do you do?" A thought— "Are you the caretaker?"

"In a way." Mr. Rebeck got up and went inside the mausoleum. He came out a moment later, holding half a baloney and a small container of milk. "Supper," he explained, "or a very late lunch. An old friend of mine brought it." He leaned against a cracked pillar and smiled at Michael, who had not moved.

"Death is like life in a lot of ways," he said thoughtfully. "The power to see clearly doesn't always change people. The wise in life sometimes become wiser in death. The petty in life remain petty. The dead change their addresses, you see, not their souls.

"I've always thought cemeteries were like cities. There are streets, avenues—you've seen them, I think, Michael. There are blocks, too, and house numbers, slums and ghettos, middle-class sections and small palaces. They give visitors cards at the entrance, you know, with their relatives' streets and house numbers. It's the only way they can find them. That's like a city, too.

"A dark city, Michael, and a crowded one. And it has most of the qualities of the other cities: companionship, coldness, argument. There is no love, of course, no love at all, but there isn't so much of that floating around outside either.

"There is loneliness, though. The dead are very lonely for a while, very bewildered, very frightened. The gap that separates them from the living is as wide as the gap that separates the living from each other; wider, I think. They wander as helplessly through the dark city as they did through the cities of stone, and finally they find a quiet bed and try to sleep.

"I like to help them. I like to be here when they come, to calm them and ease their spirits. Someone to talk to, you might say. People have gone mad looking for someone to talk to. We talk, or we sit and play chess—I hope you play—or I read to them. Very little things, Michael, and only for a little while. Soon they drift away, and where they go I cannot follow. They don't need me then; they don't need anyone, and this pleases me because most of them spent their lives trying not to need.

"So I keep them company for a while, these friends of mine. I sometimes tell them that I am the mayor of the dark city, because the word at least is familiar to them, but I think of it more in the nature of being a night light, a lantern down a dark street."

"Charon," Michael said. "Charon and coins on the tongues of the dead."

Mr. Rebeck smiled. "I used to think so," he said. "But Charon was a god, or a demi-god. I'm a man." He chuckled softly. "I used to be a druggist."

"I was a teacher," Michael said. "A history teacher. I liked it very much." He thought of something and asked, a little awkwardly, "Can you see me? I mean, am I visible?"

"I see you," Mr. Rebeck said. "You look like a man, but you cast no shadow and I can see the sun behind you."

"A kind of tracing of a man," Michael said bitterly.

"It doesn't matter," Mr. Rebeck said. "In three weeks or a month you won't even need to take the human form any more."

"I won't remember it, you mean."

"You won't want to remember it."

"I will!" Michael cried out fiercely.

Mr. Rebeck spoke slowly. "I make you the same promise I make everyone, Michael. As long as you cling to being alive, as long as you care to be a man, I'll be here. We'll be two men together in this place. I'll like it, because I get lonesome here and I like company; and you'll like it too, until it becomes a game, a pointless ritual. Then you'll leave."

"I'll stay," Michael said quietly. "I may not be a man, but I'll look as much like one as possible."

Mr. Rebeck spread his hand and shrugged slightly. "I said it wasn't so different from life." He hesitated and then asked, "Tell me, Michael, how did you die?"

The question startled Michael. "I beg your pardon?"

"You look very young," Mr. Rebeck said. "I was wondering."

Michael grinned widely at him. "How about premature old age?"

Mr. Rebeck said nothing.

"I have a wife," Michael said. "I mean, I had a wife."

"I saw her," Mr. Rebeck said. "A beautiful woman."

"Lovely," said Michael. He was silent.

"Well?"

"Well what? My lovely wife killed me. Poisoned me, like salting the soup."

He saw the shock on Mr. Rebeck's face and enjoyed it. He felt very human. He smiled at Mr. Rebeck again.

"I would like to play chess," he said, "before sundown."

3

"We could go for another walk," Mr. Rebeck said.

"I don't want to go for another walk. We've walked all the grass off this place. Where we walk the bare earth follows. Like locusts."

"But you like it. You said you did."

Michael thought hard about scowling and was pleased when he remembered the feeling. "I do like it. But I don't like watching you get tired."

Mr. Rebeck started to say something, but Michael cut him off. "Because I can't. I can't get tired, and watching you breathe as if you were drinking the air bothers me. So let's not walk anywhere."

"All right," Mr. Rebeck said mildly. "We could play some chess, if you like."

"I don't want to play chess." Michael remembered petulance. "You have to make the moves for me. How do you think that makes me feel?"

Mr. Rebeck gazed at him pityingly. "Michael, Michael, you're making this so hard."

"Damn right," Michael said. "I don't give up easily." He

grinned at Mr. Rebeck. "If I can't drink vodka and tomato juice any more I'm not drinking anybody's nepenthe. No chess. I don't like chess, anyway."

"I could read to you."

"Read what?" Michael asked suspiciously. "I didn't know you had books."

"The raven steals a couple for me down on Fourth Avenue every now and then," Mr. Rebeck said. "I've got some Swinburne."

Michael tried very hard to remember if he had liked Swinburne, and felt something only a doorstep away from terror when the name made no sound in his head. "Swinburne," he said aloud. He knew Mr. Rebeck was looking at him. My God, he thought, is it all going, then? Frantically he grabbed for the first familiar thing at hand, which happened to be his office number at the college; 1316, he thought, trying to curl up into the number, 1316, 1316, 1316. When it suddenly became 1613, he said quickly, "Swinburne. Yes, I know Swinburne. Didn't he once do a very long poem on the Circe theme?"

It was an old trick, one he remembered from every discussion and bull session he had ever taken part in: If you don't know, make it up. Nobody ever admitted he didn't know a quotation, or a book or an essay on something. The rule also had a corollary: If you're not sure, it's Marlowe.

He rationalized it, as he always had. He might very well have, he said to himself. How would I know, now?

"Circe?" Mr. Rebeck frowned. "I never read it. But that doesn't mean anything," he added, smiling shyly. "There's a great deal I haven't read."

"I'm not sure it was Swinburne," Michael said. "It might have been somebody else."

"The one I was thinking of was 'The Garden of Proserpine.' You know." He quoted the lines, a little haltingly, but with an eager savoring of the words.

From too much love of living,
From hope and fear set free,
We thank with brief thanksgiving
Whatever gods may be
That no life lives forever;
That dead men rise up never—

"I remember," Michael said abruptly. "I don't like it."

"I'm sorry," Mr. Rebeck said. "I thought you might."

"Pat," Michael said. "Very pat. Anyway, Swinburne wrote it while he was alive." He looked up and saw the sun walking slowly up the sky like a tired old man. It interested him, and he stared hard at it. While he looked, Swinburne passed quietly out of his mind forever, unloved and unhated.

"Let's play chess," he said.

"I thought you didn't like chess."

God damn you, Michael thought. He spoke with exaggerated clarity of diction. "I like chess. I am very fond of chess. I'm crazy about chess. Let's play some chess."

Mr. Rebeck laughed and got up. "All right," he said and started for the mausoleum door.

"We can use a pebble for the black rook," Michael called after him.

Mr. Rebeck was digging absently in his hip pocket. He stopped and smiled at Michael a little ruefully.

"For nineteen years," he said, "every time I come back here I reach for the key to let myself in. The lock's broken, you know, but I always expect to find myself locked out."

He pushed the door open and went into the mausoleum. Michael sat down with his back to one of the white pillars; rather, he imagined himself sitting down and, for all practical purposes, he was. He had felt himself losing touch with the physical over these last three days, and it frightened him. Whenever he wanted to walk or smile or wink he had to remember very sharply what walking or smiling or winking was like. Otherwise he remained still, completely out of contact with his body-memories, a raindrop of consciousness hanging in the air. That had happened two days ago, and Michael remembered it.

His memory was still good, and his imagination clear. He felt human and bored, and the very boredom relieved him because it was such a human emotion.

Mr. Rebeck came out of the mausoleum, carrying a chessboard backed with torn green oilcloth. He sat down beside Michael and began to drizzle chess pieces. Three fell out of his shirt pocket, another five from his right pants pocket, and so on until the set was complete, with the exception of the black rook.

None of the pieces were from the same set. Most were made from various yellowing woods, a few were red plastic, and two, a black bishop and a white rook, were carved from a sullenly beautiful mahogany. Their bases were weighted and felted, and where the other pieces wobbled, staggered, and sprawled all over the chessboard, these two stood facing each other from behind opposing lines; and when the wind or Mr. Rebeck's knee scattered the other pieces, the bishop and the rook nodded gravely to each other.

Michael liked looking at the chess pieces. They made him laugh without the rubber-band sound that had been creeping into his laughter over the last three days.

"Motley bunch," he said to Mr. Rebeck, "aren't they?"

"The raven stole them piece by piece," Mr. Rebeck said, "and it took him quite a while because I made him steal them from department stores. He wanted to get them from the old men in the park, but I feel better this way. The black rook was beautiful too, but I lost it and I don't know where it is. Probably still around here somewhere." He held out his two clenched hands to Michael. "Want black or white?"

"White," said Michael, pointing at Mr. Rebeck's right hand. Mr. Rebeck opened the hand and a black pawn rolled out. He began to set up the pieces, humming softly as he did so.

"Where did the raven pick up the chessboard?" Michael asked suddenly.

Mr. Rebeck looked up. "I don't know. He staggered in with it one morning, and when I asked him where he got it he just said he'd been a good boy." He finished setting the pieces in place. "It worries me sometimes. I try not to think about it."

He began the game by moving his king's pawn two squares forward. "I'm very orthodox," he said. He had said this twice during the eight games they had played previously, but Michael did not remember it.

"Make mine the same," Michael said. "I'm not proud." Mr. Rebeck leaned forward and duplicated his own move on Michael's side of the board. He considered his own pieces at some length and finally jumped his knight two squares in front of his king's bishop. Michael made the same move with his queen's knight, and they settled down to the game.

They played quietly. Mr. Rebeck swayed back and forth over the board, moving for both of them, his breathing becoming harsher as the game went on. Michael burrowed into the luxury of wrapping his whole mind around one subject to the exclusion of all others. On the ninth move there was a quick flurry of pawn-exchanging, and again on the fifteenth, when one of Michael's knights and both of his bishops swirled angrily around a pawn of Mr. Rebeck's and left it untouched. Two moves later Michael vengefully picked off one of Mr. Rebeck's knights; after that the game moved slowly and warily.

Suddenly Mr. Rebeck's whole body jerked erect. At first Michael thought of a puppet with all its strings drawn tight; then he rejected the inanimate image and thought of a small wild animal. Mr. Rebeck even seemed to be sniffing the air.

"What is it?" Michael asked.

"There's a woman over there," Mr. Rebeck said tightly.

Sandra's footsteps pattered on the floor of Michael's skull again. "Where?"

"Behind that clump of trees—near the very big mausoleum. She hasn't seen us. That gives us time."

He began to gather up the chess pieces, putting them hurriedly back in his pockets.

"Hey!" Michael said. "Wait a minute."

Mr. Rebeck stopped trying to fit a king into an already overloaded shirt pocket. "What?"

"Just wait, that's all. What are you so afraid of company for? I think it would be nice."

"Michael," said Mr. Rebeck, "for God's sake."

"Never mind that. Why the hell do we have to hide when somebody comes along? Do you do that all the time?"

"Most of the time. Come *on*, Michael."

"What sort of a life is that?"

"Mine," Mr. Rebeck snapped with a kind of driven fierceness, "and I manage. If just one person gets suspicious and reports me to the gatekeeper, they'll throw me out of here. And I can't go outside, Michael. Not ever."

He faced Michael across the chessboard, breathing quickly and hoarsely. Michael was about to say something, or thought he was, when Mr. Rebeck gasped shortly and whispered, "Now you've done it." The woman had mounted the slope of the low hill and stood looking down at them.

"Good," Michael said. "I concede the game. You were winning, anyway." Looking straight at the woman, he called, "Hello. Good morning."

The woman was silent and straight upon the hill.

"Good morning," Michael called again.

"She can't hear you," Mr. Rebeck said.

"She must be deaf, then. I shouted loud enough."

"Not loud enough," Mr. Rebeck said without looking at him.

"You hear me," Michael spoke very softly.

"I'm different."

"Can she see me?"

"No. At least I don't think so."

"She might be able to see me?"

"Maybe. I doubt it, Michael."

"Call her, then."

Mr. Rebeck remained silent.

"Call her," Michael said. "Call her. Please call her."

"All right," Mr. Rebeck said. He turned to look up the hill at the woman and called, "Hello." His voice cracked a little.

"Hello," the woman called. Her voice was high and clear. She began to descend the hill, placing her feet firmly and carefully.

Mr. Rebeck turned to Michael. "Do you see? Do you believe now?"

"No," Michael said. "Not yet."

Mr. Rebeck's voice was pitched low to keep his words from the approaching woman, but the words hissed out of his mouth like steam. "She can't see you and she can't hear you. Believe me, I know. The living and the dead don't talk together."

"I want to talk to her," Michael said. "I want to hear her voice. I want to talk to somebody alive."

One quick look Mr. Rebeck gave him; then he turned to face the woman, who had now come to the edge of the plot of grass that surrounded the mausoleum. "Good morning," he said.

"Good morning," the woman said. She was dressed in black, but without a veil. In her late forties, Michael thought. Then he made it the early forties. He had always been a bad judge of women's ages, and the black dress might add a few years.

The most arresting feature of her face was her mouth. It was wide and full-lipped, and there were little soft lines around the corners. When she spoke, the whole mouth became alive, jumping and twitching and gesturing like a dancer's body; occasionally curling back and down to reveal small white teeth.

"A lovely day," said Mr. Rebeck.

"Beautiful," the woman answered. "It should stay like this, is all I ask."

"Oh, it will," Mr. Rebeck said. He fancied he detected curiosity in the dark eyes, and added, "It was such a lovely day I couldn't stay indoors."

"I know," the woman said. "I was up in my house this morning and I said to myself, Gertrude, such a day you should share with somebody. Go and see Morris. So I came right down, Morris shouldn't think nobody remembered him on such a day. Morris is my husband," she explained, seeing Mr. Rebeck frown slightly. "Morris Klapper." She pointed back up the hill toward a great marble building that shone in the sun. "You know, Morris in the big house."

Mr. Rebeck nodded. "I know the name. I've passed the building. It's very impressive."

"All marble," Mrs. Klapper said, "even inside. Morris liked marble." Had she been crying? Mr. Rebeck wondered. He could not tell.

"It's a very beautiful building," he said. He pointed to the Wilder mausoleum. "This is a family plot. They were friends of mine."

He watched Mrs. Klapper inspect the building. For the first time in nineteen years he felt a little ashamed of it. They should have at least replaced the glass in the grating; and he himself could have polished the lions' heads. But the angel was still in good condition. She must see the angel.

"Excuse my saying so," Mrs. Klapper said finally, "but they don't keep it up so good."

"There aren't any caretakers any more," Mr. Rebeck said. "The family died out."

"I'm sorry," Mrs. Klapper said. "Believe me, I'm sorry. I know what that's like." She sniffed, a full-sinused, healthy sniff. "A year and two months now Morris is dead, and I still keep leaning over to wake him up in the morning."

"Some things last a long time," Michael said. He spoke loudly and clearly, but he did not shout. Not until Mrs. Klapper turned away from him. Then he yelled the words, wishing that he could feel them clawing their way out of his throat.

"Be quiet, Michael," said Mr. Rebeck hoarsely.

Mrs. Klapper came a few steps closer. "What did you say?"

"Nothing," Mr. Rebeck said. "I just said that you don't forget some things."

"Sure," said Mrs. Klapper. "Some things you remember. Like a husband, or an operation. You know, you have your appendix out and they put it in a little glass bottle and show it to you, and after that you can't stand to look at spaghetti." She took a few more small steps in on the grass. "Like you."

Mr. Rebeck blinked. "What about me?"

"You remind me of Morris," Mrs. Klapper said. "I mean, you don't look like him or anything. When I came down here and saw you playing that"—she pointed to the chessboard lying on the grass—"I thought to myself, My God! There's Morris!" She was silent for a moment. "You were playing by yourself?"

"He was playing me," said Michael, "and getting hell beaten out of him." Which was untrue, but it didn't seem to matter.

"I was trying to solve some chess problems," Mr. Rebeck said. He took the look in her eyes for one of disbelief. "I know this seems like a silly place to play chess, but it's quiet and you can concentrate more."

"You and Morris," Mrs. Klapper said. She sniffed again. "You and Morris. Morris used to do that all the time, take his chessboard and go off in a corner by himself, and if you say, 'Morris, it's time for dinner right away'—'Sha, sha, I have to figure this problem.' 'Morris, the meat's getting cold'—'*Sha, sha*, I'll be there in a minute.' 'Morris, you want maybe a sandwich?'—'*Sha, sha*, I'm not hungry.' " She sighed. "A crazy. But go forget him."

"I know," Mr. Rebeck said.

Michael chuckled. "How?"

"Believe me," Mrs. Klapper said, "he'll know I don't forget." She looked around. "Is there a place you could sit down? My feet are coming off."

"I've only the steps to offer," Mr. Rebeck said. "They're pretty clean."

Mrs. Klapper looked at them. She shrugged. "Clean, unclean," she said, "here comes Klapper." She plumped easily down on the top step and let out a gusty sigh. "*Vey*," she said, "my feet were absolutely coming off." She smiled warmly at Mr. Rebeck.

"I'm a little tired myself," Mr. Rebeck said. He felt himself blushing. "I live a long way from here."

"I'll be damned," said Michael, squatting next to Mrs. Klapper. "You've got blood left."

Mrs. Klapper patted the space at her side. "So sit. What are you, a boy athlete? At your age, a man should sit down anywhere he feels like it."

"Thank you," Mr. Rebeck said. He sat gingerly next to her, suddenly wondering, At my age? Do I look that old? How old does she think I am? He wanted to stand up again, but he felt himself committed.

They sat silently for a while. Mrs. Klapper had slipped off one of her shoes and was sighing softly and contentedly. Mr. Rebeck wanted to say something to her, but he couldn't think of a thing. It made him angry with himself.

Suddenly a scream like Hell's star tenor on a good day rang and burst inside his head. He leaped to his feet with a cry of real physical pain and looked wildly around him for the scream's source.

Mrs. Klapper remained seated, but she slipped her shoe back on and looked at him in some alarm. "You feel all right?" she asked.

"I h–heard something," Mr. Rebeck stammered, "a scream. . . ."

"Funny." Mrs. Klapper stood up too. "I didn't hear a thing."

"I heard a scream," Mr. Rebeck said, and then he saw Michael, sitting cross-legged, shuddering with silent laughter. "Michael!" he said before he thought.

Michael opened his mouth and pointed down blackness into his throat. "Testing," he said. "Just testing. I wanted to see if you were on the job."

"Who?" Mrs. Klapper's brows drew together, as if for protection.

Mr. Rebeck wiped his forehead. "I'm sorry," he said softly. "I'm awfully sorry. I thought I heard someone."

He expected Mrs. Klapper to break into either laughter or full retreat. Instead, he saw her face relax into understanding. "Your friend, huh?" she asked.

"I beg your pardon?" said Mr. Rebeck, thinking in cold-bellied terror, *Does she see Michael?*

"Your friend," said Mrs. Klapper, pointing at the mausoleum. "The one buried in there."

"Oh," said Mr. Rebeck. He thought quickly. "Yes Michael Wilder. Very old friend. It hit me very hard when he died." Mrs. Klapper was nodding steadily. He went on. "Every now and then I'm sure I hear him calling me."

"Nice," said Michael. "Very nice," After a moment he added, "I'm sorry I did that."

"I guess it sounds a little crazy," Mr. Rebeck added.

Mrs. Klapper sat down on the steps again. "Listen," she said firmly, "half the world is crazy that way." She paused. "Me too," she said finally.

Mr. Rebeck sat next to her. "Your husband?"

"Uh-huh," said Mrs. Klapper. "Morris. A lot of times I hear him calling, 'Gertrude, Gertrude,' like he'd lost his key again, or he couldn't find the light switch in the bathroom. A year and two months and I still hear him."

"I guess that must happen to a lot of people," Mr.

Rebeck said. "You don't want to believe somebody's really dead."

"No," Mrs. Klapper answered. "For me it's different. Maybe for other people it's like that." She nibbled the tip of one black-gloved forefinger, a trait, Mr. Rebeck thought, that he would never have associated with her.

"Morris died funny, you know," she said slowly. Mr. Rebeck said nothing. "We've got a nice apartment—a terrace with a little garden. We rented it, the agent said, 'Look, you got a nice little terrace, you can have dinner on it.' So we had dinner on it, except when it was cold. Anyway, that time we're eating dinner, and I see Morris doesn't look so good. So I say, 'Morris, you don't look so good. You want to go inside and lie down?' And he says, 'No, Gertrude, finish the meal, it shouldn't be a total loss.' I say, 'Okay, Morris, if you feel okay,' and I dish him some corn. Green Giant—on the cob Morris doesn't like it. It gets in his teeth."

"You don't have to tell me this," Mr. Rebeck said. "You don't even know me."

"Gallant," said Michael. "Sneaky, but gallant."

"Excuse me," Mrs. Klapper said. "I want to tell you. It's a relief, and I don't feel so much like I'll bust any more, and besides I won't be seeing you again, anyway." Mr. Rebeck knew it was true, and it made him oddly sad.

"So Morris finishes the corn, and I say, 'Morris, you want some more corn?" and he opens his mouth to say something and *boom*!" Mr. Rebeck jumped. "Right over the back of his chair he falls." Mrs. Klapper swept her arm in a wide semicircle.

"You know what I do then?"

Mr. Rebeck shook his head silently.

"I yell," Mrs. Klapper said bitterly. "I sit there in my chair and I yell. I spent five minutes maybe of Morris's life yelling. Then what do I do?" She swept her arm around again. "*Boom*! Out like a light."

She looked down at her lap. Mr. Rebeck noticed with a

strange objectivity that a seam had opened on her right glove.

"Maybe he wakes up," she said in a low voice, "and calls me, 'Gertrude, Gertrude.' He was always losing the key to the apartment. Maybe he lies there calling me, and I don't hear him."

"Don't say that," Mr. Rebeck urged. "You can't possibly know."

"You know what I did for two days after that?" Mrs. Klapper asked. "I went around saying, 'Morris, you want some more corn? Morris, you want some more corn? Morris, you want some more corn?' Like a Victrola and the needle got stuck. Two days. They had a nurse living in the house. She slept in the living room."

She fell silent, unweeping, staring straight ahead. Michael didn't want to say anything. Mr. Rebeck did.

Presently she turned her head and looked at Mr. Rebeck. Her mouth twitched a little at the corners.

"They say Kaddish for Morris every Sabbath," she said, "over at Beth David. After I'm dead they'll be saying Kaddish for him. Every Sabbath until the sky falls." She leaned toward Mr. Rebeck, her breath warm and not unpleasantly sharp. "You think I'd forget Morris? You think I'd forget?"

"No," Mr. Rebeck said. "I don't think you would."

She leaned back, smoothing her black dress over her knees. Mr. Rebeck stared hard at the word WILDER over the mausoleum entrance until it blurred and flowed before his eyes. All I can think of to say, he thought, is "I like you," and that seems silly. Not to say inappropriate.

Presently Mrs. Klapper began to laugh softly. She laughs like a river, Mr. Rebeck thought, listening to the slow, rolling chuckle. She looked up at him.

"The nurse dyed her hair," she said, punctuating the words with laughter. "And she dyed it so lousy. Different patches black, red, and sort of brownish-blond. She looked like a box of crayons."

They laughed together then, the three of them, Mr.

Rebeck's laughter high and chortling; Mrs. Klapper's rich; Michael's dark and silent.

"You think I'm terrible, laughing like this?" Mrs. Klapper asked finally.

"No," Mr. Rebeck said. "No, I don't. You should see how much better you look now."

He hadn't meant that exactly the way it sounded, and he began to amend it, but Mrs. Klapper smiled.

"You have to laugh," she said. "Sooner or later, you have to laugh. How long can you cry?"

"Years," said Michael. Mrs. Klapper shook her head, as if she had heard him. "Sooner or later," she said, "you have to laugh."

She looked at a small gold wrist watch and got up quickly. "I have to go," she said. "My sister's bringing her daughter over for dinner. A little kid she is, my niece, a first-grader. Beautiful." She stretched the word until it twanged. "I better go make dinner."

"I'm going that way myself," Mr. Rebeck said a little timidly.

Mrs. Klapper laughed. "You don't even know which way I'm going."

"Lecherous old man," Michael said. "Control the clammy hands, Tarquin."

Mr. Rebeck felt himself flushing again. He took a wild shot. "The entrance near the subway," he said quickly. There had to be an entrance near a subway. Cemeteries were built like that.

Mrs. Klapper looked at him in surprise. "How did you know?"

"Well, it's the way you're going. There isn't any other entrance that way." Please God there isn't.

Mrs. Klapper nodded. She took a few steps away, stopped, and looked back at him. "So if you're coming," she said, "come."

His mood compounded of equal parts of fright and exhilaration, Mr. Rebeck got to his feet. He looked over at Michael a little appealingly.

"Don't let me stop you," Michael said. "Go dance your life away. Toil not, nor neither spin. I shall sit here and meditate." He waved a hand in the direction of Mrs. Klapper. "Just vanish. I always do."

So Mr. Rebeck took a few steps and found himself at Mrs. Klapper's side.

Michael watched them walk off down the winding path that led to Central Avenue. He felt a little sorry for Mrs. Klapper, sorrier for Mr. Rebeck, and sorriest of all for himself. Immersed in this feeling, he wandered contentedly around the little clearing, soaking in the feeling through what he remembered of his pores, letting himself become logy with sorrow.

A small blackhead erupted in the noon sky. Michael watched it spiral down toward him with a certain lazy interest, until, against the withered sun, he recognized the raven. He had grown used to the bird's regular visits and he enjoyed talking to him. The raven's mocking humor reminded him vaguely of a man whose name he no longer remembered, but with whom he had played cards.

The raven made two gliding passes at the clearing, missed both times, and finally let himself drop ungracefully to the grass. "Damn place ought to have a runway," he grumbled. He carried a small precooked beef tongue in his claws.

"Salutations, bird," Michael hailed him.

The raven ignored him. "Where's Rebeck?"

"Our mutual friend," Michael said, "has gone off with a lady."

"I thought that was him," the raven said. He dropped the beef tongue on the grass. "Tell him I'll bring some milk tonight, if I can get it." He peered at Michael. "What's biting you?"

"I'm desolate," Michael said, "and so should you be. We've been deserted. You're flesh and I'm air, but we are now united in mutual grief, maudlin sorrow, *Weltschmerz*, and bloody damn lonesomeness. I hail you again, winged and lonesome brother."

"Speak for yourself," the raven answered amiably. "I've had my breakfast."

Mr. Rebeck and Mrs. Klapper walked along the road, past the frozen fountains of the willow trees, and Mrs. Klapper talked about the place where she lived, and about the old woman who sat in front of her house on warm days, and about her niece, who was beautiful, and her butcher, who gave you bad meat unless you were a friend of his, and about her husband, who had died. They stopped sometimes to look at the high, empty houses and to admire the angels and children that watched over them, and the swords and sphinxes that guarded them. Then they walked on again, and Mr. Rebeck spoke once in a while, but for the most part he listened to Mrs. Klapper and took pleasure in her words.

He wondered why this should be, why the things this woman was saying should delight him so, particularly when he barely understood them. He knew very well that the great majority of human conversation is meaningless. A man can get through most of his days on stock answers to stock questions, he thought. Once he catches onto the game, he can manage with an assortment of grunts. This would not be so if people listened to each other, but they don't. They know that no one is going to say anything moving and important to them at that very moment. Anything important will be announced in the newspapers and reprinted for those who missed it. No one really wants to know how his neighbor is feeling, but he asks him anyway, because it is polite, and because he knows that his neighbor certainly will not tell him how he feels. What this woman and I say to each other is not important. It is the simple making of sounds that pleases us.

Mrs. Klapper was talking about a little boy who lived on her block. "Eleven years old," she said, "and every time I meet him with his mother, he's written a new poem. And

always she says to him, 'Herbie, tell Mrs. Klapper your new poem.' She hits him until he says the poem. Eleven years old he is, last March.''

"Are the poems any good?" Mr. Rebeck asked.

"What do I know from poems, I should give an opinion? They're all about death and burying people, always. This from a boy eleven years old. I feel like telling her, 'Look, keep him away from me with the obituary column. He writes a poem about a bird, about a dog, bring him around.' But I never tell her. Why should I hurt the boy's feelings? I see them coming, I cross the street.''

She said, "Look, here we are already," and Mr. Rebeck looked up to see the black gate.

The gate was of cast iron, set into turreted pillars of sand-colored concrete. Dark green ivy covered it, twined a little thicker than ivy generally grows, and cast-iron snakes with patient eyes pushed their resigned way through the ivy. It was topped with a row of blunt spikes, and it stood open. Mr. Rebeck could see the street outside.

"Here we are already," Mrs. Klapper marveled. "Such a short walk when you're talking to someone."

"Yes," Mr. Rebeck said.

The gate had held up well over nineteen years, he thought, much better than he himself had. The black paint had cracked in several places, and the rusted metal showed through. But it was a strong gate still. He had shaken it one night and rasped his hands on the mouths of rust, but the bars had not shivered, nor the lock rattled. That had been—how long ago? Twelve years, fifteen. All he remembered was that he had wanted to get out of the cemetery, and the gate had been locked, because it was late at night. He had shaken at the gate all night long, and cut his hands badly. But when the morning came, and the gate was opened, he did not go out. He hid in the lavatory and ran cold water on his bleeding hands. Then he went back to his mausoleum and slept.

"Well," Mrs. Klapper said. "You take the subway?"

He mumbled something affirmative, thinking, I should never have come with her. How can I tell her that I cannot pass the gate, that I live in this place? She would not believe me. She would think I was joking, or mad. I made a mistake when I asked to walk with her. I don't know why I did it.

"So come on," Mrs. Klapper said. She tapped her foot and smiled at him. "What are you waiting for? The subway should come to you?"

Yes. That would be a fine idea. If it did, I would get on it. We would go underground, and I would never see the gate, or know that I had left the cemetery until we climbed up a flight of stairs cut out of the ground, and people were all around us. I could manage that, if the subway came to me. And if I were with someone.

Looking at his thin wrist, he had an idea. He crooked his left arm in front of him and said, "Why, I've lost my watch."

"What's this?" Mrs. Klapper asked. "You lost something?"

"My wrist watch." He tried to smile ruefully, but only one corner of his mouth moved, and that twitched like something cut and in pain. "I know I had it on when I came in, and now it's gone. I must have dropped it somewhere."

Mrs. Klapper was properly sympathetic. "What a thing to happen. Was it very valuable, your watch?"

"No," he said, determined not to make this too much of a lie. "But I've had it a long time, and I was very fond of it. It kept good time."

"Tell the man there," Mrs. Klapper suggested, pointing toward the caretaker's office. "Give him your address, he'll let you know when he finds it."

Mr. Rebeck shook his had. "I'd better go back and look for it. Somebody might pick it up. Or it might rain."

"Ai, you'll go hunting all over the cemetery, it'll take hours. You'll break your back. You want I should come with you?"

Say no. Say no, or you'll have to lie to her again. And you're a terrible liar, and nineteen years out of practice.

"Don't bother," he said. "It's not worth it. I think I know where I dropped it. It's a very long walk."

"Well, I hope you find it," Mrs. Klapper said. "Get the man to help you if you can't find it by yourself."

They shook hands.

"It was very nice talking to you," Mr. Rebeck said. "I'm sorry we can't continue it."

Mrs. Klapper shrugged. "So maybe we'll meet again. You come around here a lot?"

"Yes. I like walking here."

"Me too. Anyway, I come to see Morris sometimes. So maybe we'll run into each other."

"Maybe," Mr. Rebeck said. "Good-by."

"Good-by. I hope you find your watch."

He did not wait to see her walk away. Instead, he turned quickly from her and walked back up the wide road, looking at the ground as a man would if he had lost something small and valued. Only when he reached the top of the hill did he turn and look back. She was gone by then.

I hate lying and saying good-by, he thought, because I am not very good at either.

4

The three people who had not left the cemetery stood over the grave. One of the men was less paunchy than the other. The woman's nails were broad and curved, the color of old milk.

"She was such a good girl," the woman said hoarsely. The men nodded.

"Not exactly," said Laura Durand. She sat on the grass next to Michael and looked at the three people. "I was just tired."

" 'Good' is the only word for her," said the younger man. He had a clear, precise voice. "The only word that really fitted her."

"All my life," said Laura, nodding.

"So young," the woman said. She swayed a little, and the old man put his arm around her.

"I was twenty-nine," Laura said, "pushing fifty. I told people I was thirty-three because it saved questions about why I liked books."

"And so pretty," the younger man said in his typewriter voice. "So alive, so vital."

"Oh, Gary," Laura murmured a little sadly. She turned to Michael. "I looked like an elementary-school teacher."

Gary patted the woman on the shoulder a good deal and craned his neck to look at his wrist watch.

"He wants to go back to the bookstore," Laura explained. "He gets nervous if he's away from it too long. Two years ago he had appendicitis, and they operated right on the Social Sciences counter."

"We were more than mother and daughter," the woman keened. "We were friends. Isn't that so, Carl?" The old man tightened his grip on her shoulders.

"Yes, Mother," Laura said softly. "Friendship's better than nothing." She half rose, then relaxed again. "Can I speak to them?" Michael shook his head.

"She was a wonderful worker." That was Gary again. "Efficient. Always there when I needed her. I don't know how I'm going to get along without her now."

"You'll manage, Gary," Laura said. "The world's full of me." She glanced at Michael. "I had a crush on him for a while, the kind of crush you get when you get fed up with square dancing at the YWCA. He never knew, and it went away gradually, like athlete's foot."

The old man spoke for the first time. His voice was low and slightly accented. "It is time to go, Marian."

"I don't want to leave her." The mother was weeping now, quietly and steadily. Gary took a handkerchief from his breast pocket and gave it to her.

"Gary always has a handkerchief," Laura said, smiling. "Matches, too."

"We had better go," Gary said, making a vague motion to the old man over the woman's bent head. "They probably close up soon."

"I don't want to go." Michael watched the tears slipping from under the handkerchief with a kind of greediness. He had not seen anyone cry for a long while.

"Marian—" the old man said again.

"Wait a little. Please wait a little."

"Go away!" Laura was suddenly on her feet, her arms pressed tightly against her sides. "Go away, damn it!" It looked to Michael as if she might cry herself, but he knew better. He remained seated, his legs crossed, and thought that she had nice hair.

The people were going away now. The woman was still crying. Gary and the old Carl flanked her, walking slowly and staring straight ahead. They looked, Michael thought, as if they had just seen a play they hadn't cared for, whose author was sure to ask their opinion the next morning. He watched them walk, observing through death-honed eyes the way their feet slid and scuffed through the scattered gravel; watching Carl put his hands in his pockets and take them out a few seconds later, over and over again; frowning with Gary when a pebble got into his shoe. The pebble felt very real against a hastily summoned up instep-memory as he watched the younger man shake his foot in a sidewise pawing motion. And he sighed with Gary when the pebble finally lodged under the arch of his foot.

Laura cried out suddenly and started to run after them. Her hands were stretched in front of her, as if she were about to fall, and she ran constrictedly and without grace.

"It's no good," Michael called after her. "You can't touch them"—but she had stopped already and was walking very quickly back toward him. Her hands were opening and shutting slowly, but she was quite calm.

"I don't know why I did that," she said, sitting next to him again. "I knew it was useless."

"Don't admit it," Michael said sharply. "Never admit it."

Laura looked a little puzzled. "I don't mind." She looked around her. "Are these foothills of Heaven? I'm sure I'll go to Heaven. I've been dull enough."

"This is the Yorkchester Cemetery," Michael answered, "and Heaven and Hell are only for the living."

"A pity." Laura tried to pluck a blade of grass, and Michael winced for her when her fingers went through it.

She showed no emotion, except for closing her hands and pressing them into her lap.

Michael vaguely remembered a very old book, its binding hanging in strings. He associated a quotation with it and felt a disproportionate pleasure in doing so. " 'Into Paradise,' " he said slowly, " 'go those aged priests and those old cripples, and the maimed, who all day long and all night cough before the altars. With them I have nought to do.' "

Laura looked up, smiling, and snapped her fingers silently. " 'But in hell will I go,' " she quoted triumphantly. " 'For to hell go the fair clerks and the fair knights . . . there go the fair and courteous ladies—' " She frowned and shook her head slightly. "I forget . . ."

" 'There go the fair and courteous ladies,' " Michael picked up, " 'who have friends, two or three, together with their wedded lords. And there pass the gold and silver, the ermine and all rich furs, harpers and minstrels, and the happy of the world.' "

Laura finished the last line with him. "I read that," she said, "when I was seventeen or eighteen and terribly sad. Where did you read it?"

"My wife liked it. She used to quote it all the time."

Laura was silent for a moment. "Funny. I know that by heart, and yet when I tried to remember it just now I felt it slipping out of my mind, squirming when I reached for it as if it were something wild I'd captured."

"Hang on to it as tightly as you can," Michael said, "as long as you can."

"I never hang on to things," Laura answered. "I'm in favor of setting things free." She rose and walked slowly over to her grave. "Don't I get a stone?" she asked. "I thought everybody got a headstone."

"I haven't got one either," Michael said. "I think it comes later. The ground has to get used to you."

"My stone will be small and very plain. Marian believes in simplicity. Just my name and my two big moments:

'Laura Durand. 1929–1958.' And a line of poetry." She hesitated and then smiled. " 'Hail to thee, blithe spirit.' I'd bet
on it."

"Give thanks. You might have gotten, 'I will arise and
go now.' "

"Oh, Mother's Poetry Club isn't up to Yeats yet," Laura
said. "Not till the week after Hopkins."

She reached out to touch the mound and pulled her hand
back. "Am I there? My body, I mean?" Michael did not
answer, nor did she turn to him. "How strange."

"How did you get out so fast?" Michael asked. "I took
a pretty long while getting out, but you sprouted like a
geranium before the funeral was even over."

"A nice image," Laura said.

"Thank you. You should have heard me when I was
alive." He waited for an answer. It was long in coming.

"Maybe you weren't quite ready to die," Laura said. "I
was way overdue."

Michael said nothing. They moved aimlessly away from
the grave, walking without purpose, without destination,
without consciousness of motion, but always with grace.
Michael turned his head to watch Laura move. The grass
did not bend under her feet, nor did the few fallen leaves
crackle indignantly. A small wind lifted the leaves and the
marshmallow-colored spores of a broken milkweed pod,
but not her hair.

Laura spoke very quietly, never once turning to him. "I
represent," she said, "five minutes of wasted effort on the
part of either God or my father. Death isn't so much of a
change. It's as if I lived high over a noisy city and couldn't
sleep because the window was jammed and the auto horns
reached over the windowsill. Now I've shut the window
and the horns have fallen back to the street. I'm very sleepy
and I want to go to bed." Michael heard her laugh softly.
"That's not a bad image, either. A little overwrought,
perhaps."

"I've wedged the window open," Michael said.

"Only in your room," said Laura, "and not for long."

They stood looking at each other, each seeing a gray film over a small portion of the world.

"I've been dead for two weeks," Michael said, "and I've learned a couple of things. The big difference between the dead and the living is that the dead don't care about anything."

"That explains a good deal."

Michael missed the sarcasm. "Yes, it does. Caring about things is much more important to the dead because it's all they have to keep them conscious. Without it they fade, dwindle, thin to the texture of a whisper. The same thing happens to people, but nobody notices it because their bodies act as masks. The dead have no masks. They left them behind."

"Go on."

"A man I met told me all this a while ago. I didn't understand it at all then. I do now. What he didn't tell me was that, if you struggle, you can stay awake. It's like freezing. You have to keep walking up and down and stamping your feet. Otherwise the cold gets you."

"Here, too," Laura whispered, looking away from him. "I thought it might be warm."

"That's the easy way," Michael said. "That's what all the others did; wrapped themselves in the earth and fell asleep. All of them. I woke a couple up and tried to make them talk to me, but their talk was like snoring." His tone was full of contempt. "They've forgotten everything. Their minds have turned to sand. I still remember. I've forgotten a few things, but important ones I keep."

"Yes. It probably takes longer to forget the important things."

Michael shook his head. "No. It's a sort of weeding-out process—like picking out ten books to be cast away with. You'll see." He smiled, mentally admitting the conscious effort it was but hoping that the girl did not notice. "I'm glad you're here. We can make things easier for each other. That's part of being alive."

Laura turned abruptly and began to walk slowly back toward her grave. Michael followed, puzzled. "Where are you going?"

"To sleep," Laura said over her shoulder. "That's part of being alive too."

"Wait a minute!" Michael called. "Don't leave me alone!"

"Why not? That's another part of life. The big one. You can't have forgotten that—it's too important. If you want to be alive, you have to accept all the parts. You can't choose and you can't reject what doesn't please you. That's the privilege of the dead."

"You have to fight!" Michael shouted after her. "I know that now. Giving up the fight is death."

Laura stopped and faced him. "Death is not having to fight any more, either for yourself or for other people. I don't care what you do with your afterlife. You can take woodworking courses, or play correspondence chess, or subscribe to a lot of magazines, or start a repertory theater. Just do it quietly. I'm tired, and I've been up much too late."

Michael ran after her and caught up with her at the grave. She was standing quietly, looking at the grass. "What killed you?" he demanded. He felt clumsy and exceedingly pompous, but he also felt himself washed in anger, and the feeling was familiar and very pleasant. "Were you bored to death?"

"I was hit by a truck," Laura said, "and all of a sudden everybody realized that I was dead. Go away, whatever your name is—"

"Michael Morgan."

"That's fine. Go away, Michael Morgan, and write a letter to the editor. Fight the brave fight. The result is the same as the cowardly fight. The brave fight is just a retreat with publicity. You'll have a fine time. I'm going to sleep."

She lay down on her grave and promptly began to experience difficulty in disposing of her arms. She folded them on her breast, spread them out in the position of a crucifix, kept them to her sides, and finally crossed them on her stomach. She closed her eyes and almost immediately opened them again to look up at Michael.

"Now what? Do I just lie here, on top of the blankets, as it were, or can I get back into my coffin?"

"You can't go back," Michael said coldly. "Once you're out, you're out. Just lie there and think how nice it is without those damn birds waking you up every morning."

Laura smiled and closed her eyes. Michael turned and walked off. He thought he heard her say, "Good night, Michael," but he kept walking, furious at the contentment in her voice. He was sure he heard her laugh.

Out of sight of her grave, he sat down on a stone. He was so angry that he forgot what sitting down was like and got all snarled up in midair. On the fourth try he made it and sat with his remembered chin in recalled hand. He remembered the size and shape of his hands pretty well, but he had never taken much interest in his face and, as a result, its remembered corners and angles varied considerably from moment to moment. Right now his chin was more pointed than it had been, and more angled from his jawline, but he had forgotten.

She took the easy way out, he thought. Fall asleep— forget everything—be nothing. That's not my way. He thought of the athletes and Big Men on Campus he had known during his college career. The athletes towered over him on the stairs and talked to one another in short, heavy sentences, and he felt properly scornful of their gum-chewing acceptance of life, their C's in the two-credit psychology courses they took, and, most of all, their laughing, ring-waisted girls. I'm bound to a higher road, he had told himself, and possessed by a much more demanding mistress. He spent a few wistful seconds imagining the mistress. The Big Men chatted pleasantly in the halls, in the cafeteria, speaking of dances, pep rallies, student productions, elections, and fund-raising drives. They were neatly dressed, they belonged to honorary fraternities, and when they were asked questions in classes they managed somehow to make a speech out of the answer. The football players greeted them as equals; *they* greeted the football players as inferiors but fine fellows nevertheless. And when they graduated public-relations firms and advertising companies snapped them up as if they were after-dinner mints.

Phonies, Michael had thought and, sitting on the stone, thought again. False and phoney. Not for me, boy. I'm awake. I'm conscious. I know that life is strange, surprising, cruel, merciless, real, earnest. Check one. Let them be applauded, subsidized, loved; I've got my integrity.

He had used the word "integrity" often in college and managed to irritate a good many people with it. Most of them were professors. One, an associate in the English Department, had snapped, "Morgan, you have no more knowledge of the meaning of that word than a barracuda."

Michael had been indignant. "It means being true to yourself, whatever yourself is," he retorted. "And I like to think I'm true to myself."

"Mmmm," said the professor thoughtfully. "Well, cheat a little. A bit of adultery would do you a lot of good."

He had been sure of no one's honesty but his own and prided himself on the honesty with which he admitted the honesty of his reasoning. Now he wasn't quite sure. "For a wild minute there," he said aloud, "I thought I had the answer to death." He thought of the girl.

Remembering Laura Durand smiling on the grass of her grave, familiar and at ease with death, he felt tired and as sick of himself as he had ever felt after fighting with Sandra. I must be a bit of a manic-depressive, he thought wearily, and then descended into happy self-abasement as curiously as if he had been going down a stone stairway into a cellar nightclub he had never before visited. He decided, among other things, that he had not only been a fool to enlist in the Korean War, he had been something of a hypocrite to come out of it alive. He had about concluded that he would go and say good-by to Mr. Rebeck, whose patience he now regarded as Christlike, if pointless, and then find his own grave and let the straining muscles of his memory go limp, when he saw Laura walking slowly toward him.

First he felt like springing up and running to meet her. Then he thought he would wait for her to reach him and then say, "The bathroom's back near the entrance"—oh, real heavy, real Sinatra. Don't come sneaking around *me,* lady. This is Michael Morgan, as pure as mountain spring water, as unforgiving as God. Finally he sat where he was, looking at the ground as if he had lost something.

Her legs came gradually into his field of vision and stopped. She was looking down at him, he knew, and he waited impatiently for her to say something. He wondered if ghosts ever had nervous breakdowns.

"Hello, Michael," she said finally. He looked up and blinked in surprise. Admirable, laddy, admirable. These honored dead have not died in vain.

"I didn't hear you coming."

Laura smiled faintly. "The dead make good neighbors." She paused. He did not budge. Budge thee not, boy. As immovable as Kafka's doorman.

"I don't want to go to sleep right away," she said. "After all"—fumbling for words—"I've got time enough. I thought—if you weren't doing anything"—neither of them laughed—"we could walk a little. I don't know this place at all—" She faltered under what Michael fondly believed was an unwinking glare. "All right. I couldn't fall asleep. I'm still conscious and I might as well do something with it. Will you come or not? It doesn't matter to me."

Michael got up and began to walk toward the Old Rich section of the cemetery. "Come on," he said.

Laura came up alongside him. "Where are we going?"

Michael spoke so low she could barely hear him. "I know. I do know now. The dead can't sleep." He looked inquiringly at her, and she nodded.

"When I closed my eyes—it didn't make any difference. It was just as if I had them open."

"We don't sleep," Michael said. "We doze from time to time. The ones I talked to were just pretending to have been asleep. Pretending—to themselves more than me." He quickened his stride.

"Where are we going?"

"To see a man."

"A ghost?"

"No, a man. I wasn't sure till just now."

"Would you have believed me?" Mr. Rebeck asked. He sat on the steps of the Wilder mausoleum, looking thin and fine-boned in an old black-and-white-checked bathrobe.

"Probably not," said Michael. "You could have tried, though."

"Good heavens, you had enough trouble believing you were dead. And I didn't convince you of that—you convinced yourself." Mr. Rebeck hesitated, arranging his words as if they were a gin hand: "In our society, you have two choices, two possible beliefs. Either you go somewhere after you die, or you don't. Either you sing very loudly through eternity, or else you sleep quietly until the world crumbles away around you and you go sailing on through space, unwaking and unwakened. Neither belief is true, but you have to find that out for yourself."

"I was hoping for sleep," Laura said. "My last word on earth was probably 'Hurrah!' "

"You'll drowse," Mr. Rebeck answered, "and that's almost like sleeping. In time, sleep won't mean anything to you because you'll lose the concept. You won't know whether you're awake or asleep, and it won't really matter." He paused. "And you're still on earth. There isn't any special world for the dead, only cold rooms the living grant them out of respect for their used bodies. There is only earth."

He realized that a certain oracular solemnity had been

wedging its way into his words, but he could think of nothing to say to relieve its weight. Looking at the man and woman, he thought tiredly that things always became complicated in the end; webs became tangled whether the spider's intent was to deceive or not. He liked this man and woman very much, and he wished they wouldn't make him phrase things he himself wasn't sure of until he spoke them. He was neither God nor the First Gravedigger—and then there was Mrs. Klapper.

Laura was saying something. A mellifluous name, he thought. I wish she were far away, so I could call her.

"How long will it take?" Laura was asking.

Mr. Rebeck blinked. "I beg your pardon?"

"Forgetting. Disintegrating. Letting things go."

"Oh, I see." Of course, Michael would have told her. "It depends. A month seems to be about average."

"A month? What happens then?"

"I don't know." Of course I don't know. I'm not the Answer Man. He wondered if that program was still on the radio. Probably not. He should have asked Mrs. Klapper.

"I can wait," Laura said.

Michael laughed. "You'll have to."

Laura looked at him as if he were something half-eaten and discarded. "What a wonderful Messiah you'd have made."

"True. My first miracle would have been raising you from the dead. With a steam shovel probably."

"You're like an old man in a small town," Laura said, "who used to be somebody important and still hangs around the place where he used to work, making speeches on holidays and playing at still being important."

"Maybe," Michael said tightly. "But I'll sit on your grave each Christmas and sing carols to you."

"Oh, for God's sake," Mr. Rebeck thought, "shut up!"

Not until he saw the astonished looks on their faces did he realize that he had said it aloud. Committed, he charged on. "What difference does it make which of you remembers his name longer? You're both dead. That may be the only thing you have in common, but it's a big one. You make my head hurt. If you feel like bickering so much, go off and yap among the stones. Death ought to be a quiet, easy thing, like love. You spend your time yelling that you won't sleep or that you can't sleep, when you don't even know what sleep is."

He saw the childishly startled looks on their translucent faces and suddenly could think of nothing else to say. He had not shouted at anybody for a very long while, and his voice sounded echoey and cavernous. A crazy image of bats nesting in his cheeks and hanging head down from the roof of his mouth scuttled across his mind, and he very nearly giggled.

"I've been here quite a long time, you know," he added. Then he sat and looked away because he was finished speaking.

Laura started to say something but called it back. She made a small, meaningless gesture to Michael, who nodded and leaned forward, hoping that Mr. Rebeck would look up at him. "Why did you come here?"

Mr. Rebeck did look up then. "I died, like everybody else," he said; then, seeing Laura wince, added, "No, that's too easy to say and not really true." He looked at Michael. "I told you I used to be a druggist, I think."

Michael nodded.

"I had a nice drugstore," Mr. Rebeck said. "It smelled. I mean, it was clean but it smelled nice. Like gunpowder and cinnamon, with a little chocolate, maybe. I had a bell that rang when somebody opened the door, and it rang for whatever a person needed, whether it was on his prescription or not. And I had a pair of scales that could weigh a man's heart. I didn't have a soda fountain, but I had a jar of candy to give the children when they came in to buy cough syrup or razor blades. Coltsfoot candy, they called it. I don't know why. It came in long yellow sticks. I don't think they sell it any more. I had everything any other druggist in New York had, and a little wolfbane besides."

A small breeze had sprung up, and Mr. Rebeck pulled his bathrobe closer around him and put his hands in the pockets.

"Once a man asked me to make a love potion for him. He was a good man, but very ugly, with a scarred face. He was a fighter, I think, because of his ears, and because he used to come in and have coffee with me and talk about boxing. There was a girl who used to come in and sit with us sometimes. She looked a little like you, Laura, only her hair was blond. A very smart girl. The man asked me to make up something to make her love him. He was ashamed of his face, you see, and he thought it would be so easy for me to do, like whipping up a malted. I couldn't do it, of course, not really, because it's illegal, and I didn't know how anyway. But I told him I would, only it wouldn't make her aggressive, just receptive. He'd still have to do the asking, face or no face."

He smiled, thinking about it. "She was a very nice girl, and I think she loved him anyway. But after that, everybody started to come in, asking for love potions and horoscopes and lucky charms and wanting to know what their dreams meant. People are unhappy, you know, and they'll try anything to change their luck. They acted as if I were a witch or a tame warlock, pleading with me to make their children well or make their husbands quit drinking. I told them I couldn't do it, that I wasn't a magician, and some wept and some cursed me. Those were very sad curses, without much strength. So I made a very big mistake. I said I would try.

"I thought, I am a druggist. I try to help sick people. These people are sick also, in a different way. Perhaps I could help them in a different way. And I tried, which was wrong, because there isn't any magic in the world. But they needed me, I thought, and a man must be needed. So I ground up harmless little herbs and told them to sprinkle them in their food, and I told them to sleep with little bags of flour under their pillows and their dreams would be good. I was a witch doctor, a witch doctor in New York. I hadn't meant to be, but I was. And, to make matters worse, I wasn't a very good witch doctor. Sometimes I was lucky, sometimes I guessed right and the child got well, or the number was the right one. But not very often. The people who didn't believe in all this mumbo-jumbo stopped coming, and the people who did believe stopped coming because it wasn't very effective mumbo-jumbo."

Mr. Rebeck's hands twisted the belt of the robe around and around each other, but he was still smiling faintly. "Only the really dedicated crackpots remained, and a druggist is probably the one man in the world who can't find some use for them. But I served them because they were lonely and they believed in me. I was their prophet, a prophet fallen on evil days, perhaps, but not without honor. So I felt a little important sometimes."

He began to laugh quietly, in genuine amusement, smoothing his thin hair with a brown hand. "I knew something was going to happen sooner or later. What I was doing was illegal for anybody, and twice as criminal for a druggist. If a new customer came into the store—which did happen every once in a while—I'd have to brace myself against the counter to keep from running. Policemen always frightened me when I was young, and besides I was afraid I'd lose my license if anybody started checking up on me. And there wasn't anything else in the world I was equipped to do."

He settled back against one of the cracked pillars that fended off the sky from the Wilder tomb. "And then the funniest thing happened, the most logical thing in the world. I went bankrupt." Mr. Rebeck, having a good sense of the dramatic, paused for a moment and then went on. "I couldn't pay the rent, I couldn't pay for my stock, I couldn't pay for upkeep, I couldn't pay for electricity, and I couldn't pay the lawyer who told the court I couldn't pay for anything. When I left that court I'd have gone over the hill to the poorhouse, except that the city didn't have a poorhouse, and I didn't have the carfare."

"And you came here?" Laura had not taken her eyes from his face.

"No," said Mr. Rebeck. "Not right away. I was still young, you know, about Michael's age. I thought, Jonathan, you've got your whole life ahead of you, and you can't very well spend it living off oranges and cigarette butts. So I got a job as a clerk in a grocery because they let me sleep in the back of the store. I worked there for a couple of months and saved up some money and bought some new shirts. Then I went for a walk one night and passed the place where my store used to be. They had built a chain drugstore there. A big, clean drugstore with a counter made of green marble."

Now he did look away, clasping his hands tightly together. "And I thought," he said very softly, "how funny it all was. Because they were doing the same thing I'd been doing, only with advertising. Their signs said, 'We will make you beautiful, we will make you smell good, we will cure your kidney stones and your hemorrhoids and your bad breath and your dandruff and your bad manners. We will smooth your skin and pluck away forty pounds as if we were removing a wart—which we also do very well— and people will want to talk to you. Come unto us, all ye that are ugly and ill-tempered and alone—' " He paused. "It's wrong to promise magic to people. It was wrong when I did it, and it was wrong for this clean new drugstore. I walked a long way that night, thinking many philosophic thoughts which, fortunately, I don't remember." He laughed shortly and fell silent.

"And then?" Michael's voice jerked Mr. Rebeck's head around sharply, as if there had been a string between them.

"Then," Mr. Rebeck answered calmly, "I got drunk enough for a wedding and a wake put together and I wandered in here, singing to myself—they just latched the gate in those days—and I fell asleep on the top step here and slept for a day."

He shrugged. "And there you are. I stayed. At first I thought I'd just rest for a while, because I was very tired, but the raven brought me food—" He grinned suddenly. "The raven was there when I woke up, waiting for me. He told me he'd bring me food as long as I stayed, and when I asked why, he said it was because we had one thing in common. We both had delusions of kindness."

Mr. Rebeck yawned. "I'm tired," he said, almost apologetically, "and I want to go to bed." He stood up and stretched, and the bathrobe tightened around his thin body.

"I told you death was like life, Michael," he said sleepily. "It doesn't make very much difference whether you fight or not." He turned to Laura. "Except to you. Each man's death is his own concern, and whether he sleeps or doesn't sleep is of less importance than how he accepts it—or how he rationalizes it." He walked slowly to the mausoleum door and turned. "Good night."

"Good night," they said. "Good night."

He closed the door, took off his robe, and lay down on a mattress made largely out of small cushions arranged in a pattern that kept him reasonably comfortable. He pulled a blanket over himself and lay quietly on his back, staring at the ceiling.

Someone spoke his name, and he realized that Michael was in the room. He had wondered how long it would take Michael to realize that no physical barriers affected him now. "Yes, Michael?"

"Would you do me a favor?"

"Probably. What is it?"

Michael's voice was hesitant. "Could you tell me—could you tell me how this girl looks?"

"Laura?"

"Mmm-hmm. I'm just curious."

"You can't see her, I gather?"

"Just as a sort of general outline. Hair, shape—I know she's a woman, but that's about it."

"Yes," said Mr. Rebeck. He was silent.

"Well?"

"Oh. Well, she's dark. Her eyes are gray, I think, and she has long fingers."

"Is that all?"

"Michael, what difference can it make now?"

"None," said Michael after a moment. "I was just curious. Sorry I bothered you."

"Good night."

Michael was gone. It will be a nice summer. Mr. Rebeck said to himself. I've needed company.

He thought about the autumn. He had never liked the season, partly because looking ahead to it spoiled the spring a little for him. I look too far ahead, he thought, because I am afraid of suddenly coming face to face with things. He had never been able to enjoy the Christmas holidays in his childhood because they seemed to skid him helplessly toward the long January.

But the night was warm and scented, and he dismissed the autumn. It will come, he thought, as it always does. But first, the summer.

5

Mrs. Klapper had set the alarm for nine-thirty, and now she waited patiently for it to ring. She lay on her side, facing away from the clock, her legs drawn up and one arm under the pillow. The blankets had been pulled so tightly up to her chin that they had come loose at the end of the bed and her feet were uncovered. She crossed her ankles and rubbed her feet against each other, but her feet remained cold, and she felt oddly vulnerable.

Rolling over on her back, she flung out an arm and became aware, as she did every morning, that nobody was there to be hit and snarl a complaint out of a half-dream.

The bed was too big, she thought. She'd go down to Sachs today or tomorrow and trade it in. "What do you need with a double bed, Klapper?" she demanded of the ceiling. "You expecting guests?"

The alarm clock made a small, self-satisfied click, and Mrs. Klapper tensed in expectancy. But the alarm did not ring, and the clock hummed innocently to itself. "So ring already!" Mrs. Klapper relaxed disgustedly. "It's by now ten o'clock, ten-thirty. What do you want, I should send you an engraved invitation?" The clock expressed no preference.

"Ai, the wonders of science," said Mrs. Klapper and turned groaningly over to look at the clock face. Her eyes looked cautiously out through her heavy lids, like two sentinels spying out enemy territory. She brushed her hair away from her face and looked closer at the dial. "You're supposed to glow in the dark, you know," she reminded it conversationally. "So glow a little." She finally made out the time to be nine-fifteen.

Mrs. Klapper fell back onto the pillow. "Fifteen minutes. I still got fifteen minutes." She was silent, then turned back to shout at the clock, "So what do I do for fifteen minutes? Tell myself jokes?" She turned over and burrowed into the pillow.

She could always get up, of course, she thought. It would at least give her the pleasure of shutting off the alarm. The idea delighted her. She reached out an arm toward the clock and then pulled it back. There wasn't any rush.

If I don't get up, she thought, I'll get such a headache. That nearly got her out of bed; she feared pain and endured it, when it came, with the stoicism of the deeply afraid. She pushed the covers back and started to sit up. Halfway erect, she changed her mind. And if I get up, all I got to look forward to is not getting a headache. Big deal. She lay down again.

An urge possessed her to look over her shoulder at the clock and find out how many minutes she had to go before she could get up in honesty. But that would have been a moral victory for the clock, and Mrs. Klapper knew the value of moral victories. She collected them. So she lay motionless, one arm lying heavy on her thigh, and thought quite directly about the strange small man in the cemetery. She had thought about him a lot during the twelve days that had passed since she had visited her husband's tomb.

The small man bothered her because she could not come to any definite conclusion about him. A gentleman, she had decided tentatively. A gentleman with a screw loose. But the decision did not satisfy her. Mrs. Klapper had met gentlemen with screws loose before; Morris's law firm had seemed to specialize in them. The man she had met was not one of these.

This clock was electric and guaranteed noiseless. Actually, it made a small humming sound that Mrs. Klapper found infinitely annoying. Ticking she understood, and she loved the sound for the memories it brought back of the nights when she and Morris had lain side by side on the low bed with the thin mattress and there had been no sound but the jagged ticktock teeth biting pieces out of the night. Sometimes, if she listened for a long while, the ticking had seemed to speed up, to rush and thunder through dark tunnels in search of something just ahead, something that would be waiting only a little farther on, hunched and glowing redly. Then she would grasp Morris's arm, as if it were a banister on a long and crooked stairway, and pull herself close to him, holding him so tightly that he would move sleepily and say, "Gertrude, a little air here, please. You are not married to an accordion."

And then it would be all right. Morris was there, solid and warm and complaining, and the clock was just a clock, and she would just lie awake for a minute more, breathing deeply and quietly, and then she would turn in to face Morris and go to sleep—

The alarm went off, buzzing like a dentist's drill, and Mrs. Klapper sprang out of bed and pounced on it, shutting it off. Then she sat on the edge of the bed and said, "Hell," in an abstracted tone. Her head did hurt a little.

She got up and went from window to window, opening the blinds to let the sun flow into the big room. Standing in the sunlight, blinking a bit, she stretched and yawned with the same sensual appreciation of a good stretch and yawn that animals and children have. "A little exercise maybe, Klapper?" she asked herself aloud. "Bend down and touch your toes." Looking incuriously at her bare feet, she decided against it. "Silly way to start the morning."

Wandering slowly in the direction of her dresser, she caught sight of herself in the full-length mirror set into the closet door. She began to take off the faded blue pajamas. "*Vey Gott*, Klapper, you look like a bunch of bananas." She opened the closet quickly and looked inside for a slip.

Mrs. Klapper dressed slowly, picking her clothes carefully. It was hot already; wherever she turned, she could feel the sun on the back of her neck. She made a mental note to take a shower that night, and to wash her hair as well. As she dressed, she sang a small song about a girl whose mother offered her a choice of husbands-elect, all of them rich, successful men, but who refused them all to marry a penniless rabbinical student. "Dope," she said at the end of the song, as she always did, but, as always, she said it with kindness.

Dressed, her face washed—she had worn no makeup since Morris's death—she went into the kitchen to boil a couple of eggs. She set the timer for fifteen minutes, because she liked her eggs hard and firm, and because it was fifteen minutes during which she could move quickly around in the kitchen, running water and shutting it off, lighting small fires on the stove and then turning them off, ferreting in the refrigerator and cupboards, planning her meals for the rest of the day, and sometimes the days beyond. The dining room was quiet and much too big, and she did not like eating there any more. She continued eating at the too long table, however, because she was very much a creature of habit. Habits were secure and comforting and lent a certain purpose to the day.

She made toast as an afterthought and brought it and the eggs into the dining room. After setting them on the table, she went back into the kitchen for a container of milk. Mrs. Klapper ate with gusto, for she enjoyed food.

While she ate, she thought about Mr. Rebeck again. His abrupt leave-taking at the cemetery gates bothered her. So maybe he did lose his watch, she reflected. This happens. She stabbed the last of the boiled eggs with her fork. But to walk all the way back to find it, and not knowing if maybe you dropped it along the way or lost it on the subway or left it home—this, believe me, is crazy. She shrugged, spreading the toast with cherry preserve. So maybe he's got a wife, he doesn't want to go home just yet. Don't be nosy, Klapper.

Did he have a wife? Mrs. Klapper bit off a piece of toast, liking the crunching sound. Since when does a married man go wandering around a graveyard like he's taking inventory? A married man goes to a graveyard, he goes to see his wife's relatives. Maybe he wasn't married, then.

He did look like Morris, she thought. Morris was a little bigger, maybe, and his eyebrows were bushy, like the tails of angry cats, but the eyes were the same, and the shape of the head. Morris crouched over whatever he was doing, whether it was playing chess, reading a book, or preparing a brief. She had teased him about it, saying, "Morris, you keep on sitting like that, you will go to your grave hunchbacked. A special wing they'll have to stick onto your coffin."

Morris had given that slight laugh of his that you could miss if you weren't listening closely and said, "I like to think of myself as looking like a question mark." And now, seeing this small man playing chess all by himself, hunched over the board as if he were about to spring on it—

"Stop it, Klapper," she said sharply. "You are a grown woman. An overgrown woman, if I may say so." She poured a glass of milk, gulped it hastily, and took the dishes back into the kitchen.

After washing the dishes, which she did with much unnecessary splashing of water and fiddling with the faucets, she opened the broom closet near the refrigerator and took out a broom and a dustpan. She was not a good sweeper. The motion utilized in sweeping is not a particularly natural one, nor is it usually graceful, and the quality of the sweeper can almost always be judged directly from his form. Mrs. Klapper swept the floor as if she were expecting it to wince under the broom. She hated dustpans because whenever she squatted down and choked up on the broomhandle to sweep the dirt into the pan there was always a little dust left over at the rim. She would move the pan back and, subvocalizing curses, attack the dust again. But there would always be a thread of dust left on the floor, and she would finally rise with a snort of disgust and sweep the dust under the refrigerator.

Her sweeping finished, she looked at the wall clock. "Ten-forty," she said. "Good. See, it goes faster than you think. You got to keep busy." She remembered her sister's saying that to her. Maybe she ought to visit Ida today. Anyway, she ought to go out. She put away the broom and pan and went to look out of the window.

"Ai," she said softly, "such a morning." The sun was high and hot, dazzling her with its reflection off thousands of windows. She turned and walked slowly into the living room. It was a big room, lined on three sides by Morris's bookcases. Mrs. Klapper had had it refurnished a month ago and was sorry about it now. The new chairs and the new sofa were plump, springy, and ungiving. They could not be pounded or worn into comfort. As soon as the momentary brightness they had brought into the house was gone, she had wanted the old ones back.

"So what do I do today?" She leaned against a bookcase and ran her hands idly over Morris's books. They were always "Morris's books." Mrs. Klapper did not read much, nor had Morris, after a few teasing attempts in the first years of their marriage, ever made any serious efforts to get her to read. She had liked to be read to, but she always fell asleep, and Morris had smiled, patted her affectionately, and played chess with himself.

"I got to go shopping." She counted on her fingers. "Let's see—I got to go by Wireman's and get a loaf of bread, and some milk, and baking powder maybe—" She frowned. There must be something else. Wireman's was just two blocks away.

"If I go to Ida's I go past the butcher near the subway, and I could stop in and get maybe a pound chopped meat and a couple lamb chops." She *would* go to see Ida, then. "My own sister, you'd think I'd say hello once in a while. We're like strangers." Ida, the older of Mrs. Klapper's two sisters, had never married, and Mrs. Klapper had never felt right about bringing Morris over for supper. During the twenty-two years of her marriage she had snatched an awkward, silent lunch with her sister no more than twice a year.

Always, she remembered, always the look in the back of her eyes. I talk to her, I make jokes so she laughs and says, "Ai, Gertrude, everything changes but you"—and always, in back of the laughter: *This one also has a man, and I got nobody.* A look like that, you choke on your celery. What can you say?

Now, she thought, it might be all right to go to Ida.

The living room had always been Morris's domain, just as the bedroom had been hers. Each had intruded into the other's realm with something of the arrogance and curiosity of king visiting king. Morris was dead, but the room was still loyal to him, and the stranger pictures on the walls stared at her with the hatred of the conquered. She left the room quickly and went to the closet to get a light coat.

So I'll go see Ida, she thought, rummaging in her purse to make sure she had enough money, and we'll have lunch and talk about things and maybe take a walk in the park, and then I'll say, "Look, Ida, I got all this food; I got a whole pound chopped meat and nobody but me to eat it. Come on home with me and we'll make hamburgers and schmooze like we used to."

The idea pleased her. She won't go till late, she thought. That well I know Ida.

At the door she paused and muttered, "*Sei gesund,* Morris." She had never been able to break herself of the habit of saying "Be well" to her husband before she left the house, nor did she really want to; but she whisked the door shut behind her as she always did to keep herself from waiting for the soft "*Geh gesund*" from the living room.

Outside the air was warm and dry, and she breathed it with real pleasure as she walked slowly toward the grocery. Early summer in New York is at its most beautiful in the mornings, but few people ever notice it. The children go away to summer camps, and their parents' two weeks off usually come in late July or early August, when the days are sticky with boredom. Only old people know these early summer mornings, old people and the men who sell ice cream in public parks. They know these mornings well and love them desperately because they cannot last—these people who know that nothing lasts. The vendor buys an ice-cream cup from himself and sits down on the grass to eat it, or at least he thinks about doing it. The policeman sings to himself and stops to talk with the candy-store man, who has come out to get a little air before the wind becomes hot and sour. They talk about going swimming or going to the ball game, but it is enough for them to be there on the street corner talking to each other about it. And the old women move their chairs to follow the sun and do not speak to each other at all. They will in the afternoon, but that will be a different season, a different world. Now, in the morning, they stare across the street and do not blink when the cars go by.

Mrs. Klapper knew some of these women, but she did not nod to them as she passed the line of folding chairs. In a vague sort of way, she had always felt a certain contempt for them. She thought of them as *yentas*. Some of them aren't any older than me, she thought, and they sit there like stones and don't knit or read the papers or anything. What kind of way is that to live? You got to keep busy, keep moving, visit people. She walked faster, pleased with her decision to see Ida, and turned into Wireman's Dairy Grocery.

Wireman was behind the counter, a small pear-shaped man in a gray sweater and brown slacks. His eyes were black and sleepy, and he kept them fixed directly on whomever he was talking to. The skin on both sides of his wide face was slack and sagging, giving the effect not so much of jowls as of a face relaxing and crumpling like a robe thrown carelessly into a corner. He had been established on the corner before Mrs. Klapper and Morris had moved into the neighborhood, and she could not remember him as looking any different then or as changing notably during the twenty-two years. His wife, his children, his store had all grown, aged, and expanded during the time, but Wireman remained Wireman. She always wondered how she looked to him.

"So," he said when she came in. "So how are you today?"

"Just fine," Mrs. Klapper said. "How's your wife?" She nodded to his daughter, Sarah, who was sitting on an empty milk-bottle crate, reading a magazine.

"Who can complain?" Wireman shrugged. "She's on her feet, she eats. More you shouldn't ask from God."

"You hear from Sam lately?" Wireman's son had married six months before and moved to the West Coast.

Wireman looked quickly over his shoulder into the back of the store. When he turned back to her his face had gone dead. "No. What can I do for you?"

"A loaf rye bread," Mrs. Klapper said; "should be seedless. Also two bottles milk and a can of baking powder."

As Wireman turned to go to the back of the store, where his refrigerator was, Mrs. Klapper suddenly became freezingly aware of the way he walked. His shoulders were humped under the gray sweater, and he walked with small steps, one foot sliding ahead of the other and the other foot hurrying to catch up. His hands made very small pawing motions at his sides, and he looked as if over the years the air in which he moved had gradually changed to water.

"So old," Mrs. Klapper said aloud, and then realized that

Sarah must have heard her. She looked guiltily at her; the girl nodded and kept reading her magazine.

"So, Sarah," she said because she could not bear the silence. "How are you doing?"

"Fine," said Sarah. How old was she—eighteen, nineteen? She was fat for her age, pimpled, and, Mrs. Klapper had always suspected, the brightest in the family.

"When you getting married already?" she asked loudly and was completely disgusted with herself when she saw the anger in Sarah's eyes. What do you care? she demanded of herself. Why is everybody around here so interested when everybody's getting married?

Sarah Wireman smiled determinedly. "Not right away, Mrs. Klapper." Her voice was completely without inflection, and Mrs. Klapper knew that she had given the same answer to a great many other old women while her father was getting their orders. She didn't want Sarah to lump her with those women, but she knew she had a long time ago, and she kept talking, thinking that there must surely be a sentence to remedy the situation.

"Well, you'll pretty soon be an aunt," she announced, thinking, Klapper, shut up! Just keep the mouth shut, please.

The girl's smile was as straight and thin as a dagger. "I sure hope so, Mrs. Klapper."

Shut up, shut up, Klapper! What are you becoming? She turned away from Sarah and stared hard at the Wheaties, Kix, and corn-flakes packages that lined one wall of the store. She could hear the girl's soft sigh of relief, and she herself sighed as if she had just gotten off an elevator in which she and a stranger had carefully not looked at each other. Then Wireman was shuffling in with her bread and milk and baking powder, putting them on the counter, and adding up her bill, mumbling the sums to himself as he wrote out the total. "You want I should charge you?"

"Yes," Mrs. Klapper answered. Wireman put the order

in a brown paper bag and stuffed the bill in after it. She took the bag and started for the door.

"Tell your wife I said hello." She closed the door behind her, cutting off Wireman's short reply.

Having decided to visit Ida, she hoisted her bag into the crook of her left arm and set off down the block. The sun restored her good humor, and in two blocks' walking she had almost forgotten the weary politeness in Sarah Wireman's voice.

A figure was coming up the street toward her, but it took her a while to identify it because she was looking into the sun. When she finally recognized Lena Wireman she winced. *Vey*, she thought, now comes the heavy artillery. Maybe if she hoisted her shopping bag up in front of her face, Mrs. Wireman might not recognize her. But she had no real hope for this; she was one of the few women in the neighborhood who bothered to speak to Mrs. Wireman, and Mrs. Wireman knew her own.

She was a thin woman who had once been fat. Skin hung loosely on her forearms, between her knuckles, and around her elbows. The flesh was orange-white and seemed almost transparent. She always wore flat-heeled white shoes, having admired them on nurses, and tied her hair on top of her head in a knot about the size and shape of a prune. Once she had worked in the store with her husband, but for the last ten or twelve years she had sat in a metal-and-cloth chair in front of the store when it was warm, or on a milk-bottle crate inside the store when it rained. She never went across the street to sit with the old women in their folding chairs, and she always arranged her own chair so that she sat with her back to them.

"Hello," she called to Mrs. Klapper when they were twenty yards apart.

Mrs. Klapper lowered her shopping bag. My God, what eyes. She sighed, preparing herself for at least a ten-minute harangue. Be polite, Klapper. Somebody's polite to you and you're polite to somebody else and so the world goes around. She arranged her face in a wide smile of welcome.

"Lena!" she exclaimed. "How are you? You look wonderful!"

Mrs. Wireman shrugged and said, "Ahh," which meant that she was resigned in the face of chaos. "All right. How are you doing?"

"Ah, so-so. I just came by your husband's."

Mrs. Wireman's eyes were the very pale gray of an old egg; they were large eyes with wide rings of white, and she narrowed them now to look up at Mrs. Klapper. "How come you don't come around so much no more?"

"What are you talking about? I do come around." With her free hand Mrs. Klapper pointed at the package. "I got to eat too, like everybody."

The grocer's wife shook her head firmly. "I remember every two days, regular, I say to Avrom, 'Get the milk and eggs ready now so, comes Gertrude Klapper, you shouldn't keep her waiting.' Now all of a sudden, two days, three days, four days, no Gertrude Klapper. What are you, a stranger? You saving your money?" She looked accusingly at the younger woman. "You buying someplace else?"

No friend like an old friend, Mrs. Klapper thought wryly. Aloud she said, "Lena, twenty years I been buying at your place, I should change now? What is it with you? I got food in the house, I don't come in for a couple of days, suddenly it's by you a run on the bank." She spread her feet a bit and settled her weight; she'd be here a while yet. "Remember, I'm just buying for me now, I don't eat for two people, Lena."

Mrs. Wireman lowered her eyes. "All right, forgive me, I forgot about Morris. Excuse me."

"That's all right," Mrs. Klapper said. "It's over a year already."

To herself she said, Morris, forgive me that I should even

think of forgetting you, but I am not going to talk about you to this one.

"So when you going away, Gertrude?" Mrs. Wireman was looking at her again.

"Going away?" Mrs. Klapper blinked in real bewilderment. "Lena, what is this? Who's going away?"

"Every day I say to Avrom, 'Gertrude is all by herself now, so why is she putting her money in the bank? Why doesn't she take a trip somewhere, go maybe to Florida? She's got a little money, she should use it now, go somewhere.'"

"Lena—" Mrs. Klapper began.

"I got a cousin"—Mrs. Wireman did not so much cut her off as run her down—"I got a cousin went to Florida, Miami Beach." She leaned closer to Mrs. Klapper. "She was there two weeks, *bang!*" She snapped her lean fingers. "Married like that. A rich man, too."

Well, you asked for it, Gertrude, Mrs. Klapper told herself. Next time, maybe you'll lay off Sarah. She took a deep breath. "Lena, I am not going anywhere, Florida or anywhere."

Mrs. Wireman squinted her eyes even more. "What are you saving up for, a big house with nobody in it? Better you should take a trip, have a good time."

"Lena, I don't want to go anywhere. I live here, I cook, I keep the house neat, I go for walks, I got you to talk to." God forgive you, Klapper! "Why should I go somewhere where I don't know anybody? Don't be in such a hurry to go rushing me off to Florida. I like it here."

"Look, look, how angry she gets!" Mrs. Wireman smiled, exposing long, wide teeth. "So who's rushing you? Just say a hello to your old friends once in a while."

Mrs. Klapper sighed. "I tell you, I'll drop in, a day or two, and we can sit and talk." She thought of a way to change the subject. "You can tell me about Sam, how he's doing."

The thin, orange and white face hardened into an

expression of disgust. "About Sam and the bitch he married, I'll tell you nothing. Anything else we talk about. Not Sam."

"She looked like a nice girl, Eleanor." Mrs. Klapper remembered Sam's wife as a tall, pleasant-faced woman who had tried to help out in the store before she and Sam were married.

"A bitch," Mrs. Wireman said flatly. "Strictly no good, believe me." She looked at Mrs. Klapper as if daring her to say something in Eleanor's defense.

"I got to go, Lena," Mrs. Klapper said finally. "I got some more shopping to do." She began to edge around Mrs. Wireman, who made no move to let her pass. "Look, I'll come over soon, and we'll sit outside and schmooze a little, okay?"

"All right," Mrs. Wireman answered. "But you think about what I said, about Miami Beach."

Mrs. Klapper was safely past her. "I will, Lena. Take care of yourself."

"*Sei gesund,*" Mrs. Wireman said, turning to go.

"To your pretty daughter," Mrs. Klapper called after her, "say a hello for me."

Mrs. Wireman did smile then.

"Ya," Mrs. Wireman said, and went up the street. She walked faster than her husband, but her shoulders were hunched and crooked.

Mrs. Klapper stood in the middle of the sidewalk and watched her until she was gone. Then she half turned to go on down the block, stopped, and began to walk back the way she had come. She walked very slowly, taking small steps.

She could hear little Schwartz, who drove a fruit truck, crying his wares in the distance. His voice was high and musical, but he was too far away for her to make out the words. A woman she knew smiled as she passed and said, "Hello, Gertrude." Mrs. Klapper nodded and hurried past, not wanting to stop and talk.

To laugh at the Wiremans, she thought, this is easy. Lena is stupid, she knows from nothing, she's fun to talk to like a flounder. Wireman knows nothing but the store. His feet are flat from standing up all these years; sitting down he's forgotten. To both of them, money is God on earth. Sarah—she did not want to be hard on her—all right, so Sarah is smart. What good does it do her? In such a family, to be born smart is a curse. Better she should never have learned to read. She sighed. But I feel for them. Do me something. I feel for them. Am I so smart I should laugh at Lena? Am I so popular I should sit with the old women and say, "Lena Wireman sits by herself, good. Just so she don't sit with us"? Who are they? Her husband runs a store, he sells things to people. Are they so useful? Am I?

Mrs. Klapper was not an introspective woman, or, usually, a very analytical one. Thinking about Lena Wireman irritated her, and she walked quickly when she passed the grocery again, having no desire for a return match. She saw Sarah through the window for a second and wondered if she had seen her go by.

Some other time I'll go over to Ida's, she decided. Today I don't feel like walking. The baking-powder tin, atop the loaf of bread, caught her eye, and she tried to remember why she had bought it. I could bake a cake, maybe, and then call up Ida and say, "Look, come on over, we'll get fat together. Who can eat a whole cake?" She nodded. First she would bake the cake, then call Ida.

Passing the line of chairs—Morris had once called them "Murderers' Row"—she recognized old acquaintances. Sitting, as always, under the green awning of the corner candy store, which spot was hers owing to both seniority and squatter's rights, was a tiny gray-haired woman named Lapin. She had been old when Mrs. Klapper had moved into the neighborhood, and guesses as to her exact age ranged between eighty and one hundred. She was a dried-up comma of a woman, but Mrs. Klapper liked her and had found her good company.

"Hey, Lapin," she called loudly, Lapin's first name was Bella, but nobody ever used it. "Lapin, look up, say a hello."

Lapin looked up slowly from her omnipresent knitting needles and hank of black yarn. "Hello, Gertrude," she said in a surprisingly deep voice. "So how are you?"

"Managing. You look fine, Lapin."

The old woman tapped her chest. "I got a rattle in here two days now, and in my stomach it's all the time growling. Sit down already."

Mrs. Klapper shook her head. She had time, but the idea of taking even a temporary place in the row of chairs always frightened her. "I got to go in a minute, Lapin. Eat a little, so your stomach won't growl so much."

Lapin shook her head. "I been talking to the rabbi. He says at my age I got to be prepared. Why should I stuff myself? Any day—*boom!*" She smiled at Mrs. Klapper. "Any day."

"God forbid," Mrs. Klapper said. "You will outlive me and the rest of the buzzards. The rabbi too."

"Any day." Lapin's voice sounded a little petulant. She beckoned Mrs. Klapper close with a long-nailed forefinger "But I'm ready, believe me. When I die the House of Sages will say Kaddish, regular like Rosh Hashonah."

Mrs. Klapper knew what question was expected of her. "So what about your nephews? Better the family should say Kaddish."

Lapin's mouth twisted, and she wrinkled her nose. "Kaddish they don't believe in, my nephews. For their children they wouldn't say it." Her face relaxed again. "For me the House of Sages will say Kaddish."

For at least thirty years, Mrs. Klapper knew, Lapin had lived off the sums her three nephews sent her every month. She needed very little to live, and so she kept a steady current of five-dollar bills flowing into the House of Sages.

Once or twice Morris had been prevailed upon to send ten dollars in her name, and Mrs. Klapper had done so more often than she had let Lapin know.

"The House of Sages will give me a good funeral," Lapin said contentedly.

"Lapin," Mrs. Klapper said, "I only got a few minutes. Talk about something else, please."

The old woman went on, her eyes closed. "I will be buried in my robes." She had fallen into Yiddish. "And there will be some earth from Israel in the coffin."

"Why is it with you always funerals?" Mrs. Klapper asked a little nervously. Lapin kept on in Yiddish, her voice low and droning.

"And I will live in a beautiful house of my own. I will live forever. I will live in God—"

"So?" Mrs. Klapper's voice was harsh and querulous. "So how many floors will there be in this house, Lapin? And who will be the landlord?"

Lapin seemed to withdraw into her shawl. "Don't make fun. I don't care how many floors."

Mrs. Klapper regretted her words. "I'm sorry, Lapin. So have a beautiful funeral, live in a beautiful house. You got it coming."

The black eyes stared at her, and Lapin pointed the long forefinger. "*You* come to the funeral."

"Me?" Mrs. Klapper recovered quickly. "All right, Lapin. I'll come."

"Tell my nephews I said they should give you a ride to the cemetery." Lapin was staring absently down the street. "The rabbi will tell everybody how holy I was."

"Sure, Lapin. I got to go now. Take care." Mrs. Klapper had almost turned the corner when she heard the old woman call, "Gertrude!"

She turned and walked back to Lapin's chair. "So?"

"I was thinking," Lapin said slowly. "The funeral."

Mrs. Klapper waited, but Lapin said nothing. "What were you thinking, Lapin?"

"For you it's all right." Lapin turned her head stiffly to look up at Mrs. Klapper. "You come to the funeral, you say good-by, Lapin, you cry, you go home. You go home and have supper." She kept knitting her black yarn. "Me, I got to stay there. You'll all go home and have supper and leave me there."

Mrs. Klapper muttered something, patted a bony shoulder, and fled.

She almost ran the rest of the way home, stopping only in the lobby to catch her breath before she rang for the elevator. A straight-backed bench stood near the elevator door; she sank into it as if it were a hot bath. Her breathing became slower and shallower, and she gradually unclenched her hands that clung together in her lap. "Hoo-boy!" she said aloud. "What a morning!" The elevator arrived, and she stepped into it.

Lapin's predictions of and plans for her own death were nothing new to Mrs. Klapper. They were issued on a regular basis, like weather forecasts and stock-market reports. Morris had laughed at them, referred to them as "the ghetto preoccupation with a superghetto," but Mrs. Klapper had been brought up in a house and a neighborhood where even the mention of death was warded off with a "God forbid." A certain pride was to be taken in the knowledge that your children or your relatives would see that you were buried properly and with all honor, but Mrs. Klapper felt that Lapin was overdoing it a little.

Still, she reflected, entering her apartment, what else has Lapin got to talk about? Her nephews throw dice, the loser should go visit her; the rabbi comes over to tell her the House of Sages will give her a good funeral; what else can she talk about? At least it's not gossiping all day long like the others. She kept seeing the long row of chairs and the old women leaning to one another like bushes in the wind.

Don't worry, Klapper. She hung up her coat and walked slowly into the kitchen. For you there is also a seat waiting in Murderers' Row. Drop in any time. She put the milk in the refrigerator and wandered into the living room.

"So now what?" She looked defiantly at the books and paintings. "It is now twelve o'clock and I'm back where I was at eleven. Any suggestions?" But the living room belonged to Morris. It had no intention of suggesting anything.

Mrs. Klapper had, as a child, woven sturdy legs and a lot of curiosity into a real talent for getting lost. Even as an adult she was perfectly capable of getting lost in Brooklyn or Queens. If there was one emotion she could recall in totality it was the feeling of standing on a strange street under a five-o'clock sky, making tentative, trotting casts in one direction after another, knowing that each was the wrong one. She had always been afraid to ask people, for they looked gray and thick-fleshed, not at all like the people of the Bronx, and they went by without looking at her, except the children, who knew she was lost and delighted in it. There were no familiar subways, and the buses were colored differently and had strange numbers. So she might remain, as balanced between forces as the hub of a wheel, for half an hour or an hour before she called home and her father—later on, Morris—came and got her. So she remained in the living room, her hands at her sides, seeking a reason to move from the dark square of rug on which she stood.

She thought again of Jonathan Rebeck and wondered if he had found his watch. A watch is a small thing, she thought. You could look for days. Remembering that she had planned to call Ida, she went to the telephone, lifted the receiver, and slowly replaced it in its cradle.

So I call Ida and I say, "Ida, come over because I'm an old woman and I don't know what to do with myself." She watched the second hand sidling around the face of the kitchen clock. What do you do tomorrow, Klapper? Better start counting your relatives.

As she turned from the telephone, her glance fell on the small framed photograph of Morris she had kept hanging in the foyer. She stared at it, remembering the long jaw and the high, prominent cheekbones, the cattail eyebrows and the wisps of hair that clung to his head as scraps of meat do to a gnawed bone. Morris had been fifty-nine when he died, but his face was strikingly smooth and unlined, as if wind and water had rolled over him for thousands of years, whittling and polishing his face, eroding away the scars of human anger; not so much a face at peace as a face from which the marks of war had been worn away.

I could go down to the cemetery, Mrs. Klapper thought, and maybe keep Morris company a little. She toyed with the telephone dial but did not lift the receiver again. I got no place else to go. A few more days like this, I'll go looking for Lena Wireman, we'll sit down on boxes and talk about how lousy people are. This I don't need.

She headed for her closet. Besides, it's quiet, and I could maybe think about what I should do for the next thirty years.

After a long deliberation, she chose her new light wool coat and went into her bedroom to look at herself in the mirror.

"Hmmmm," she murmured in admiration. "Beautiful, Klapper. Like a young bride. Only—" She took off the coat and went back to the closet. "Only a young bride would not be going out to a cemetery. Act your age, Klapper."

A little regretfully, she put on a dark spring coat and went to the mirror again. "Nu, it'll do. To a cemetery you don't wear a trousseau." She smiled at the mirror and sighed. "Be a little honest with yourself, Klapper. With Morris also."

She turned off the light and went from room to room, making sure that all the lights and gas jets were off and that all the faucets were shut. Finally she stood in the hall with the door open and looked back at the darkened apartment.

"Morris," she said softly, "I feel a little bit guilty because I'm not sure if it's just you I'm coming to see." She hesitated. "Morris, I would bring you something. I would do something for you, only I can't think of anything you need."

Mrs. Klapper closed the door behind her and walked to the elevator.

6

The raven was tired of flying. He had been all over the Bronx that morning, trying to find a restaurant that sold ready-made sandwiches. All the cafeterias were jammed with the lunch-hour crowd, and the Automat represented a problem in logistics that the raven had never quite solved. Finally he twitched a roast-beef sandwich out of the hands of a telephone linesman before his victim had even unwrapped the waxed paper. The telephone linesman was not a philosopher. He threw a rock at the raven. The rock missed—the raven had a sense for these things—and clipped a policeman above the kidneys. The policeman was also not a philosopher.

But it was a long flight out to the Yorkchester Cemetery, and the raven's wings ached. He found himself struggling to keep from losing altitude, and the roast-beef sandwich was getting heavier with every flap of his tired wings. He flew under the Broadway El, and this was a terrible blow to his pride. The raven held trains in deep contempt and usually went out of his way to fly high above them, matching their speed as long as he could, shrieking insults after them for as long as he could see them. When he was much younger he had loved to chase the Lexington Avenue Express underground at 161st Street and scream what he thought of a worm that fled into the earth without the slightest gesture of defiance, for all it was a glandular monstrosity.

His adolescence ended abruptly on the day when he flew down the tunnel in pursuit of a great worm that shrieked with terror. Even now, winters and moltings later, he refused to talk about it.

Flying wearily over the cemetery gates, he caught sight of a small pickup truck a little ahead of him. He recognized it; the cemetery's caretakers used it to travel back and forth from the distant corners of the cemetery to the main office by the gates. It was rolling along the paved path at an easy twenty miles per hour; and, looking at it, the raven fought against a sudden impulse to hitch a ride.

He had never done such a thing before. Because he was too arrogant to walk, too heavy for telephone wires, and too unpopular for bird sanctuaries, an amazingly large portion of his life had been spent in the air. He felt no particular pride in having been born a bird, and he subscribed to no avian code of ethics, but he had never seen a bird make use of human transportation, and pioneers made him nervous.

The decision had to be made quickly. His wings felt like flatirons, and the truck was pulling farther and farther ahead. The raven glanced quickly around, saw nobody, hesitated, felt oddly guilty, said, "Ah, screw it," raised one last small chinook of flapping, and fell, gasping, into the back of the truck.

He lay on his side for a few minutes, content simply to breathe and feel the ache slowly go from his folded wings. Then he stood up carefully and looked over the tailgate at the road spinning away behind the truck. He had no way of appreciating the truck's exact speed, but he knew that it was far faster than his normal cruising pace, and he laughed in the sun at his own epochal cleverness.

"By God," he said aloud, "this is the way to travel. Damned if I ever fly another stroke." He turned, hopped up on the front rim of the truck body, and craned his neck to see through the narrow glass slit at the back of the cab.

There were two men in the cab. One was a huge dark man named Campos, who slouched on the seat with his feet stretched out in front of him, his hands in his pockets, and his eyes half closed. The driver was a medium sort of man named Walters, who had a cold and kept taking one hand off the wheel to wipe his nose on his sleeve. He talked incessantly, frequently glancing eagerly at the silent Campos to see if he was paying attention. Campos's cap was pulled down over his eyes, with the visor nearly resting on the bridge of his nose, and he seemed sound asleep.

"A real good guy," Walters was saying, "and a hell of a driver, but not very bright. He used to drive for some perfume company up around Poughkeepsie, and he was always picking up guys. Hitchhikers, you know. Anybody he saw walking along the road, he'd stop and pick them up. Anybody at all. He used to come rolling into Pough-keepsie with eight or nine guys on board. They'd sit in back with their legs hanging out, or up front with him. It looked like they'd all get together and chartered him. So finally— You listening, Campos?"

Campos remained immobile, but the brim of his cap quivered.

"So anyway," Walters went on, reassured, "one day he picks up these two tough kids in Fishkill, and they beat the hell out of him, dumped him off, and stole the truck. Kind of spoiled his outlook."

He grinned at Campos. "He wouldn't pick up nobody, from that day to this." Campos did not move. Walters sighed loudly. "You try to be a good guy," he said, looking straight ahead, "but they get you sooner or later."

Campos gave a small noncommittal grunt. Walters nod-ded. "Sooner or later, boy." He looked out the window, took a deep breath, and sneezed. "Beautiful day. Beautiful goddam day."

The truck jounced over an unpaved section of road, and Campos slipped even lower on the seat. Walters looked at him a little nervously. "Someday you're gonna break your ass doing that." Campos grunted again.

"All right," Walters said. "I don't give a damn." He sneezed again and drove in silence for a few minutes. Then he turned hopefully to Campos again and asked, "You catch the game last night?"

He was off before Campos had even shaken his head. "They lost, five to four. Cepeda hit two, but Kirkland struck out with two on in the ninth." He spat out of the window. "The bastards gave them the game, anyway. They made four errors. Wagner dropped a fly ball and Spencer threw one into left field. . . ."

He described the game with the sad relish of the messenger to Job, blinking his pale eyes rapidly as he talked. Beside him, Campos slumped in his seat and grunted and nodded now and then, and he might have been nodding to Walters or to something else.

Walters sniffed, wiped his nose on his sleeve, and began to sing Perry Como's latest. He chanted the song as if he weren't sure of the tune, and he appeared startled when Campos stirred beside him, sat up a little, and said, "You got it wrong."

"Better'n any goddam Puerto Rican," Walters said delightedly.

"Cuban, you bastard," said the big man without rancor. He slipped down in his seat again and looked out of the window.

In the back of the truck the raven had been joined by a small red squirrel who had dropped out of an overhanging tree as the truck passed under it. The squirrel was thin, with large bright eyes, and he sat on one of the chains that held the tailgate shut and demanded, "What on earth are you doing?"

"Making a good-will tour," said the raven, who disliked squirrels even more than pigeons. "What does it look like I'm doing?"

The squirrel drew his front paws close against his furry chest. "But you're a bird!" he said in amazement. "Why aren't you flying?"

"I've retired," said the raven calmly.

The truck took an exceedingly tight curve, and the squirrel nearly lost his balance on the chain. He recovered himself with a small squeak of alarm and stared at the raven. "Birds are supposed to fly," he said a little querulously. "Do you mean you're never going to fly again?"

It had come very gradually to the raven's attention that the motion of a truck on a gravel road is quite different from flight. There was a faint murmur of discontent from his stomach, distant as heat lightning still. "Never," he said grandly. "From here on in, I'm a pedestrian."

The truck hit two ruts in succession, and the raven lay down quietly and glared at the squirrel, who had balanced himself twice with a graceful flick of his tail.

"Personally," the squirrel continued, "I don't know that I'd care to fly. Unnatural method of locomotion, after all. Tiring, dangerous, exposed to all manner of injuries. Oh, I can see your point in wanting to get out of the business. But, after all, it's what you were born for. Just as I was born to be a squirrel. Fish got to swim and birds got to fly. God made them, high and lowly, and ordered their estate." He coughed apologetically. "Those last two lines weren't mine, I'm afraid."

"You could have fooled me," said the raven.

"All lives are composed of two basic elements," the squirrel said, "purpose and poetry. By being ourselves, squirrel and raven, we fulfill the first requirement, you in flight and I in my tree. But there is poetry in the meanest of lives, and if we leave it unsought we leave ourselves unrealized. A life without food, without shelter, without love, a life lived in the rain—this is nothing beside a life without poetry."

The raven lifted his head from the floor of the truck. "If I was a hawk, I'd eat you in two bites," he said weakly.

"Certainly," agreed the squirrel promptly. "And if you were a hawk it would be your duty to eat me. That is the purpose of hawks, to eat squirrels, and I may add, gophers. But if you ate me without any appreciation of your own swift-plummeting stroke and without a certain tender understanding of my mad, futile flight toward my tree, where my wife and family dwell—well, you wouldn't be very much of a hawk, that's all I can say."

He drew himself erect on the tailgate, as if he were facing a firing squad, having just rejected blindfold and cigarette.

"It's people like you who make things tough for the non-combatants," said the raven bitterly. He got up and walked to the back of the truck to look over the tailgate. The truck was approaching the ungardened path that led to the Wilder mausoleum. Remembering the roast-beef sandwich, he went back and picked it up rather awkwardly in his beak.

"Are you getting off here?" the squirrel asked. The raven nodded.

"Well, it's been very interesting talking to you," the squirrel said earnestly. "Do drop in if you're ever in the neighborhood. We have little get-togethers every Saturday night. If you're ever free some night—"

But the raven was gone, flapping heavily on stiff wings down the narrow path to the mausoleum. Turning his head, he saw the truck careening on its way. As soon as it was out of sight, he dropped to the ground and began to walk determinedly along the path.

I didn't want to walk, he thought, with that furry little bastard yapping at me. Squirrels get so damn enthusiastic about things.

The gravel skidded under his feet, providing very little for his claws to grasp and making his legs ache. The casually dashing feeling he had enjoyed on the truck before the motion began to affect his stomach was gone, and in its place came a mental picture of a somewhat carsick black bird stumbling along a slippery road that hurt his feet. It was an utterly undignified image, and the raven winced and put it from his mind. The raven believed, grudgingly and inarticulately, in dignity.

But he kept walking. Once he looked up and saw a swallow coasting down the sky. His wings jerked involuntarily, tugging like children at his body, but he did not take off. He walked on the gravel road and thought about the squirrel.

Goddam organizers, he thought. You get something good going, and somebody comes along and organizes it. He told himself that this was inevitable, the way of the world, but it bothered him. The raven would have been in favor of a movement in the general direction of chaos, consternation, and disorganization, had he not known that such a project would require the most organization of all. Besides, there would undoubtedly be a squirrel running it.

"Saturday-night get-togethers," he muttered into the roast-beef sandwich as he limped along. "Tiny little hot dogs with toothpicks through them. Crap." His feet hurt quite a bit, and the sandwich was getting heavy again.

Michael Morgan made no sound on the gravel, and when he said, "Good day, bird," the raven dropped the sandwich and sprang almost four feet straight up. He turned in the air so that he was facing Michael as he came down and he was cursing even before he hit the ground. "What a thing to do!" he cried furiously. "What a sonofabitching thing to do!" Michael slapped his thighs soundlessly, and from his throat came surfs of laughter as silent as lightning.

"I didn't know you'd take it that way." He gasped, putting out his hand to silence the angry bird. "Really I didn't. I'm sorry. I apologize." He looked closely at the dusty raven. "What makes you so touchy today?"

"I've had a tough morning," the raven said sullenly. He felt that he had acted foolishly. But he hated to be caught off guard.

"You dropped something," Michael said, pointing at the

sandwich with a transparent foot. "And why in God's name are you walking?"

"I had a flat."

"Tell me why you're walking. I'm curious."

"Mind your own goddam business," the raven answered, but he said it absently and he did not seem to be thinking of Michael.

"Do you know what I think?" Michael folded his arms and grinned. "I think you've forgotten how to fly."

The raven looked at him in amazement. "I've what?"

"Of course," Michael went on cheerfully, "Like playing the piano. You know—you play beautifully, you don't even need sheet music. Then you look down at your hands and think, How did I do that, how am I doing this, what am I to do next? And then everything goes bang. You forget how to move your fingers, how to pedal, even how the piece goes. That's what's happened to you, my friend. You've thought too much, and now you don't remember how to fly."

"Go haunt a house," the raven said. He picked up the roast-beef sandwich once more and began to walk on. Michael matched his pace, talking as he did so.

"It comes from being around ghosts too much, lad. Very bad for you. You start becoming one, by osmosis, as it were. You start to forget things, the way they do. You move slowly, the way they do, because nothing in the world can rush you. Oh, you're well on the way, boy, forgetting how to fly. A few more days and you can join our chess club and have Mr. Rebeck push the pieces around for you."

The raven stopped walking and looked at Michael for a moment with something approaching pity. Then he put the sandwich on the ground and looked directly at Michael again.

"Watch me," he said. He took two quick steps and went into the air.

The wind dizzied him and made him a little drunk. He

cleared a tree by a few inches, turned, and seemed to slide down an invisible tightwire to a smaller tree. Then he flew almost straight up for twenty or thirty feet. At the top of his climb he fell off on one wing and began to spiral gradually down like a sleepy leaf. He glided in small, angled circles without beating a wing until he was no higher than Michael's head. Then he made an ungraceful movement of his wings, seemed to skid a little, and was roosting in a tree off to the left, breathing hard, with his heart stuttering delightedly.

He shook his head slightly, winked maliciously at Michael, and rose from the branch with a jump that was very nearly a dance step. The air was as warm as wedding cake as he fell, volplaning directly at Michael's feet. Michael stepped back nervously, wondering if the ground would cleave before the strong beak like the Red Sea or if it wouldn't, and how the raven felt about the matter, if he gave a damn at all. And then there was a quick swirl in the gravel and pebbles scattering and a black feather on the ground, and the raven was circling overhead with the roast-beef sandwich in his beak.

The sandwich had had a pretty tiring morning itself, and as the raven circled triumphantly the worn wrapping tore, and the sandwich fell from the raven's beak, turning over and over. Michael raised his hands to catch it, and then lowered them and held them behind his back.

But the raven fell beside the sandwich, turning his head to judge its descent so that they looked like two meteors comforting each other. Then a branch broke the sandwich's fall for a moment; the raven struck and was gone, over the trees and down the path. Michael smiled with just the right touch of casual sadness and followed.

Laura saw the raven first from where she sat with Mr. Rebeck on the grass in front of the mausoleum. She had been sitting there when he had come out to stand on the steps and yawn. He had been inordinately pleased to see her and had gone back into the mausoleum to dress as fast as he could, because he felt somehow that she might be gone when he returned.

But she was there, sitting on the grass and looking curiously at the sun. He had not seen her since the time she had come with Michael, a week ago. June then, it was July now, a New York July, full of rust-colored mornings and shining noons that hurt the eyes. People came less often to the cemetery, and the roses went brown on the graves before they were replaced.

She had not come again, and he had wondered. Now he went over and sat down beside her.

"Hello, Laura," he said. "Where have you been?"

"Here and there." Laura moved her hand very slightly and was both here and there. Mr. Rebeck saw her so— sitting, with the sun shining through dress and bone and body, making her look like a pen-and-ink drawing; and walking among the olive-colored ferns that grew all around the cemetery, encircling it as cattails do a stagnant pond. She smiled at him now, and he saw her the night before, standing close to the snake-laced gate, smiling.

"I see," he said, and he did.

"I came to visit you," Laura said. "I came to sit and hear you talk to me."

"Delighted to have you. What should I talk about?"

"Something alive. The theater, or subway fares or labor unions, or books, or baseball, or foreign relations, or the going price of bananas. Talk to me, please, about anything at all, so long as it's alive."

Mr. Rebeck's brows consulted each other as he tried to think of a subject, but Laura interpreted the frown as an expression of puzzlement and went on, "Because I'm going to have to make a choice very soon, and I want to be sure it's the right one."

She paused, and her hands moved in her lap like captured butterflies. "Death has been very good to me," she said finally. "Do you know what I can do now?" Mr. Rebeck shook his head.

"I can think myself places. I can go back and forth across this cemetery seven times, from gate to gate, and be back here before you can snap your fingers. I can ride in the caretakers' truck, in a space barely big enough for two people, and hear the men talking. All I have to do is let my body drop from me as if it were a wet bathing suit, and then I'm me and I can go where I want to go."

"Except out of the cemetery," Mr. Rebeck said.

"How did you know?"

"It works that way for all ghosts. You can go anywhere, except away from the place where your body is buried. I suppose there's a reason for it."

"I thought it was just me," Laura said. "I thought perhaps you had to want to go back very badly before the gate would let you pass."

She looked past him, and he knew that she was staring at the lion-heads on the mausoleum door. "It doesn't matter. There's nothing I want to see. I like it better this way. Nobody can see me, you know. Not even you, unless I want you to. I've sat and watched you for hours"—Mr. Rebeck started—"and you read, and sometimes you have put your book down and looked at me and didn't know I was there. You were humming to yourself."

"I can see you now," Mr. Rebeck said.

"Sometimes I put my body back on. But not as often as I used to. It feels tight on me and makes me walk slowly. It always did. Someday, someday soon, I may just leave it and not come back."

"Where is the choice, then?"

Laura's hands stopped moving in her lap, and she looked away from Mr. Rebeck. "Because I might be wrong," she said softly, "and Michael might be a little bit right, even if he is a fool."

She turned back to Mr. Rebeck. "This is very much like the last minute before you fall asleep at night. You close your eyes and everything seems to be rushing away from you, and you're sinking backward and down—like a subway when you're in a local and an express goes by so fast that your train really appears to be going backward. You just let yourself fall with it, and it's easy and comfortable and quite wonderful. But you keep yourself awake until you make sure that everything's all right; that the lights are out and the door is locked, that you did everything you meant to do that day, that nothing's left unfinished.

"Well, I don't feel right. I keep thinking that I've left a door open somewhere." She put a hand out to touch his own, and Mr. Rebeck felt a cold breeze drying the July sweat on the back of his hand before she moved away.

"Do you want me to talk about live things now?" he asked. "I've remembered something."

"Yes, please," said Laura. And Mr. Rebeck sat with his legs tucked under him and his eyes holding the delicate tracings of iris and pupil and eyelash that had been Laura's eyes, and he told her about a zoo he had visited more than twenty years before. He told Laura about a hippopotamus that would munch on the same tiny square of chocolate for almost an hour, rolling it around in its mouth with its eyes shut tight; and an immensely fat orangutan that sat sleeping in a puddle of its own flesh; and a monkey that tossed itself carelessly around the cage like a spool of red ribbon; about two white wolves; and about the people that had been at the zoo. He made them up for her; they weren't too good because it had been a long time, but Laura seemed satisfied. Suddenly she pointed over his shoulder and said, "The raven's coming—and Michael."

Mr. Rebeck turned his head and saw the raven in the sky and Michael coming slowly down the path, stepping on twigs and not breaking them.

The raven seemed reluctant to land, but he finally did, dropping a battered roast-beef sandwich into Mr. Rebeck's lap just before he touched the ground. He seemed a little unsteady on his feet, Mr. Rebeck thought, but his eyes glittered and he carried his head like the cocked hammer of a gun.

"All I could get," he said, gesturing at the sandwich with his beak.

"Just one?"

"Things are tough all over."

"I was joking." Mr. Rebeck unwrapped the torn waxed paper. "This will be fine." He pulled a strip of meat from the sandwich and offered it to the raven, who shook his head. "Uh-uh. Found a robin's nest this morning."

Mr. Rebeck ate the meat himself, but Laura made a small sound of horror. "You ate—" She could not finish.

The raven turned to look at her. "Morning," he said cheerfully. "Didn't notice you."

Laura remained still, but she seemed to have drawn miles away from the man and the bird. "You ate a robin's eggs—"

"Egg," said the raven. "More than one egg in the morning and I get the hiccups." He made a casual grab at a grasshopper, headed it off with his beak a couple of times, and then let it escape into the grass.

Laura's hands cupped around each other, as if she were shielding something blue and fragile. "But they're so pretty, and so harmless!"

"So?" The raven canted his head slightly to one side. "And a hen's Public Enemy Number One?"

"It's not the same thing. It's not the same thing at all."

"Damn right it isn't. Nobody ever says, 'Look, it's spring! I just saw the first hen.' You ever hear a song about when the red, red hen comes bob, bob, bobbing along? Hell, you give a smart bird like the buzzard half the publicity a robin gets, and he'd be the national bird inside of a year."

His voice dropped back to its normal range. "People root for the goddamnedest birds. You see a robin murdering a worm, and right away it's 'Hold the fort, redbreast! Help is on the way! Wait'll I find my old army rifle and we'll fight the monster off! You and me, bird! Shoulder to shoulder! To the death!' But you seen an owl having breakfast off a field mouse and you form a committee to march on Washington and make them pass a law saying from now on owls can only eat cabbage and apple pie.

"Take a worm now. All right, they aren't brilliant, but they work hard. Your average worm is a nice enough little guy, a kind of small businessman. He's quiet, he's good for the soil, he doesn't bother anybody, he leads a good, dull life—and the poor bastard is a three-to-one bet to wind up on the end of some kid's hook if the robins don't get him. And that's all right, because he's slimy and he can't sing either. But a kid shoots a robin with a slingshot and forty years later he writes in his autobiography how he didn't know the meaning of death till then. Or you take squirrels." His eyes brightened perceptibly. "The way I feel about shooting squirrels—"

"But you eat worms," Laura pointed out.

"Sure. But at least I don't call in the photographers."

Michael reached them then, and Mr. Rebeck was suddenly aware of the disparity between his walk and Laura's. Laura moved like a dandelion plume on a day wrinkled with small winds, barely touching the ground. When she did, it seemed accidental and meaningless, for she left no footprints even in the softest earth, and no pebbles sprang aside from her feet. Whether she stood on the ground, on a tree limb, or on a rose's smallest thorn, she was separate from the ground or the branch or the thorn.

Now Michael, Mr. Rebeck thought, Michael walks slowly because he is busy remembering how it felt to walk. He must build his road as he walks along, and it cannot be pleasant for him to realize that the road rolls itself up behind him with every step he takes. He steps hard, banging his feet against the ground, hoping to feel the pain that comes when you do that, as if you'd stepped on a lighted cigar. But there is no pain, and he leaves no footprint to tell where he has gone.

Aloud, he said, "Good morning, Michael."

"Hi," Michael said. He looked at Laura. "Hello, Laura."

"Hello." On seeing him approach, she had planned to add something like "Still fighting good fights?" But she also saw the way he walked and the desperate tangibility he strove for that made him look even more unreal, a shape superimposed upon the world, and she said nothing. What can life possibly have been to him, she wondered, that he clings to it so? She felt a bit jealous.

"Hey, Morgan."

Michael turned quickly to the raven. "Yes?"

"Knew I had something to tell you," the raven said. "They set your old lady's trial for August eighth."

Michael's heart might have skipped a beat here, or pounded like a drum, or raced like a mile runner, or done any of the other things so popular among hearts, except that Michael had no heart now, not even the most smudged carbon of one, nor ever would again.

"My—old lady?" he asked, slowly and quite foolishly.

"Sandra." It would have taken a stronger man than Mr. Rebeck to keep his mouth shut. "Your wife, Michael."

"I know who she is!" Michael shouted at him. He hadn't known he was angry until he answered, and he hadn't meant to shout so loudly. But they were all looking at him.

"I remember," he said. "What about her?"

"Saw a couple of papers," the raven said. "All over the front pages. She looks a little worried."

Michael was thinking about Sandra. He had not thought about her for nearly a week. That is, he had thought about her a good deal, but somewhat in the way one thinks about an aching tooth. It's there, of course, and the sound teeth ache with it in four-part harmony, but it can be lived with and taken as much for granted as all the other parts of daily life. The idea is to keep from touching it with your tongue. And, like the heart and the sphincter muscles, the tongue can be disciplined. It just takes will power and a lot of free time.

"I didn't even know she'd been arrested," he said to the raven.

"I'd have told you before, only I don't read the papers much, and then it's just the sports section. They indicted her right after they buried you, and it's probably been front-page stuff since."

Laura was looking from one to the other of them, frowning slightly. "I don't think I understand."

The raven favored her with a swift, golden-eyed glance. "Don't feel bad. Nobody does."

"But why is Michael's wife on trial?" Laura persisted. "What did she do?"

"Poisoned the hell out of me," Michael said briefly. He did not look at her. "I told you about it."

"No," Laura said. "No, you didn't."

"Of course I did. How do you think I got here—overeating? I told you, all right. You just forgot."

To the raven he went on, "Has she been in jail all this time?"

"Uh-huh. They don't allow bail for first-degree murder."

"Sandra in prison," Michael said tentatively. "Odd sound. Is she just going to plead guilty and get it over with?"

"Can't," said the raven. "Not for first-degree murder. She's got to plead not guilty or they won't play. They got rules, you know, like everybody else."

"Not guilty!" Michael stared at the bird. "Is that what she's going to tell the jury?"

The raven scratched at the earth restlessly. "I'm not her lawyer. I just read a couple of papers."

"Ah, she can't get away with that!" Michael was outraged now. "She poisoned me good and proper."

"Well, the cops think so," the raven said. "Most of the reporters too. I'll bring you a paper tomorrow. You got a real good press."

Michael did not seem to hear him. "What can she possibly claim? Accidental death? She'd never get away with it;

they'd want to know where she got the poison and how it got into my drink."

"They found the poison in her dresser or someplace like that," the raven told him. "She says she doesn't know anything about it. Didn't buy it, didn't even know it was in the house."

"Life is full of surprises."

"You know it," agreed the raven. He worried an itching leg with his beak. "She's not gonna claim it was accident, though. Not by the papers."

"What then? An act of God?"

"No." The raven lunged at another grasshopper and batted it, stunned, to the ground. He took an unconscionable time devouring it, and Michael became impatient.

"What is it, then?"

The raven finished the grasshopper and said, "Suicide." Then he hunted through the grass for more insects, because grasshoppers are like peanuts. Nobody eats just one at a time.

7

They were all looking at Michael. Mr. Rebeck, Laura, the raven—they were all looking at him. He felt as if he had told a joke and they had missed the punchline and were leaning to him, waiting for the kicker, the all-illuminating kicker that is found only in jokes; or as if someone had asked, "How you doing?" and the spring-and-strap arrangement in him that always answered that question for him had rusted and broken and he would never again be able to answer perfunctory questions the way other people did. He hoped that Mr. Rebeck would say something, and then he thought he had better speak to the raven before Mr. Rebeck did say something. So he shook his head slowly to show that he was amazed and more than amazed and he said to the raven, "She says I killed myself?"

"Uh-huh." The raven had found another grasshopper. "She says you had a nightcap together and you went to bed, and when she woke up, there you were."

Michael tried not to look at Laura. "That's crazy! Why should I have killed myself?"

"I'm not your mother," the raven said crossly. "Look,

all I know is I read the papers. So here she is and they say did you? She says no. They say ho-*ho*. So she goes on trial August eighth." He turned to Mr. Rebeck. "I got to pull out. Anything you want me to take?"

Mr. Rebeck produced a half-pint milk container. "Thank you very much for the sandwich."

"Pleasure was mine," the raven said. "Also the flying around. See you." His wings began to beat.

"Wait a minute," Michael said. "Could you find out?"

"Find out what?"

"Don't act stupid," Michael said shortly. "About Sandra. What's happening in court. Could you keep an eye on the papers? I'd like to know how the trial's going."

"Guess so." The raven took off lightly, swung in a long ellipse, and came soaring back over their heads. Skidding on a thin breeze, he banked and banked again, trying to keep within earshot.

"I'll keep an eye out. Maybe bring back a paper, if I can get one."

"Thanks," Michael called. And then the raven was gone, flying at right angles to the wind. The milk container swung from his claws, and sometimes he did a sideslip for no reason that Mr. Rebeck could see. But his wings beat easily and strongly, carrying him higher than the trees.

Michael watched the raven for as long as he could see him, and did not turn even when the bird was out of sight. To his right, he knew, Mr. Rebeck sat and looked at him, with his chin on his fist and his eyes puzzled. He would ask no questions, Michael knew; he would be very polite and wait for Michael to open the subject. And if Michael didn't, he would talk about something else and never mention Sandra again. There might be strain and awkwardness between them for a while, and it would all come from Michael. He would be placed in the uncomfortable position of a man whose privacy is genuinely respected, and he hated Mr. Rebeck a little for it.

But behind him he could hear Laura's laughter rushing

and tumbling in her throat long before it spilled into the space between them, and he spun on her as she laughed and said, "Something's funny?"

"Everything," Laura said happily. She laughed the way the few ghosts who remember how cry: quietly and incessantly, because there are no tears to dry up, no throats to ache, and no faces to be spoiled. There is nothing really to stop that kind of crying, that kind of laughter, and Michael thought that the slow force of it might bend him until he snapped.

"Stop it," he said angrily. "She has to plead something."

Laura kept laughing at him. He looked over at Mr. Rebeck. "She can't plead guilty—and she wouldn't if she could. They'd put her in jail for life."

Laura stopped laughing quite suddenly, and where her laughter had been there was the glossy silence that hangs in the air after a train has gone by. "And if they find her guilty now?" she asked.

But Michael was thinking of Sandra in prison, and he said nothing.

"They'd kill her," Laura said, "the way they do. It's quite a gamble, if she's guilty."

Michael still said nothing, and Mr. Rebeck stirred and got up. "Maybe she'd rather be dead," he said slowly. "She might not want to go to prison."

"Nobody does," Laura said impatiently. "But women don't just throw their lives away like that. Women are real gamblers. They only bet on sure things."

She looked again at Michael, who would not look at her. "Wouldn't it be funny," she said thoughtfully. "Here we've got Michael Morgan, running back and forth in his grave, stamping his feet, telling everybody he loved life so much that they had to amputate him from it. A murdered man, crying for justice. Everybody within the sound of his voice is suitably impressed." She laughed again. "Me, too. I thought he was a fool, but he howled so loudly and made so much fuss that I began to wonder. And now, after all—"

up!" Michael said. "Just shut up. You don't know you're talking about."

"And after all," Laura went on, "it turns out that maybe he performed the operation himself. Well, fine. Hurray. Good for him. A consummation devoutly, and so on. You done good, boy."

"Sandra," Michael said huskily, "I mean Laura, shut up and leave me alone. I didn't kill myself. Before God, I didn't kill myself."

But Laura's voice skimmed on, not laughing now; even shaking a little, but clear and pitiless, and he could no more stop it than the strongest wire fence can stop the most casual breeze. "And now he's terribly embarrassed about the whole thing. He wants out. He figures if he shouts loud enough, maybe he'll wake himself up." She essayed to laugh again, but the quaver in her voice tripped it up. "God damn you, Michael, for a little while, maybe only a few minutes, you really had me going. You were a symbol of the indestructibility of life or something. A real Greek challenge to death. Man Against The Night. Wherever you go, darling, I'll be with you. Curtain. Everybody files out, uplifted, and the orchestra plays the big tango number from the second act." She sighed. "Oh, well, never mind, Michael. You just locked yourself out, that's all."

She got up and brushed her hands down the sides of her dress, although no grass clung to it. "Good-by, Mr. Rebeck. Thank you for talking to me. Good-by, Michael." She began to walk away, and sometimes her feet touched the ground and sometimes they didn't.

"Woman!" Michael's shout bounced, burst, and bloomed inside Mr. Rebeck's head and hurt a little. "Damn and blast it, I didn't kill myself! I had no intention of killing myself. I was too bloody arrogant for suicide. It would have been like murdering God or drawing mustaches all over the Sistine Chapel. Why should I have killed myself? That's what she can't get around, that's what they'll get her on. We had a nightcap, we went to bed, and I woke up dead. That may be indigestion. It's not suicide."

Laura had stopped walking when he first shouted, but she did not turn. Michael made an abbreviated gesture of head-scratching and said suddenly, "Anyway, my grave is in church ground. I was a Catholic, you know. Not a very good one, but I never left the Church. I think I was too lazy. Would they have buried me here, in hallowed ground, if they thought I'd committed suicide?"

Then Laura did turn. "I don't know," she said slowly. "I hadn't thought of that."

Michael took a few steps toward her and stopped. "I didn't kill myself. I know that as well as you can know anything in this place, where all your thoughts crumble and go. It's just not the sort of thing I'd do."

"As the mother said when her son ran amuck and chopped up two old ladies, a bus driver, and the head of the fire department."

"No, not like that. Listen to me, Laura. When I was eighteen or twenty, I knew everything except what I wanted. I knew all about people, and poetry, and love, and music, and politics, and baseball, and history, and I played pretty good jazz piano. And then I went traveling, because I felt that I might have missed something and it would be a good idea to learn it before I got my master's degree."

He smiled a little at the silent Laura and turned slightly to get Mr. Rebeck in too. "And the older I grew, and the farther I traveled, the younger I grew and the less I knew. I could feel it happening to me. I could actually walk down a dirty street and feel all my wisdom slipping away from me, all the things I wrote term papers about. Until finally, before I lost everything, I said, 'All right, I'm sorry. I was young and I had a girl and I didn't know any better. It's not easy to stay properly ignorant. I apologize. Leave me a few things to know, just enough to get home on, and I'll be content with these and not bother anybody. I've learned my lesson. Maybe I'll write a book.'

"And then the little went too, and I found myself alone in the middle of the world, without a doubt the most stupid man that ever scratched his head. All the things I thought I knew about people, about myself, they were all gone. All I had left was a head full of confusion, and I wasn't even sure what I was confused about. Nothing stayed still. So I said, 'What the hell, I'm a fool,' and that seemed reasonable enough. So I went home and became a teacher."

"Because you couldn't do anything else?" Laura asked. "I've heard that before. I never really believed it."

"No, because I felt safe. It was nice being back in college. I knew about colleges. I figured that I'd stay for a while and teach and try to learn a few things. And when I was whole again, and wise, why then I'd be off again to wherever it was I was going.

"Only I got to like it. I liked it very much. And so I stayed. I compromised, I suppose. You can say that, if you choose. But I felt comfortable, and after a while I felt wise enough to find my way home at night. There were always books to read and plays I hadn't seen, and in the summer Sandra and I—" he caught himself, hesitated, and went on—"we'd drive up to Vermont. I used to write articles during the summers, sort of historical essays. I was going to make a book out of them. And sometimes I'd make up poetry in the bathroom."

He waited for Laura to say something, but she was silent, and he continued, "So I had something to do, something I'd done, someplace to go, and something to look forward to. That's a reasonable way to live. I enjoyed myself living. I had a good time. How much else can you ask for?"

"A lot more," Laura said softly, "if you're greedy. I was greedy once."

"So was I, but that was a long time ago. You're greediest when you're born, and after that it's downhill all the way. Live to be two hundred and you wouldn't demand anything.

"Live to be two hundred and you couldn't use anything."

They were looking directly at each other now and paying no attention to Mr. Rebeck. But he leaned against a tree and watched them. He dug his fingernails into the bark of the tree, and little shreds of it came away under his nails. An ant ran over his shoulder and disappeared into a crack in the bark.

"I'm going to say something a little cruel," Michael said. "I don't mean it that way, but that's how it's going to sound. Do you mind?"

"What difference does it make? Go on."

"Well, here you are," Michael began. He tried to cough, but he had forgotten how it felt and it came out as more of a whistle. "I mean, you seem happy. Happier than you were. Or, putting it another way—what I'm getting at is, you didn't have the hell of an exciting life, did you?"

"No," said Laura. Her smile was too tolerant, Mr. Rebeck thought, too wise, too *tout comprendre est tout pardonner*. "Not very exciting. Dull, if you like. It doesn't hurt."

"Well," Michael said. He tried again. "Well, but just the same, you didn't kill yourself, did you? You didn't go running to meet that truck as if it were the mailman—or a lover, for that matter. And when you saw it coming, no matter how bored you were, no matter how damn dull everything was, you tried to save yourself, didn't you?"

The smile was sliding off Laura's face, like mascara in the rain. She started to say something, but Michael went on, without noticing. "You threw yourself away from death, not at it. That's the human instinct. You didn't make it, but that's not the point. The thing is, when it came down to die, *yes*, or die, *no*—and you had time to choose—you tried not to die. With less reason to live than a lot of other people, you chose life. Right?" He winked triumphantly at Mr. Rebeck and would have jammed his hands in his pockets except that he had long since forgotten what pockets were like.

Laura stood quite still. She seemed, Mr. Rebeck thought,

a little less sharply outlined than she had been, a little fainter to the eye, a little more wind-colored. She turned away, pivoting on one foot the way a bored child will, and now there was nothing in her moving of the skipped stone or the paper airplane.

"I don't know," she said. Michael could barely hear her. "No. I wouldn't—I don't know."

"Let it go, Michael," Mr. Rebeck said under his breath, or perhaps he only thought the words and did not say them. Michael did not seem to hear him at all.

"You wouldn't have killed yourself," he said. "Oh, I'm sure you thought about it. People think about everything in their lives. But you put it off until morning, and in the morning you had to get up and go to work. People do that. Me too." He made a sweeping, generous gesture with his arms. "But I never found myself alone at the right moment. And neither did you."

"I don't know, I don't know," Laura said. There was a moment in which she and Michael stood still, poised and waiting but immobile, like weathervanes on a bland summer morning, and Mr. Rebeck leaned against the tree and felt the rough bark under his light shirt and willed them and himself just so forever. Then forever passed and the enchantment expired, and Laura began to run.

There was no sweep to her flight, and nothing feathered or hoofed about it. She ran like a woman, from the knees down, her hands a little in front of her, and her shoulders slightly stooped. And as she ran she seemed to grow fainter, like a soap bubble blown at the sun.

Michael shouted her name, but she kept running until the foliage of a cherry tree caught her up. Then he was silent. His right hand kept closing and opening, and he stared at the cherry tree.

Presently he went over to Mr. Rebeck's tree and sat down. "All right. Be fatherly. What did I do?"

"I don't know," Mr. Rebeck said. "She's very upset."

"That's fine. I'm upset too." He thought of the Thurber

cartoon and grinned. "We're all upset. But how come she's more upset than I am? She didn't kill herself."

"Are you sure? She isn't."

"Of course I'm sure. That kind don't kill themselves. They live in hope, waiting for a phone call, or a telegram, or a letter, or a knock on the door, or running into someone on the street who will see how beautiful they really are. They think about killing themselves, but then they might not be able to answer the phone."

"I wonder," Mr. Rebeck murmured. "Surely some of them—"

"Oh, sure, some of them do. They get tired of second-class mail with the address mimeographed and pasted on. But not that one. She wouldn't kill herself. She can afford to play with the idea because nobody's trying to prove she did. Now me, I've got troubles. If anybody's got a right to be upset, I do."

Mr. Rebeck turned his head to look down at him. "Michael, are you still sure your wife poisoned you?"

"Sure? Hell, I'm just surprised she used poison. Sandy always impressed me as the meat-cleaver type."

"What happened? Do you remember?"

"Up to a point," Michael said. "We went to a party that night, I think. I don't remember who gave it, but I'm pretty sure there was a party. I don't think it went too well. When Sandra and I got to snapping at each other we didn't care where we were. Once we had a real throat-grabber at the Met and they threw us out. Very politely."

"Why did you fight so much?"

Michael shrugged. "Anyway, we came home from the party and maybe we made peace and maybe we didn't." He grinned suddenly. "I think we did both. I remember Sandra made us a couple of drinks, and that was usually a kind of peace offering. But then she went off to the bedroom and I slept in the living room, so there must have been a real shooting war on." He drew up his knees and looked across the clearing where the path ended. "We weren't what you might call a twin-bed family."

"You loved her very much," Mr. Rebeck said.

Michael took it as a question. "Uh-huh. At odd moments. She wasn't the sort of woman you could love for any extended period of time." He shook his head sharply. "So. I went to my celibate couch and I fell asleep fast. *That* must have made her sore. Then—and this I remember very distinctly—I woke up and I was sweating frog ponds. My stomach felt as if I'd swallowed somebody's hot plate."

He looked up at Mr. Rebeck. "Right away I knew Sandra'd poisoned me. I didn't think I'd eaten a bad egg or something. I tried to sit up and I couldn't, and I thought, The bitch did it. The bitch really did it. Then I passed out—died—and when I came to they were singing 'Gaudeamus Igitur' or something over me. The rest is here."

Michael rose and paced a few steps with the peculiar stamping gait that Mr. Rebeck had noticed earlier. "I remember everything as if it were happening now. I tried to forget it, the way I forgot the poetry and whether I ever got to be a full professor, but it stays. She may get away with saying I killed myself. I wouldn't be too surprised if she did. But I know she killed me as surely as I know I'm dead."

Mr. Rebeck straightened up slowly. "Well, we can follow the papers and see how the trial comes out."

"I don't care how it comes out. If they find her guilty, fine. It won't bring pleasant old me back to life, but fine. If they decide she's innocent—well, I know better, and that's always a consoling feeling." He was standing in the middle of the clearing now, with his back to Mr. Rebeck. "Still, we might as well see how it goes. What the hell."

He turned around suddenly. "But I'd like to know what sort of reason she'll give for my committing suicide. She's a fertile-minded wench, but this is for the big money."

"Could she say you'd been—oh, depressed lately?"

Michael snorted. "That was what we fought about. I

wasn't depressed. She thought that any man in my position ought to be depressed. My position—she made it sound as if I were tied to some Indian rotisserie." He swung away again and prowled restlessly to the foot of the mausoleum. "Maybe I was, in a way. But Sandra was dancing around the stake, yelling like hell and pouring on the kerosene."

For a moment Mr. Rebeck thought he winced. His image rippled slightly and seemed to fade. Then it was whole again, as if it were a reflection on water and a stone had broken it.

"She didn't mind me being a teacher. Don't think that. She just wanted me to be an important teacher. She was getting a little bored with cooking dinner for me and a few students, and playing the *Threepenny Opera* record in the living room afterward. A hungry woman, my Sandra. Wanted me to realize myself, to be everything she knew I could be. A hungry woman. Very sexy, though. She had beautiful hair."

He was silent then, standing in front of the dirty white building, throwing no shadow on the barred door.

What a fine spot for a few words, Mr. Rebeck thought, from a wise and understanding man. I must write away for one. Perhaps I could put an advertisement in the paper. The raven could figure out something. We could have a wise and understanding man in residence. Somebody ought to.

Michael was looking straight in front of him. Now, without turning his head, he said quietly, "Your lady's coming."

"What?" Mr. Rebeck asked. "Who's coming?"

"Way the hell down the path. Can't you see her?"

"No." Mr. Rebeck came slowly to Michael's side. "No, not yet. Tell me."

"You know the one. The widow. The one who's got a husband buried around here."

"I know her," Mr. Rebeck said. He stood on tiptoe and strained his eyes. "Yes, I do see her."

"Probably coming to visit her husband again," Michael said. He glanced sideways at Mr. Rebeck.

Mr. Rebeck bit a knuckle, "Oh dear," he said. "Oh. Lordy."

"You seem nervous. Anticipatory, one might say. Shall I go away somewhere and count my toes?"

"No, no," Mr. Rebeck said quickly. "Don't do that." He began to take shuffling steps backward, still watching the small figure that approached.

"Taking rather the long way around to visit her husband, isn't she?"

"Yes. I was just thinking that."

"If you're trying to hide behind me," Michael said, "it seems a little pointless."

Mr. Rebeck stopped moving backward. "I wasn't hiding. But I wish I could think of something to say to her. What can I say?"

"Something beautiful," Michael replied carelessly. He began to drift off slowly, like a lost rowboat. "Something crippled and beautiful."

"I wish you'd stay," Mr. Rebeck said.

"I thought I'd go and see about Laura. You've got company. She may want some." He grinned at Mr. Rebeck over his shoulder. "Just be darkly fascinating."

Mr. Rebeck watched him wander along the path. His head was high, higher than he usually carried it. Sometimes he kicked lightly at a pebble or a spring-rotten twig, but not as if he expected them to move. Mr. Rebeck found himself holding his breath as Michael approached Mrs. Klapper, half expecting to see the woman blurred for a moment, as when a thin pulling of cloud passes over the sun. Later he did not remember having had this feeling, but he was to have it several times more and not remember those times earlier.

But the two figures met on the path that was only wide enough for one, and neither gave way; nor did the woman become bleared or the ghost less transparent. He thought that Michael said something in Mrs. Klapper's ear as they passed each other, but he had no time to wonder what it might have been. For Mrs. Klapper saw him then and waved. She began to walk faster, smiling.

Michael also waved to him, a casual gesture like the flicker of a distant flag, and then vanished beyond the cherry tree. Mr. Rebeck waited for Mrs. Klapper and thought, Maybe she will just say hello and isn't it a fine afternoon and go on to where her husband is buried. That would be the best thing, certainly the best thing for you. He leaned against his tree with his hand behind him and one foot braced on a root and tried to look sanguine, that having always been one of his favorite words.

Mrs. Klapper stopped at the edge of the clearing and peered at him a little uncertainly. Then she came a few steps toward him and said, "Well, hello!"

"Hello," Mr. Rebeck replied. "I'm glad to see you." That was true, but he wondered immediately if he should have said it, became Mrs. Klapper hesitated before she spoke again.

"We keep bumping into each other all the time, don't we?" she observed finally.

"It's our habits, I think. There can't be too many people who spend their summer afternoon in cemeteries."

Mrs. Klapper laughed. "So where can you spend an afternoon now? The parks are full of kids. They play around, they yell, they set off firecrackers, they fight; it's better to take a nice quiet nap in a washing machine. A cemetery is the only place you can hear yourself think."

"I used to go to museums a lot," Mr. Rebeck said. He would have made it, "I go to museums a lot," but he was afraid that she might ask him which museums he went to, and he couldn't remember their names any more.

"Morris again." Mrs. Klapper saw the puzzlement on Mr. Rebeck's face. "I mean Morris was also crazy about museums." She sniffed. "For twenty-two years I went to museums with Morris. Once a week it was 'Gertrude, let's go to a museum; Gertrude, it's a beautiful day, let's go to the Metropolitan, they're having a big exhibit; Gertrude, here's a museum, let's stop in for a minute.' Excuse me, I have been to museums. I don't want to see any museums for a while yet. Maybe later."

She was looking up the hill to her husband's tomb, and her voice had become a little softer and slower. Mr. Rebeck looked down and concentrated on his right foot, which pressed hard on a mound of root. The light rain of the night before had made the root a little slippery, and Mr. Rebeck's foot skidded a trifle. Suddenly angry, he threw all his weight on his right leg, stamping his foot against the dark, slick bark. For a moment only he remained balanced; then his shoe squealed off the root and he lurched forward. Mrs. Klapper took a few quick steps toward him, but he was on his feet, muttering, "No, no, no, I'm all right," and waving her away.

"Woops," Mrs. Klapper said helpfully. "You slipped a little."

"I lost my balance." Let that be a lesson to you, Rebeck, he thought. You are not debonair, and it's a great mistake to pretend that you are, a mistake that may hurt you the way it has hurt other people who thought they were graceful and sanguine. Sanguine. He sighed briefly for the word, as for a vagrant love, and then let it go.

He wished that Mrs. Klapper would say something. She looked very nice in her spring coat. Not beautiful, he thought; beautiful is a word for young people. Beauty is a phase you grow through, like acne. Mrs. Klapper was handsome. Striking. As striking a woman as he had ever seen. But he knew that she had dressed up to please the memory of her husband, and, admiring, he was a bit wistful. She had probably looked forward for days to her tryst with her husband, planning what to wear, what time to come, how long to stay; wondering if the weather would be good and how bad it would have to be to make her stay home; carefully counting out the subway fare, whatever it was now, into her coat pocket before she left the house; keeping track of the subway stations the train passed, because each one brought her that much closer to where her husband was. He wondered how many stations away she lived.

She had not brought flowers. He wondered about that too. Most people swamped the headstone in flowers until it was completely hidden.

"I was coming to see my husband," Mrs. Klapper said then, as if she had known what he was thinking.

"I know," Mr. Rebeck said. Mrs. Klapper turned away from him again to look up the hill, and he thought she would leave then. Indeed, she began to move slowly toward the hill and she did not turn back.

She might at least say good-by, he thought, and he was about to say something like "Don't let me keep you," when Mrs. Klapper turned around. She stood with her legs planted solidly and she held her purse with both hands.

"You could come," she said, "if you're not doing anything."

"I wasn't," Mr. Rebeck answered. "I was just wandering around." He could feel the sudden sweat on his wrists and he wondered if he was frightened. His stomach felt cold.

"Visiting your friend," Mrs. Klapper said.

Mr. Rebeck remembered his supposed acquaintanceship with the Wilders and nodded. "Yes," he said. "It's a quiet place, and we were good friends." He wanted something to lean against, but he stretched his arm behind him and could not find the tree.

"If you're going to see your husband," he went on, "maybe you'd rather go alone. I mean, I wasn't doing any-thing"—might as well get that in—"but maybe you'd rather go by yourself."

"I don't like going by myself," Mrs. Klapper said. "A little company never hurt anybody." She smiled, her mobile mouth as quick as a whitecap on the sea. "You're worried Morris would mind?"

"It isn't exactly that," Mr. Rebeck began. "I just thought—"

"Morris wouldn't mind. Come on." She half extended

her hand to him and then let it drop to her side. "Come on, we'll talk like two friends and make a little noise. Quiet is all right, but enough is enough. Around here it gets too quiet sometimes."

The cold feeling was suddenly gone from Mr. Rebeck's stomach, and in its place a small but earnest thimbleful of wine radiated warmth, like a sun born unexpectedly into a frozen universe. He felt unhooked from himself, dislocated, and he listened with interest to himself saying, "Thank you. I'd like that very much."

Together they walked slowly up the gradual hill beyond which the white house over Morris Klapper loomed and dwarfed the scrubby trees that surrounded it. Neither spoke, nor did they look at each other. Their bodies walked on, while their minds stood a few minutes behind them in the clearing before another house and mused over a still moment when one offered and another accepted.

The building grew great before them, pillar and scroll, marble and iron, far bigger than the Wilder mausoleum, and still the foundation could not be seen. Mr. Rebeck, having just made the pleasant discovery that Mrs. Klapper was smaller than she looked, was practicing looking down at her.

"It's very big," he said. He had never learned to like mausoleums, especially large ones, but he tried hard to get an admiring tone into his voice.

"I wanted it big," Mrs. Klapper answered. "I wanted everybody should know who's buried here." She stopped for a moment to shake a pebble out of her shoe. "You know, I didn't have to give him a big funeral. I mean in his will it didn't say anything about it. His partner said to me—Mr. Harris, his name is—he said, 'Look, Gertrude, all Morris wanted was a little tiny funeral, with maybe a couple of friends and no speeches, please.' He said, 'Gertrude, believe me, we used to talk about it and he didn't want you should fire cannons over his grave or hire a Grand Rabbi.'" She raised her eyebrows at Mr. Rebeck. "Down on his knees, practically. So I said, 'Mr. Harris, I want you to know I appreciate your efforts in Morris's behalf'—just like that—'only I think I knew my husband a little bit better than you did, excuse me, because I was married to him. Morris is going to have a big funeral,' I said, 'with a lot of people, and he is also going to have a big house, marble, the way he wanted it. Maybe you don't want to pay for such a big funeral, Mr. Harris—all right, I'll pay for it. Don't tell me how to bury my husband,' I told him. 'When you die, God forbid, you can have a little tiny funeral and not invite anybody and have a house the size of a cheesebox, but don't tell me how to bury my husband.'"

She was walking faster as she finished, and breathing a bit harder. Mr. Rebeck had to take three short steps to fall into the rhythm of her stride again.

"We could walk a little slower if you're tired," he suggested. Mrs. Klapper looked at him for a moment as if he had suddenly stepped from behind a bush and grabbed her arm. Then she smiled.

"No," she said. "I'm fine." But she did slow her pace, seemingly as unconsciously as she had quickened it.

When they finally topped the low hill they met a man and a woman who greeted them as saviors and asked if they knew where a particular grave was located. And Mr. Rebeck made a mistake, as far as his role of quiet-seeking visitor was concerned. He told them.

He gave the directions carefully, never once noticing the sudden wonder in Mrs. Klapper's eyes. The couple were tired, and angry with each other, and quite lost, and it pleased him that he could help them. So he was quite thorough: he told them the road they must take and the paths they would have to take to reach the road, and he told them to count the marble angels along the way and turn right at a certain angel, and he told them that the grave they sought was very close to the path and would be easy to find. The man and woman were very grateful, and the woman turned around as they walked away and waved at Mr. Rebeck. He waved back.

When he turned around again he met Mrs. Klapper's eyes and knew that he had made a tactical error. There was speculation in her stare, compounded with wonder and a certain amount of awe. She had never looked at him like that before, and the fear that is never far from the hearts of affectionate people returned to his own. He had not considered the effect his casual knowledge of the cemetery might have on her, because he had not even thought of it as knowledge. Someone had asked him for directions, as they had occasionally over nineteen years, and he had known the way. Now, at best, she would mark him as unusual, a freak perhaps, at all events a man with a gimmick memory. She would be amused—she seemed easily amused—but from that time on, she would think of him as a little less than human. That would be the best that could happen. At worst, she would not be amused. She would ask questions, and he would have to lie to her, as he had once before. This depressed him; he did not want to lie to her again, and he knew how poor a liar he was.

He turned away before the couple were out of sight and looked at the mausoleum with his hands in his pockets and his head tipped back. "Well," he said with what he hoped was a calculating but quite unprofessional air. "Well, this certainly is a big house." That was safe. That wouldn't take nineteen years of living in a cemetery to figure out. A man could just look at it and see how big it was. "It certainly is," he said again.

Behind him, Mrs. Klapper said, "I hope they find the place they were looking for."

"Me too," said Mr. Rebeck. "I may very easily have given them the wrong directions. I wasn't at all sure."

"Oh?" Mrs. Klapper was standing at his side now. "You seemed pretty sure."

"Well, you know how it is." Mr. Rebeck smiled hope-

fully at her. "A man hates to have people think he doesn't know his way around."

Mrs. Klapper smiled back. "Believe me, I understand."

There was a long silence, during which Mr. Rebeck looked at the Klapper mausoleum with frantic admiration and Mrs. Klapper rummaged for a handkerchief in her purse. It took her a while to find it because she was looking at Mr. Rebeck, and when she did find it she held it in her hand for some time and then stuffed it back into her purse.

"One headstone," she said quietly. "That's what gets me. A mausoleum, all right, a mausoleum I could see. But one headstone out of a thousand, five thousand, this takes a very good memory."

"I've got a very good memory," Mr. Rebeck said. It was to be the living-room sorcery then. "I can take a deck of cards and—"

"I know you've got a good memory," Mrs. Klapper said absently. "This must be a real blessing. Me, I'm always forgetting things. Did you ever find your watch?"

The question was asked in such an expressionless tone of voice that it took Mr. Rebeck a moment to realize that it was a question at all. When he did realize it, he answered hastily, without looking at his forearm.

"Yes," he said. "I found it right along Fairview, about a mile from the gate. It must have dropped off while I was talking to you and I didn't even notice it."

As he spoke he looked down at his wrist. It was brown, like the rest of his arm, and covered with fine black hairs. He did not look up immediately.

"I left it home today," he said softly. "It had to be fixed." He raised his eyes very gradually and looked at Mrs. Klapper. "Something was wrong with it."

Mrs. Klapper looked at him for a long time, and he looked back at her. There is nothing marvelous about meeting a person's eyes, he thought. Your eyes may start to water after a bit and you may get a kink in your neck, but the soul is far behind the eyes and doesn't even know what's going on up front. So he stared back at Mrs. Klapper, directly and with dignity, until she began to blur and go out of focus.

It was Mrs. Klapper who looked away at last. She walked to the steps of the mausoleum and sat down. "All right," she said. "Forget it. Forget I asked anything. A woman shouldn't play detective. It makes people lie to her, and then she catches them lying and feels proud of herself. Forget I asked. I'm a nosy old woman and I want to know too much. Don't tell me anything."

Mr. Rebeck rubbed his hand across the back of his neck and felt the sweat there. "Mrs. Klapper—" he began.

"Don't tell me anything." Mrs. Klapper made a cutting motion with the edge of her hand. "It's better I shouldn't know. I got a very bad habit."

Mr. Rebeck rubbed his neck again and looked down at her. Quite suddenly he grinned. "Move over," he said.

Mrs. Klapper blinked at him a little bewilderedly. She moved over slightly on the mausoleum step.

"I have to think for a moment." He sat down beside her and looked at the ground. He could feel her eyes on him, but he did not turn his head.

Rebeck, he thought, you have reached one of those Crossroads people write about. As it is your first Crossroad in a good while, I think you ought to take very good care of it and examine it carefully. Not too long, though, please. There is a hypnotizing quality about Crossroads. You can stand and look at them long and long, as Whitman insisted on putting it, and forget to Cross.

He looked down at his wrist and thought, If you had been wearing a wrist watch for any length of time, there would be a white band around your wrist where the sun could not reach. Hurray for you, Jonathan. You and Mrs. Klapper ought to form a detective society.

Should I tell her now? he wondered. Why not? I've been telling everybody lately. Don't exaggerate, Rebeck. Who is everybody? Michael and Laura. Michael and Laura hardly count. They're ghosts. They know what's possible and what isn't. This woman is alive. Make no mistake about that. She is alive, and that means she can hear the truth. It does not mean that she will know it when she hears it.

You'll have to tell her sooner or later. She'll be just as incredulous whenever you do. At worst, she'll run screaming out of here, which might be very interesting to watch, but lonesome later on. At best—what would she do at best? Probably say something like "Okay, but isn't it a little silly?" What will you do then?

Maybe it is a little silly.

Get off the Crossroads, Rebeck. You are beginning to turn around in small, neat circles. A car might hit you.

Maybe it is silly, he thought again. That has nothing to do with it. A lot of serious things are silly, even to the people who do them. That's no way out.

Look at it another way. If you don't tell her, she won't ask you again, but she won't like you very much because you've made her feel nosy. Oh, she will be friendly and cheerful and all that because she is friendly and cheerful. She'll simply stop coming. Even to see her husband, if it means running into you. On the occasions you do meet, you'll smile and wave furiously at each other, the furiousness increasing in direct proportion to the distance between you. Right there you have the nucleus of one of those fifty-year friendships.

Is she that important to you? Privacy is important too, and there is less of it.

No. She is not that important. Not yet. I barely know her. She is not important as an individual. She is a Symbol.

Oh, that's fine. A Symbol of what?

How should I know? As Symbols go, though, she's very nice.

Mrs. Klapper shifted impatiently beside him. "Rebeck, pardon an old woman, but are you laying an egg?"

Whenever Mr. Rebeck thought about it later on, he was always sure that the scales were kicked over when she called him by his name. She never had before. Laura always called him Mr. Rebeck.

He got up and stretched, thumping his chest as if he were taking a shower. Then he looked down at Mrs. Klapper.

"Come on," he said. "Let's walk."

8

Hills had no meaning for Laura any more. She remembered them; in the cemetery there were roads that arched up suddenly, curved and hung, and then dipped to rise again, coiling on themselves like toads' tongues, and these she accepted as hills. Even now, if she thought hard, she could remember what it had been like to climb hills. But the actual rise and fall of land under her feet as she walked did not reach her. Roads and walking she remembered; so under her feet there were pavement and gravel and yellow-brown dirt, pebbles, weeds, grass, even the stunted star that she had been told lived at the center of the earth. Where Laura walked there existed only what Laura remembered, and Laura had forgotten about up and down. So there was no up and down now, exactly as there is no up and down in space, and Laura walked a flat, submissive road that her feet never quite touched.

Actually, she was walking up a small hill, a momentary shoulder-hunch of a road that wound through the poorer section of the cemetery. It was no potter's field; the York-chester view was that excessive poverty was just as ostenta-

tious as excessive wealth. The graves were well kept and
neat, and the ivy that covered most of them was closely
trimmed, but there were so many of them. Headstones
crowded within six inches of one another, and statues
touched elbows. There were enough Christs, Madonnas,
and angels standing in the field to people a thousand heavens, and the short grass that grew between them had a
tentative look about it.

The ragged blanket of earth had been stretched about as
far as it would go, Laura thought. Sooner or later it would
rip down the middle with a sound like fire, and the dead
would be revealed, blinking in the light, lying feet to head
and feet to head, kicking out with their legs for room to
be dead. Get your feet out of my eyes, friend, and quit that
talking to yourself. I don't want to hear you. Leave me
alone. We're dead. I don't have to be your brother now.

There were a lot of people in the cemetery today. Was it
a weekend? Didn't they have anything else to do with their
holidays but come out here and stand around a piece of
stone with their hats off? She was glad that her parents
weren't here. They had sense enough to realize that there
is a little dignity in death but none at all in mourning.

To them all—to the middle-aged man laying flowers at
the feet of a trim and perfect statue; to the pregnant woman
who had brought a wooden folding chair with her; to the
three old women who got out of a big car, wept, got back
into the car, and drove away; to the yellow-haired young
man who sat down on the grass in the middle of a family
plot and spoke politely in Italian to all the gravestones—to
them all, she said aloud, "Do you think your dead can hear
you, do you think they know you weep? They're not here,
not one of them, and if they were they wouldn't know
you. They're a long way gone and they wouldn't come
back if they could. Go home and talk to each other, if you
know how. We don't want you here. You didn't want us
when we were alive, and now we don't want you. Go
away. Tell your bodies to take you home." And although

they could not hear her, she felt for a moment that she was more than Laura, that the absent dead had truly chosen her to speak for them.

But then she saw a man standing before the statue of a boy reading a book. The boy's face had the picture-book impersonality of the Christs that flanked him, but something—the round chin, perhaps, or the big ears—made him look young and human. The unlined slickness of marble had trapped a little of that youth. On the front of the bench there was an inscription. Below it were two dates.

The boy himself was sitting on the bench, next to the statue. He was smaller than the statue and very thin and tenuous; a thin line marking a boy's shape in the air. Against the stained marble of his statue and with the sun behind him, he was nearly invisible. The man in front of his grave spoke softly and foolishly, and the boy never moved.

The man reached out a hand to touch the statue and Laura was quickly and completely jealous. She thought, Oh, this is bad, this is really bad. Leave him alone. Must you even envy dead children? You were better alive, when you didn't dare let people see how jealous you were. The familiar swelling ache was in her, for this is an ache of the mind that does not need the body to express itself.

"He comes to see you now," she said to the boy, "to show everyone how much he misses you. But he'll stop coming someday. What will you do then?"

The boy did not turn to her and this infuriated her. It was as if he too were alive and she were the only one of them who could not be heard.

"You'll sit and wait," she said. "He'll never come, but you'll sit and wait for him. People will come to see every grave in the cemetery, but not yours. You wait and look up whenever anyone passes by, but they don't come. They never come. You think you have him now, but you've no one but me, no one but Laura to talk to you and be with you. You're dead now, and you have only me."

But the man murmured softly to the statue, and the boy listened, and the statue continued to read its stone story.

"All right," Laura said. "Do you think I care?" And she turned her back on them all and began to walk up the hill that seemed as level as any other road, as all roads. . . .

Thinking again of the boy, she wondered, Why did I do that? What was it I was trying to do? Whom was I trying to hurt? Not him. Not a dead child. I used to be very good with children. It was part of my charm.

God, I was jealous of so much beauty when I was alive. It ought to stop here. This is no place for envy, for wanting to be like the soft-skinned women. We're equal now. They can't bring their good bodies here, or their smooth little faces. No one will wait for them at lunchtime, or take them at night. Their men can't see them any more, or touch them, or love them. It takes time, but we're equal in the end. There is no difference between us.

Only the difference between you and that stone boy. Someone remembers him.

Michael's grave and her own were in one of the Catholic sections of the cemetery, about half a mile from the gate. It was a middle-class section, meaning that the graves were not as closely crowded together as in the section she had left, and there were a few small mausoleums. One, by which she recognized the area when she came to it, bore a statue of a kneeling woman clinging to a cross. Laura disliked that one. The cross looked smooth and unreachable. She expected it to free itself from the kneeling woman with a quick shrug, and the woman looked as if she expected it also.

Even as she made it perfectly clear to herself that she was passing Michael's grave only because it was on the way to her own, she saw two people standing before it. She stopped for a moment, ready to hide, before she remembered that they could not see her. Then, irritated because she had forgotten this, she walked up to the two and stood beside them as they looked down at the plain square head-stone that said MICHAEL MORGAN.

They were a man and a woman. The man was short-legged and heavy-shouldered, a little shorter than the woman. He was hatless, and his face was truculent and tired. The woman was blond, and her head was small and so subtly and gradually tapered that it seemed almost out of place attached to her full-breasted body. But her waist and hips were slim, and she carried herself with the light arrogance of a Jolly Roger.

She's beautiful, Laura thought. Heavens, she's beautiful. If I were alive I'd hate her. No, I wouldn't, either. What would be the point of it? I used to hate the almost-beautiful women, the pretty women, because I felt that I could look like that if I knew what to wear and what sort of make-up to use and how to walk right. I felt that they knew something secret and were keeping it from me, because if I knew it I'd be just as pretty as they and be able to compete with them for the things I wanted. This one is on another level altogether. I'd never even think of competing with her, no matter how pretty I was. Which is damn nice of me.

"The poison is the big thing," the man said. His voice was high and hoarse. "If you didn't buy it, he did. And if I can find out just where he bought it, we've got something to go on."

The woman's voice was just the way Laura had imagined it would sound. "I don't see how you can. Every little hardware store in the country probably carries it."

The man chortled triumphantly. "Uh-uh. That's just it. You can't get it in New York."

"I don't see—"

"Look, I took the can to a couple of hardware stores, and they told me the same thing in each one. The stuff isn't marketed in New York because it's mostly for field mice. It's strychnine-based, like the standard brands, but it's sup-posed to be very effective on field mice. Who's got field mice in New York? You see what I'm getting at?"

There were flowers on the grave, roses. The woman knelt to touch one. "Where did it come from, then?"

"That I don't know," the man said. "But it's made by a little outfit in Greenwich, Connecticut. They distribute to about ten or eleven little weed-killer stores all the hell over New England. The way I figure it, if I spend the next couple of weeks chasing around up there, I might be able to trace the stuff back to wherever it was bought. And they just might remember who they sold it to. They keep records. It's worth a shot."

The woman did not rise or turn her head to him. "It's not very much, is it?"

"It's not that bad," the man said defensively. "The thing is, the stuff isn't moving very well. Most people still buy the standard brands, and this stuff just sits on the shelves. When somebody does buy some, it's a big event. Like Christmas. They remember who buys that brand."

He sighed and seemed to slump from the shoulders down. "Sure it's thin," he said sourly. "It's even thinner than it sounds. If the poison was bought more than a month ago, I'm screwed. They won't remember. But what else can I do? I told you before, I'm no Darrow. I'm just persistent as hell. I do what I can with the tools I've got, and all I've got is that poison. So I'll trace it back as far as I can, and if it doesn't work out, I'll try something else. If I can think of something else to try."

"Eleven stores make it difficult," the woman said. She straightened up, brushing dirt and grass from her skirt. "Even if one of them did sell the poison to Michael, they might not remember him."

This is Sandra, Laura realized. This is Michael's wife. She came closer to the woman and stared at her, unconsciously trying to see her less beautiful. She searched the gently pointed face for a skin blemish, tried to will the gray eyes smaller and the nose overlarge. As close as a woman has ever stood to another woman Laura stood to Sandra and, invisibly, felt nakedly ugly by comparison.

"They treating you all right there?" the man asked. He slouched as he stood there. Occasionally he would look sideways at the slim woman beside him and make an effort to straighten his slumped shoulders.

"Oh, yes," the woman said. "Very well. They're very polite." She smiled absently, looking at the grave. "I wonder what Michael would think if he knew I was in jail. Michael was always very protective."

"Yeah," the man said. "That reminds me, fighting with him at the party wasn't a hell of a good idea. The D.A.'ll have everybody who was there in court, and there won't be very much I can do about it. I wish you'd waited until you got home."

The woman turned slowly to face him. "He was drunk. You don't know how it was. He was drunk, and he made a complete fool of himself in front of the chancellor. He told jokes, and he sang, and he kept starting stupid arguments with the chancellor. All the women were looking at me, because I was his wife and I couldn't stop him, and all the men were figuring how they could get closer to the chancellor by taking his side against Michael. Everything I ever worked for went out the window that night. We'd have had to go somewhere else and start all over again. And they write letters about you when something like this happens. I know they do. All the things Michael could have been—"

The man interrupted her, harshly and deliberately. "You see why I didn't let you go before the grand jury? You get all worked up like this and you sound as if you could have killed somebody. Take it easy. You do that in court and you'll make the D.A.'s case for him. At least let's make him work a little."

"You still believe I might have killed Michael." There was a soft and plaintive dignity to the woman's voice that Laura admired, although she knew perfectly well that it was artificial. Women make better innocent victims than men, she thought. They see the drama in the role. Men see only the injustice happening to them, and they howl.

"I think you could have done it," the man said. "I'm pretty sure you didn't. But I'm never really sure of anything."

"That must be sad."

"It's kept me from being married, killed, and disbarred. It's only sad if you think there's one thing sure in the world and you have to keep looking for it. Otherwise it holds up pretty well. Keeps you from spending much time in places like this."

"Michael was my husband," the woman murmured. There was a sleepy, smug look about her eyes, the look one often sees in the eyes of women who have just given birth. "I had to come. I wouldn't have felt right if I hadn't come here today."

"Why? If you're trying to impress the D.A.'s tails, forget it. They're waiting outside. And if you're trying to convince me that you loved your husband, I'll take you home whenever you're ready."

"I loved him as much as I could." The woman stared down at the grave. "Sometimes I wonder if I'm able to give love. I don't think I am. Michael wouldn't have committed suicide if I was."

"That's getting to be a pretty fashionable position," the man said. "Used to be people wrote books about women who slept with the iceman because they were overflowing with love for humanity and they had to start somewhere. Now it's the other way around. Everybody's sorry for the woman who can't love anybody. Now she sleeps with the iceman because she's trying to destroy herself. Doesn't make a hell of a lot of difference to the iceman. Anyway, I wouldn't feel too bad about not loving your husband. He didn't love you."

The woman turned on him so fast that she kicked one of the roses. "That's not so. Michael loved me. If he loved anything in the world, he loved me. He told me so a dozen times a day. It used to frighten me because I knew I didn't deserve that kind of love. I used to warn him not to love me so much." The soft voice had gotten higher, and the narrow face was quite pale. "Don't you ever say Michael didn't love me. There's a lot you don't know about Michael, or about me."

"Ain't it the truth," the stocky man said amiably. "You ready to go now?"

"Not yet," the woman said. She had regained control of herself as quickly as she had thrown it away, but her hands were still clenched and pressed against her sides. "I just want to stand here quietly for a moment. Don't say anything. I shouldn't have let you come with me. Be quiet."

"But first, ladies and gentlemen," the man muttered, "our national anthem." The woman gave him a look of calm disgust and turned away to stare at Michael's grave. Her head was bowed and her hands, open now, seemed conscious of their futility. A breeze ruffled a loose lock of her blond hair, and she did not raise a hand to pat it back into place. All sexuality was gone from her in that moment. She might have been a nun at evening. Even the heavy-shouldered man seemed on the verge of being impressed.

Laura saw the woman's lips move to shape Michael's name, and she thought, Michael's Sandra, you're a hypocrite and you may be a murderess just as naturally. I hope you are. Forgive me that, and forgive my envy of the golden planes of your face, but I hope, and, because I hope, believe, that you killed your husband. Please understand me. I have nothing against you as a person except that you had to warn a man not to love you so much. This seems a waste of natural resources to me, whose hair was straight and dull and who danced like the Washington Monument. My attitude may seem unfair and incomprehensible, but you would understand if you had known me when I was alive. If I were on your jury I would fight to see you set free, but I know you're guilty. That's the way my mind works, or at least that's the way I remember its working.

I have to find you guilty because I'm not dishonest enough to find you ugly, and I have to dislike you to keep myself from wanting to be like you. If you knew me you'd understand.

Is that all? she wondered. Is there anything else to say? I have a feeling there is, the same feeling of something left out I've had ever since I came to this place. You try so hard to be honest with yourself and you wind up by making lies a little less pleasant to the taste.

"We can go now," the woman said.

You're forgetting the rose you kicked, Laura told her. Put it back the way it was. It just has to be straightened out a little. I'd do it myself and save you the trouble, but I can't. Would you, please? Thank you.

As if she had heard, the woman knelt gracefully and put the rose back into line with the other flowers. Her long fingers had a slight tint of lemon to them, but her nails were the same shade as the roses. A little darker, perhaps; roses after rain.

Thank you Sandra, Laura said. Good-by. She wondered where Michael was.

"How much time do we have?" the woman asked. She and the man began to walk away from Michael's grave.

"The trial's down for August eighth," the man answered. "Gives us almost a month."

"That's not much time." The soft voice sounded a little worried.

"Time enough. If there's anything for me to find, I'll have it in a month. If I can't turn up anything—" He shrugged heavily. "We can always appeal."

The woman stopped with her hand on the man's arm. "I didn't kill Michael. I won't suffer for something I didn't do."

The man's high chuckle was like sand rattling into a tin pail. He started walking again, and the woman followed him. "Why not? Why should you be different from the rest of us?"

"That isn't funny, damn you," the woman said.

They passed out of Laura's sight, although she could still hear their voices. The man's answer was amused and easy. "That's called gallows humor, lady. It'll get funnier as time passes." From that point on, the voices became blurred, partly because Laura was not listening very hard.

I suppose I could follow them, she thought. I was going to visit my own grave, after all, not Michael's. The trouble is, I don't really want to follow them. I don't want to see them. What do I want with the living? I'm not going to depend on them. If I do that I'll never forget life, never get to sleep. And I've got to stop letting myself be distracted. If I can't be alive, I want to be dead. Dead, as in dead. I don't like this in-between state. It's too much like life and not enough like it. I have to stop looking at live things and being interested in them. Even the scurrying of an ant is treachery, even a dandelion is deceitful and seductive. And that reminds me, I wish I could blow on one of those fat white dandelions. If you make a wish and blow all the fluff off in one breath, the wish comes true. I know. I was never able to do it all in one breath, and my wishes never came true.

The dead have nothing to do with dandelions, and the dead don't make wishes. I'll go to my own grave and lie down again.

Then she heard whistling, and she turned to see Michael coming down the road she had walked. The whistling of a ghost is like no other sound in a fistful of universes, because it is woven of all the whistles the ghost has ever heard, and so it usually includes train moans, lunch whistles, fire alarms, and the affronted-virgin screaming of tea kettles. To all of these components Michael had added an extra memory: the agonized yowl of a car stopping very suddenly in a very short space. It all made for a tuneless and unmelodic sort of sound, but ghosts have no interest in melody. The production of sound is all that interests them. Michael seemed quite pleased with his whistling.

"Hello, Michael," Laura said when he seemed about to pass by without seeing her.

Michael stopped and looked up. "Hello, Laura. Listen, and I'll whistle your name."

He whistled a brief passage of notes that made Laura think of a kite caught in a hurricane. It stopped suddenly, and she said, "Is that all?"

"You ought to have a longer name," Michael said. "Longer and harsher. That's the best I can do with Laura Durand." He sat down in the middle of the road and beckoned her to join him. "I've been doing this all morning—whistling up names for things. Like leitmotivs. You name it and I'll whistle it. Go on."

"Dandelions," Laura said promptly.

"Dandelions. Right." Michael whistled a few bars of a crashing march tune. "Dandelions."

"Not to me. It sounded like dinner music at an American Legion picnic."

"That's the way I see dandelions," Michael said firmly. "I'm an impressionist. If you want program music, get yourself one of those hundred-and-fifty-violin orchestras. Whistling is a very personal kind of music."

"All right," Laura said. "I leave you your integrity. Do Mr. Rebeck."

"I haven't got him yet. I've been trying on and off, but it never comes out. I'm still new at this, remember. Try something else."

For a moment Laura considered saying, "Sandra. What kind of Sandra-music do you have?" She gave up the idea only because she was afraid he might actually have a melody for the name.

At that moment Michael noticed the bright flowers on his grave. "Hey," he said. "Somebody dropped something." He got up and went over to look closely at the roses.

"I'll be damned," he said. "I've got a secret admirer."

"Your wife left them," Laura said. "She was here a few minutes ago."

Michael was silent, his back to her. She could see through to the small marble headstone shining in the sun.

"Very fresh, too," he said after a moment. "And expensive. Eight or ten dollars a dozen. I always wondered why one kind of rose should be worth more than another."

"She just left a minute or so before you came," Laura said doggedly. I'm getting mean again, she thought, and in a way it's worse than with the boy.

"I heard you," Michael said. "What do you want me to do about it?"

"I don't know. She's your wife."

"Nope. Not any more. Death us parted. We are annulled. There's a really terrifying word for you. Annulled."

"You could follow her, I suppose," Laura said. "She was walking very slowly."

"I don't want to, God damn it!" She felt oddly satisfied that she had made him shout. "I don't want to see her. I have nothing to say to her, and if I had she couldn't hear me. She was my wife and she murdered me, and my feelings are understandably hurt about the whole thing. Stop talking about her. I don't want to hear anything about her. Stop talking about her or go away. One or the other."

He had stepped on the roses in his anger. They lay unharmed under his feet, dark red, their outer petals already beginning to curl in the heat of the morning. They had not yet begun to change color. That would come later.

"I'm sorry," she said, and she was, though she did not quite know for what. "I'm very sorry, Michael."

"Forget it," Michael said.

"I get like this once in a while. I don't know why. I never used to when I was alive."

"It's all right," Michael said. "Don't talk about it. Look, are you doing anything right now?" In the same breath he said, "That is conceivably the most stupid thing I ever said, in life or in death."

"No," Laura said. She did not laugh. "I'm not doing anything special. I was just walking around."

"Come with me, then, if you feel like walking. I was heading down to the gate to look at people."

Laura hesitated before she spoke. "I usually stay away from the gate. I used to go down regularly, like going for the mail, but it's begun to depress me. The people and the guards and the cars, and the gate so easy for them to pass—I'd rather not, Michael."

"It doesn't bother me much," Michael said. "I like listening to them. But we don't have to go there."

He frowned for a moment. "I found a place a while ago. Maybe you know it. It's a wall." He glanced at her for any sign of recognition.

Laura shook her head. "I don't think I know it."

"It's right at the edge of the cemetery. A low brick wall."

"No," Laura said. "I'm a stranger here."

"Come on, then," Michael said eagerly. "It's not too far—as if that makes any difference. Come on and I'll show you. It's very nice. Looks out over the whole city—all of Yorkchester, anyway. It's a wonderful view."

"I'd like that," Laura said.

"We have to go back where the road forks," Michael said as they walked. "Then it's a straight gravel road with a big hothouse at the end of it. We turn right at the hothouse, and there it is."

"What on earth do they have a hothouse for?"

"You know that fungus-like ivy they have on most of the graves?" Laura nodded. "That's where they raise it. They raise some flowers too, in case you come unarmed."

He turned his head to look down at her. "I was thinking about flowers on graves. Isn't it the hell of a barbaric custom? Look at it logically. It wastes perfectly good flowers. They lie there and wither. Nobody should do that with flowers. And it doesn't mean anything to the dead."

"Yes it does," Laura said. "I like it when Marian and Carl leave flowers for me."

"Why? Does it make you feel that somebody remembers you?"

"No, it isn't that."

"Because they don't, you know, after a while. It becomes automatic, something done, like going to church."

"It isn't that," Laura said. "Oh, I suppose it is, a little, but I like flowers. I liked them when I was alive, and I like them now. They please me."

"They please me too, but there's nothing personal in it. Flowers on anybody else's grave please me as much as flowers on my own. I like flowers as flowers, not as symbols of loss. I know I'm generalizing and oversimplifying and, in general, talking like a college sophomore, but I'm also dead, and gestures toward the honoring of my body don't interest me these days. I'd just as soon they'd buried me with my bow and arrows and killed a horse over my grave. A dead horse on my grave would be fine. Distinctive. Be the first in your gang to get one."

"I saw a boy this morning—" Laura began, but Michael rode right over her.

"And my wife," he said delightedly. "Let them bury my wife with me. There's a useful gift to the departing warrior. Never mind the bloody flowers. Skip the bow and arrows and drag that damn horse away. I want my wife. Just drop her in with me and pat down the earth with a shovel. If you hear noises, it'll be us singing the duet from *Aida*." He grinned at Laura. "There's a personal gift. What do I want with flowers?"

"Your wife is beautiful," Laura said.

He wants to talk about her, she thought. He'd rather forget her altogether, but if he can't do that he'll talk to keep from thinking. I don't mind. I don't think I mind.

"Isn't she, though?" Michael said. There was a touch of grimness in his tone. "In many ways the ranking bitch of the Western world, but, by God, I loved to walk down the street with her. I have to admit that. We used to walk along with our arms around each other's waists—" He broke off the sentence and looked so long at Laura that she became a little nervous and was relieved when he spoke again.

"That's the nicest way of walking I know. Something secure and affectionate about it. Solid."

"I know," Laura said, thinking, I really do know, but I'll bet you don't believe it.

"Anyway," Michael said, "we were walking like that once and we saw ourselves reflected in a store window. I laughed, and she wanted to know why, and I said, 'I was just wondering, What's that bum doing with that good-looking broad?' "

"What did she say?" Laura asked.

"She said, 'I was just thinking the same thing.' We went on walking." Michael sighed. "I wish she hadn't murdered me. We got along well sometimes."

He began to whistle again as they walked along. The sound was high, so high that it would have been inaudible to a human ear. The tune was wailing and mournful, almost flagrantly so, and the total effect was of a heart-broken piccolo being parted forever from its bagpipe lover. But Michael seemed proud of it, and he whistled it contentedly all the way to the gravel path, and when he stopped it was to ask, "She really looked good?"

"Yes," Laura said. "She looked graceful. That's the only word that seems to fit."

"Graceful," Michael said thoughtfully. "It is a good word. Sums her up, in a way. She did everything gracefully."

"There are people like that," Laura said. "People who never look clumsy, no matter what they do. Everything is done just right, everything is said right. If they seemed conscious of it you'd feel better, because you could call them affected and say, 'Well, thank God I'm not like that.' But with these people it's completely natural, like a cat stretching."

She felt that she was stumbling and straining for words, but the sudden curiosity with which Michael was looking at her drove her on. It was like running downhill, arms

spread wide, hoping not to fall but expecting it momen-
tarily. She wanted Michael to understand.

"Sometimes you walk along the street and you see someone coming, somebody you know. He hasn't seen you yet,
but you know he'll wave and smile and say something as
soon as he sees you. And all at once, in the moment before
he sees you, you think, I'm going to foul this up. I don't
quite know how, but I'm going to. I can hardly wait to see
how I do it. Will I stop and stick out my hand when he
expects me to wave and pass by, and will we stand there,
a little island of embarrassment in the middle of the street,
with people jostling us and our hands sticky? Will I let go
of his hand before he is ready to let go of mine, or will it
be the other way around? What will I say when he calls,
'How's it going?' Will I just grunt like an idiot, or will I
stop and tell him? Am I brave enough to walk on and
pretend I don't see him? What terrible thing is going to
happen in the next five seconds? . . . So you wait five seconds and find out."

That was pretty good, she thought. I never said it that
way when I was alive. And he's looking at me and thinking
about it. Maybe it was worth saying.

Two white butterflies danced across the path with the
rambling abandon of ribbons in the wind. They spun
around each other, like a double star, broke apart, and fled
away down the gravel path, one close behind the other.

"Anyway, that doesn't ever happen to the graceful people," she said. "I don't know why, but it doesn't. Maybe
it's due to a gene or a lack of one."

"Stop feeling sorry for yourself," Michael said, and she
gasped with shock.

"I'm not feeling sorry for myself! I never do. That's one
of the things I learned very early—it's useless to feel sorry
for yourself, and it's ugly besides. I haven't pitied myself
in years."

"All right," Michael. "Keep up the good work."

His calm amusement angered her. "And I don't hang on

to things—life or people or objects or anything. I told you that once. I let things go. It might do you a lot of good."

"Maybe," Michael said. "That's where we differ. What I love I hang on to. With both hands, and my teeth, if I can get a good grip."

"Even if it doesn't love you?" Laura demanded.

"Even then. Especially then. Anybody can love something that loves you back. The other way takes a certain amount of effort."

"We see things differently, then," she said, and they walked on silently.

The gravel road made a gradual turn, and they saw the hothouse. Michael pointed at the greenness that crowded against its glass sides.

"See," he said. "That's the ivy. Unprepossessing, isn't it?"

Laura nodded. The ivy seemed squat and sullen in the glass house. "I wonder," she said aloud, "if that's the same type of ivy that's supposed to grow on college walls."

"Might be," Michael said. "It has the same arrogantly useless look. I wouldn't be surprised."

He pointed again. "And the wall's right over there. Can you see it?"

"Yes," Laura said. The wall was about as high as her shoulders, and perhaps seventy-five feet long. The gravel road ended in a kind of dusty hollow, and the wall fenced off the open end of the hollow. It was made of reddish-brown bricks, and it had been made with too much mortar. As they approached it they could see the hardened cement bulging and spilling thickly between the individual bricks.

Michael stopped at the wall and turned to her. "Do you know how to jump?"

"I guess so," she said dubiously. "What do you do?"

"Like this," Michael said. He flickered out of sight for an instant and reappeared sitting cross-legged on top of the wall.

"It's like thinking yourself places," he explained, "only

it's for such a short distance that you have to be careful not to overshoot. Concentrate on getting the jump just right and forget about being visible for a moment. Be careful. It's tricky the first few times."

Laura made it on the fourth try and sat beside him on the wall. "I'd feel excited and breathless," she said, "if I had any breath to lose. That's the great disadvantage of not having a body. You forget what it's like to rest when you're tired."

"You're never satisfied," Michael said, but he smiled. "Look now. Look over there."

Below the wall the land fell away abruptly to a last field of cheap, chalky headstones. Beyond the field she saw the great fence that ran all around the cemetery, and beyond the fence there was the hard grillwork of the city.

"I never saw this," she said. "I was never here before."

From where they sat on the wall they could see almost all of Yorkchester. The buildings stood up in pinkness, differing from one another only in the number of television aerials that they wore like hairpins. Between them, cars clustered in the streets like bunches of a sour fruit. The flat wind of summer slid across the city, lifting skirts without any real interest, and the people moved slowly in the streets. On the skyline there rose the proudly naked skeleton of what would probably be a housing project. There was movement on it, and Laura was sure she could hear the workmen shouting. A three-lane highway ran parallel to the city, agreeable to keeping it company for a little, but sleekly separate even when the streets of the city ran into it.

Michael saw Laura looking at the highway and said, "There was a river there before the highway. First they thinned it down to a trickle. Then they changed its course three or four times. Finally the damn thing just disappeared. Died of frustration, I think."

She could hear every sound in the city, Laura thought. She heard the car horns, and the curses in the streets, and the children crying in the heat, and the clicking of light switches in the office buildings. She heard the thrumming of the electric fans in the subway trains, and the sounds that different kinds of heels make on different kinds of pavements, and the bouncing of rubber balls against the sides of buildings, and the shrill yells of the workmen on the housing project. She even heard the clear clatter of coins in the money machines of buses.

Beside her, Michael murmured, "And the devil took Faust up on a high place and showed him all the cities of the world."

Laura reluctantly took her eyes off the city before her. "Is that Faust? There's something like it in the Bible, about Christ."

"Both, I think," Michael said. "Faust gave in and Christ didn't, that's all. The devil couldn't meet Christ's price, and so Christ went uncorrupted. There are honest people in the world, but only because the devil considers their asking prices ridiculous."

Laura laughed. "Now you sound a little like that man who was with your wife."

"What man?" Michael asked sharply.

"I don't know his name. I think he's her lawyer."

"Oh," Michael said slowly.

After a moment he said, "Excuse me for snapping at you."

"I didn't notice," Laura said. She looked out at the city again. "Anyway, this isn't exactly all the world. It's only Yorkchester."

"It's all we've got. Hell, it's more than we've got. If the devil offered it to me right now—" He left the sentence unfinished.

"Michael," Laura said suddenly.

"Uh-huh?"

She began to tell him about the statue of the boy she had seen in the morning. She told it carefully, putting in every detail she could remember, including the statue's book and the things the man had said as he stood there. When she came to the parts where she had threatened the boy and told him that nobody would come to see him, she faltered a little and looked away from Michael, but she told him everything that she remembered. He listened quietly, never smiling or interrupting her.

"I don't know why I did it," she finished. "Every time I think about it I get more and more ashamed of myself. I never did that sort of thing while I was alive, Michael, no matter what I felt. Why should I do it now? What did I think I was gaining from it?"

Michael shrugged. "I don't know, Laura. I don't know you well enough. Maybe you just got tired of being sweet and shy. This happens. It's a bastardly role to play. It doesn't matter. You didn't hurt him."

Deliberately and openly he changed the subject by pointing a third time toward Yorkchester. "Do you like it? Are you glad I brought you here?"

"Yes," Laura said quickly, glad for the opportunity to stop talking about the boy. "I love sitting and looking at it. I could sit here all day."

"I have. You should see it at night. Like a birthday cake."

"I love the sounds. Probably because the cemetery's so quiet. I found myself going in search of noises."

"Tell me some," Michael said. "What do you hear?"

"People talking," Laura began, "and traffic, and airplanes overhead—" She stopped and turned to him. "Why do you ask me? Can't you hear them yourself?"

Michael shook his head. "Not a sound. Never, since I died."

"I don't understand," Laura said slowly. "You can hear me, can't you?"

"Loud and clear. I hear whoever I'm talking to, and I hear whatever sounds you can hear in a cemetery. But I can't hear a thing from that damn city."

He smiled wryly at her puzzlement. "All the sounds we hear are sounds we remember. We know how talk and trains and running water should sound, and if we're a little off in remembering, a little sharp or flat, nobody notices. But I just don't remember how Yorkchester sounded, all in all. I didn't pay very much attention, I think."

"I'm sorry—" Laura said awkwardly.

"Never mind being sorry. You and I waste entirely too much effort apologizing to each other. Just tell me some of the sounds you hear. I'll listen."

Laura hesitated. "I don't really know where to begin. There's a pile driver working over by that new building."

"What does it sound like?" When she did not speak, he added, "It's all right. Tell me what it sounds like to you."

"Like a heartbeat," Laura said. "Very heavy and regular. A slow, slamming heartbeat."

"Uh-huh. What about subway trains? Can you tell me about those?"

"Not right now," Laura said. "I'll tell you as soon as one comes. I can tell you about buses in the meantime."

"All right," Michael said. "Fine. Tell me how buses sound."

So Laura told him about buses, and they sat on the wall all that summer day, listening to the city and the trains.

9

Somewhere between two and three in the morning, Mr. Rebeck gave up the struggle. "This is not going to work," he said. He stood up, barefooted, in a swirl of blankets and cushions and went to the open door of the mausoleum to consider the matter.

I am not going to get any sleep tonight, he said to himself. For all I know, I may have evolved beyond the need for sleep. Perhaps I will never sleep again. Well, that may not be too bad. I can spend my nights working on the very hard chess problems, the ones I have never been able to solve, and maybe I can teach myself a little about astronomy. I could start right now.

But he did not move. He leaned in the doorway, shivering pleasantly at the touch of cold iron against his skin. The night air was warm, even a trifle humid, but whenever it threatened to become stagnant a breeze disturbed it, as small bugs skitter away the dignity of a still pond. The sky was dark but completely cloudless. Tomorrow would be a very hot day, with the kind of heat that lasts long after sundown, betraying the night. The days following it would

probably be hot too; late July in New York is the time
when the hot days run in packs.

The trouble is, Mr. Rebeck thought, that if I haven't
worked out these chess problems in nineteen years of days,
I don't see what difference the nights will make. If I had it
in me to find the answers, I would have found them long
ago. And the same applies to knowing about the stars. I
could never be an astronomer. I haven't got the brains. I
am a druggist who has read a few books. I haven't taught
myself anything here. I have just remembered a few things
that bored me when I lived in a different world and changed
my clothes every day. Forget it, Jonathan, and go back to
sleep. And before you go to sleep, pray that no well-mean-
ing god ever makes you immortal.

He turned and went back into the mausoleum, but he did
not lie down to sleep. Instead he groped in a sock-cluttered
corner and drew forth his old red and black bathrobe and
a pair of battered bedroom slippers. He put them both on
and went outside again, closing the iron door behind him.

I'll go down to the gate, he thought, just for the sake of
the walk. Maybe it will tire me out and make me sleep
when I get back. Besides, I can get a drink from the water
fountain in the lavatory.

So he knotted the belt of his bathrobe around his thin
waist and walked through the grass until he felt the loose
gravel of Central Avenue rolling under his slippers. Then
he set off down the long road, trying out of habit to make
as little noise as possible. There was no moon to light the
way, but Mr. Rebeck padded along the road with the brisk
air of a man who knew what he was doing and would have
rejected the moon as an impertinence. He felt it himself.
How wonderful it is to feel competent, he thought. Every
man should know something in the world as well as I know
this road. It fits my feet. I could walk it drunk and blind-
folded and never lose my way. But I wish somebody could
see me. I wish I could show somebody how well I can walk
this road in the middle of the night. . . . And that, of

course, made him think of Mrs. Klapper. He would have, anyway, but it was more fun to let her gradually creep into whatever he was thinking. It felt more natural.

Mrs. Klapper thought he was crazy. She told him so every time she saw him. Any man who would live in a cemetery, she told him, was not only crazy but guilty of extremely bad taste. What a place for visitors to have to come! How did he get his mail? What did he do in the winter? Could he at least take a bath once in a while? How did he eat? The latter question almost led to Mr. Rebeck's complete undoing. He had begun to tell her about the raven when he realized that Mrs. Klapper's credulity had been stretched as far as it would go and would snap at the slightest mention of a profane black bird bringing him food. He quickly changed the raven to a very old friend, a childhood companion who kept him supplied with food out of respect for the lost youth they had shared. He told it very well and wished it were true.

Mrs. Klapper was not impressed. She sniffed. "Some friend. How come he doesn't say, 'Come on over to my place, I'll put you up,' he's such a friend?"

"I wouldn't think of imposing on him," Mr. Rebeck had said. He drew himself up and looked sternly at her. "I do have some pride, after all."

"Hoo-boy," Mrs. Klapper hooted derisively. "Suddenly it's pride. A proud crazy. Look how he sits up, like a general. Ah, Rebeck, you're such a *schmuck*."

But in the three weeks since he had disclosed his manner of living to her she had come often to the cemetery. For a while he had taken to sitting on the mausoleum steps in the afternoon, waiting for her to come. Recently, though, he had begun to walk down the road to meet her because Central Avenue ran uphill from the gate, and Mrs. Klapper was not built for much uphill walking. Besides, he found himself eager for the moment when she caught sight of him—he always saw her first—and waved her arm and yelled, "Hey, Rebeck! It's Klapper!" There was nothing planned about the greeting, even though it was always the same. He felt that she was glad to see him and wanted to make sure that he noticed her. For himself, the exuberant shout made him feel real, a person who clashed enough with the scenery to be recognized, and hailed, and called crazy.

Man searches constantly for identity, he thought as he trotted along the gravel path. He has no real proof of his existence except for the reaction of other people to that fact. So he listens very closely to what people say to one another about him, whether it's good or bad, because it indicates that he lives in the same world they do, and that all his fears about being invisible, impotent, lacking some mysterious dimension that other people have, are groundless. That's why people like to have nicknames. I'm glad Mrs. Klapper knows I exist. That should count for two or three ordinary people.

The road broadened, spreading to a kind of delta of pavement, at one side of which there shone the single light of the caretaker's office. Directly across from it, about thirty yards away, the far more impressive shape of the lavatory bulked in darkness. The road itself ran straight to the entowered gate, padlocked now, as it had been since five in the afternoon. Mr. Rebeck turned his eyes away from it. He never looked at the gate more than he had to.

He was very quiet, slipping into the lavatory. The first thing he did was to close the heavy door, knowing from experience that an unavoidable noise, such as the flushing of a toilet or the running of water in a sink, could not now be heard unless the listener were standing only a few feet from the door. Then he turned on the dim fluorescent light on the ceiling. There was no window on the side of the building that faced the caretaker's office, and the light was so dim that there was very little chance of its being seen under the door.

He used one of the urinals, keeping a nervous eye on the door. In his recurring dream of discovery, it was often at moments like this that the doors—there were always several doors in his dream—burst open and the faceless captors came rushing in upon him from all sides. He drank from the water fountain set near the row of sinks, opened the door carefully, and stepped outside to face the shadows that reminded him of iron dogs, frozen in wait for some quarry. He was deeply glad that they paid no attention to him. Years ago he had thought that they bared bright teeth at him in recognition and too eager welcome.

Tonight, however, a new shadow stood among the shadows, a Monster among the iron hounds. The shadow moved through them, shoving the tensely patient dogs out of its path, faced Mr. Rebeck with its hands on its hips, and said, "You!"

It had come, then. That was how they said it in the dream—"*You!*" There were more of them in the dream, and they were shouting, but it was the same word. They were aware of his existence now; he had identity in their minds, and he was almost grateful for it.

"Me?" he said, questioning his new-found status, as if he were not quite able to believe that the gift was really for him, that there had been no mistake.

"Come here," the man said, gesturing imperiously with a heavy forefinger. "I said, come here," he repeated when Mr. Rebeck did not move.

Mr. Rebeck went slowly toward him, feet dragging on the pavement. The man became huger and darker as Mr. Rebeck came closer, until at last Mr. Rebeck stood in front of him, peering up into his face with his neck slightly twisted, as if he were following the drift of a great thundercloud. The man's features—nose, mouth, eyes, chin, forehead—were all large and prominent, except for a pair of ridiculously small ears, fitting so close to his head that they were almost lost by contrast with the shock of burnt-black hair that finished one end of the man.

He pointed back toward the lavatory over Mr. Rebeck's

shoulder and asked, "You finished in there?" His voice was deep and without expression.

"Yes," Mr. Rebeck said. He thought that it was decent of the man to ask.

"Okay," the man said. He jerked the pointing arm at the lavatory. "Now you just go back there and turn off that electric light. Go on back there."

Mr. Rebeck was quite sure that he had heard him correctly. His hearing was very good for a man of his age, and he had been listening closely to this big man. When he said, "What?" it was only because he wanted the man to say the words again. He thought the man might have made a mistake, and he wanted to give him every chance.

"Go on back there," the man repeated. "Hurry up. Turn that light off. You don't leave no electric lights on here. Wastes."

"Right away," Mr. Rebeck said. He went back into the lavatory and switched off the light. Then he came back to face the big man and stood silently in front of him, still awaiting judgment, but wondering now if it might not have been derailed somewhere between the man and him.

"Good," said the big man. He stared silently down at Mr. Rebeck, who blinked and looked away, noting as he did so that the big man's left hand clutched a half-empty bottle. Whisky, Mr. Rebeck supposed, and allowed himself a quick bite of hope.

"Okay," the man said. "Now I got to go. You stay here and stay put." He thrust the bottle into Mr. Rebeck's open hand. "Here." He chuckled tonelessly. "That'll keep you here. Be right back. You just stay the hell there."

He turned around and walked quickly into a clump of bushes at one side of the lavatory. Hardly had he disappeared when the bushes crashed and chattered and the man's huge head stuck out, his eyes searching out Mr. Rebeck among the shadow-hounds.

"You think I'm kidding, buddy?" the deep voice demanded threateningly.

"No," Mr. Rebeck said, not daring to move. "I'm sure you're perfectly serious."

"Show you who's kidding," the man mumbled. He shook a drum-sized fist at Mr. Rebeck, and his head disappeared in the bushes. Mr. Rebeck stood alone and waited for the man to return.

Run now, he told himself. Keep out of the light and run. In two hundred yards he won't be able to see you. Run, fool! Has your mind finally forgotten to come home? But he stayed where he was, knowing that the man could simply wait until dawn, enlist the aid of a few guards, and run him down. They had cars and a truck. If they wanted to, they could find him in a day. There would be no dignity to it, only sweating and fear and the yells of discovery and the dragging him from wherever he was hiding, laughing at his bony efforts to escape. . . . It was quieter this way, and less painful. Running would be painful.

He looked curiously at the long-necked bottle in his hand. It was too dark for him to read the label, and he assumed it was whisky. He had drunk very little in his days in the world, and of course not at all since the monumental bat that had brought him into the cemetery. He sniffed cautiously at the open neck of the bottle and found the smell dizzying and completely strange. There was not a part of him now that remembered the aroma of whisky. He imagined that he ought to be glad.

The bushes crackled again, and the big man stood in the light, buckling his belt. His head turned slowly from side to side, like a cannon, as he looked for Mr. Rebeck. "You there, buddy?" his cannon-voice tolled into the night. "You there?" He seemed anxious.

"I'm over here," Mr. Rebeck called. His common sense gave him up as senile, locked up for the night, and went home.

"Good," the man said. He came toward Mr. Rebeck, who was sure that he could hear the ground shake.

Mr. Rebeck remained where he was, holding the bottle

as tightly as he could. A feeling of unreality shook him violently and left him feeling a little sick. "What am I doing here?" he said aloud. "I'm Jonathan Rebeck. I'm fifty-three years old. How did I get here?"

The man took the bottle from Mr. Rebeck's hand. He drank from it, his Adam's apple bobbing like a bell buoy. He wiped his mouth with the back of his hand and glared down at Mr. Rebeck. Big as a truck, big as a bulldozer, he was, and he rocked up and down on his heels and scowled at Mr. Rebeck, and his shadow moved with him on the hard pavement.

Then, quite suddenly, he scratched his head. His right hand came all the way up from where it hung by his side and burrowed into his coarse hair, digging into his scalp with a sandpapery sound. He blinked. The two gestures made him look young and uncertain of his strength.

"What'm I gonna do with you?" he asked. It was a direct question, and he waited for an answer.

"I don't know," Mr. Rebeck said. He felt suddenly angry and put-upon. "That's your job. I'm not going to help you."

"I got no more rum," the big man said defensively. He pressed the bottle he held against his thigh, as if trying to hide it. "This's all I got left. I need it."

"All right," Mr. Rebeck said. "I don't want it."

He wasn't all that big, Mr. Rebeck decided. Very big for a man, yes, but familiarity and the head-scratching had taken him out of the bulldozer class. In the light from the wide-open door of the caretaker's office Mr. Rebeck saw that the man's eyes were dark blue and, at the moment, puzzled. He felt somewhat better. He had expected the man's eyes to be colorless and no more expressive than tree trunks.

"Ah, what the hell," the man said finally. "You come with me." He went toward the office, looking back occasionally to make sure Mr. Rebeck was following him. At the door he waved Mr. Rebeck to a stop and vanished into the small building. Mr. Rebeck heard something crash to the floor, heard the man's short, inventive obscenity, and the sound of a filing-cabinet drawer sliding open. He waited where the man had left him and thought, He must be new and unsure of himself, so he has gone to call his relief. In a few minutes there will be a man here who knows what to do with trespassers. People who knew what to do always impressed Mr. Rebeck in spite of himself.

A yell of triumph in the office, another crash, and the man was in the doorway, holding up a fresh bottle. "Found the sonofabitch," he exulted. "Lying right under m' very nose." He held the bottle against his nose and giggled. "Lucky I had a very big nose. Here." He offered the bottle to Mr. Rebeck. "Here. While I think what to do with you."

Mr. Rebeck did not take the bottle. He tightened the belt of his bathrobe and demanded, "Are you the guard on duty?"

The big man nodded. "Me. On duty from midnight to eight. Then I go home."

"Well, for heaven's sake," Mr. Rebeck said indignantly, "guard something! What kind of a guard goes around offering drinks to everybody he meets?"

The big man treated the question seriously. "Don't tell me," he said. He closed his eyes tightly, screwed up his forehead, and murmured possible answers to himself.

"A generous guard," he suggested. "A dumb, generous guard. Right?"

Mr. Rebeck was a neat man and a respecter of property. The man's attitude pained him. "Damn it," he said, "for all you know I might be a thief. How do you know I'm not trying to steal something?"

Deep, rum-warmed laughter chugged out of the man. "Nothing to steal. Thieves don't come messing around cemeteries. What for?"

"Body-snatchers do," said Mr. Rebeck, unwilling to concede the point. "Grave-robbers do. Maybe I'm a grave-robber."

The blue eyes inspected him seriously. "Have to be a pretty small grave. You only got one pocket."

Somebody was going to have to awaken this man to a sense of his responsibilities. It was lucky that he had come along, Mr. Rebeck thought. He set his feet firmly and tapped his open palm with a forefinger.

"You're not supposed to make decisions," he said patiently. "You're not supposed to decide who's a thief and who isn't. That's not your job. Are you listening to me?"

"Yeah," said the man. He shook the bottle in Mr. Rebeck's face. "Look, you want this or you don't?"

"Give it to me," Mr. Rebeck said warily. He was glad that the man did not seem about to arrest him, but the man's cavalier dismissal of his duties saddened and faintly disgusted him. He thought of all the nights when he had sneaked fearfully into the lavatory, tiptoeing, desperately willing the door not to squeak, hearing his doom in every echoing step he took, afraid even to glance at the lighted building on the other side of the road because he might somehow draw the guard's attention. I could have come marching down in army boots, he thought bitterly, singing drinking songs and throwing rocks at his door, and he wouldn't even have turned in his sleep. He realized now that he had enjoyed the furtive excursions and was sorry that there would be none ever again.

He drank from the bottle, not choking, although it was his first drink in nineteen years. The chocolate-charcoal flavor of the rum warmed the back of his throat as it went down. "Thank you," he said, and offered the bottle to the big man.

The man shook his head. "Yours," he said, shoving the bottle back at Mr. Rebeck with enough force to send him staggering. "Until I finish mine."

"Well, that's fair enough," Mr. Rebeck said, and drank again. Then, remembering his manners, he held out his hand to the man. "My name is Jonathan Rebeck," he said.

"Campos," said the big man. He shook Mr. Rebeck's

hand with the taut gentleness of a man who knows his own strength and released it almost at once. "Let's sit down somewhere with this stuff."

"Very well," Mr. Rebeck said. "But I want one thing clear. You're a fine fellow, and you set a fine table, but you are the worst guard I ever saw. Let there be no pretensions between us."

"None," Campos agreed. "None of them. Only I always thought I was a pretty good guard."

"You're a terrible guard," Mr. Rebeck said earnestly. He touched Campos's arm. "I'm sorry. I didn't want to hurt you. But some things must be said."

"I'm a terrible guard," Campos mused aloud. He shrugged lightly. "Well, learn something new every day. Come on, sit down."

They sat down together in the grass in front of the care-taker's office. Campos immediately jumped to his feet and dashed into the office, returning almost instantly with a leather-covered portable radio clutched against his chest.

"My music," he explained. He put it down on the ground, turned it on, and tuned it until he found a station that played classical music. Then he leaned back against the wall of the building and grinned at Mr. Rebeck. "Great stuff," he said. "Listen to it all the time."

Mr. Rebeck settled himself beside him. "It's very pretty," he said comfortably. He held the bottle in his lap, rolling it between his palms.

"Listen to it all the damn time," Campos said. "Ever since I been working here."

"How long has that been?"

"Year now. Walters got me the job."

Mr. Rebeck was uncautious. "That's the man with light hair?"

"Yeah." Suspicion flared for a moment in Campos's blue-ink eyes. "How come you know what Walters looks like?"

The light-headed feeling of reprieve that Mr. Rebeck had been allowing himself died in his stomach with a reproachful murmur. A trickle of rum got into a cut on his lip and stung.

"I've seen him," he said, "when I was here before. I saw him driving in the truck. I think you were with him at the time."

Campos was not to be put off. His huge hand closed on the bottle that Mr. Rebeck held and jerked it away. "Don't go slopping my rum like that. How come you're in here this time of night anyway? We close at five."

"I got locked in," Mr. Rebeck said promptly. He smiled appeasingly at Campos. "You know how time flies when you're visiting someone. And before I knew it—"

"You didn't come in here running around in no bathrobe," Campos said. He pointed at Mr. Rebeck's feet. "Nor in no carpet slippers. Walters wouldn't let you. I might, because I might be listening to my music and not noticing things. You might get past me, because I don't notice things sometimes, but Walters wouldn't let you in here dressed all like that."

He ended on a triumphant upbeat, and Mr. Rebeck twisted the hem of the terrycloth bathrobe and knew himself trapped. There was nothing for it now but to throw himself on Campos's mercy, and it had been Mr. Rebeck's experience of mercy that it had a tendency to buckle under the weight of a human soul. But he was tired, and it was three in the morning, and sitting side by side in a cemetery with this strange and suspicious man was aging him rapidly. If it must be, let it be now, before the rum and the appearance of friendship were quite finished.

"I live here," he said evenly. "I live in an old mausoleum and have for a good while. Now either call the police or give me back that rum. I'm too old for this sort of thing."

"Sure," Campos said. "Didn't even realize I had it." He gave the bottle back to Mr. Rebeck, who stared at him for a moment and then drank with painful-sounding gulps. Campos patted his back when he finally choked, and helped him to sit up straight.

"See, I knew Walters wouldn't let you in," he explained, "so I figured it was something like that." He reached out to finger the material of the bathrobe. "Catch cold running around in that. Catch a real mean cold."

"No I won't," Mr. Rebeck said. "It's a very warm night."

"All the same," Campos said. He turned the radio up louder and listened intently to a string quartet. It was a Mozart piece, or a Haydn. The little Mr. Rebeck had ever known about classical music he had utterly forgotten. But he saw Campos looking at him for approval, and he closed his eyes and hummed softly to indicate that he was following the music.

"Great, huh?" Campos's face was eager for endorsement of his taste. "All them fiddles. They make me feel loose."

"Loose," said Mr. Rebeck. He was a little afraid to make a question out of it. "Yes. Loose."

"Like I was twenty and not working for anybody and I could fly," Campos said. "Like that, loose."

Together they listened to the string quartet. The music was happy on top and sad on the bottom, and it warmed Mr. Rebeck's stomach as much as the rum. He lay back on the grass with his hands beneath his head and the bottle of rum balanced on his chest and looked up through the trees at the few stars there were.

This is very pleasant, he said to himself. It seems unusual to me because I haven't done very much of it, but this may be what a man is for. It may, of course, not be. It may be simply a very nice way to spend time, with music and something to drink and a friend—although he did not know if he could honestly consider Campos a friend. He was much too unpredictable, even for a friend—no more good or evil than the wind, and just as trustworthy. Still, there was a debt between them now, and drink shared, and this often makes a good friend-glue.

When he heard Campos's cheerful "Hello," he was sure that the big man was greeting another guard, and he pressed himself flat against the earth, feeling pinned and helpless. But when he heard the familiar voice of Michael Morgan answer Campos, he sat up so quickly that the bottle of rum rolled off his chest and would have spilled its contents if Campos had not snatched it out of the air. He looked up the road and saw Michael and Laura coming down together.

They looked extremely tangible, he noticed, extremely human. Part of that was understandable—their transparence was not evident against the blackness behind them. But there was more to it than that. There was an edged clarity about them, and a new sharpness of detail about their faces and bodies, as if they had looked at each other's eyes and suddenly remembered how their own were set. They walked easily; Michael did not stamp on the earth nor Laura flinch from it with each footstep. They looked almost real enough to cast shadows or be reflected in mirrors.

But this shivered through his mind and vanished. Now he stared from Campos to Michael and heard the man and the ghost call to each other. He heard both of them laugh and could tell only that one laugh was deeper and rougher than the other. Laura saw him and called his name. He nodded stiffly in reply, feeling older than he was.

"Can you see them?" he asked Campos in a wondering whisper.

"Sure," Campos said. "What kind of a dumb question is that?" Mr. Rebeck did not answer.

Campos stood up as Michael and Laura approached and demanded, "Where you been?"

"All the hell over," Michael answered. "We've been selling beads and pottery to the tourists. It's not much, but we manage in our primitive way. Sometimes she does a little primitive dance for them while I'm filling out the primitive sales slip. Sends them away happy."

"Hello," Laura said to Mr. Rebeck. She sat beside him and put her hand on his. He could not feel her fingers, but his own felt suddenly cold.

"Hello, Laura," he said. And because he could think of

nothing else to say, he added, "I haven't seen you in a while."

"We meant to come," Laura said. "We'd have come." She followed his glance at Michael and Campos and smiled. "Are you surprised that we can talk to Campos too?"

"Very," Mr. Rebeck said. "I don't quite understand it."

"Neither do we, honestly," Laura said. "It was Michael. He ran into Campos first. I only met him later."

Michael turned his head to her. "What did I do?"

"You met Campos," Laura said. "I was telling Mr. Rebeck."

"So I did," Michael said complacently. "He was driving along in his truck and I stepped into the road and tried to put the whammy on him, because I wanted to see if there was anything to all the old ghost stories. The dirty dog ran right over me. Through me, really."

"I knew you were a ghost," Campos said. "Anyway, didn't I go back to make sure?"

"Oh, you did that. That I will grant you. To make sure you hadn't spoiled the pelt." He looked at Mr. Rebeck. "Well, it turned out that he could see me and talk to me, the same way you can. And Laura and I got into the habit of coming down to visit him when he's on the night shift. We sing to him and tell him stories. It keeps him awake."

"I see," Mr. Rebeck said. He sighed, and his body relaxed. "Excuse me for seeming startled. It's just that I always wondered if I might not be the only man in the world who could see ghosts. I know it sounds greedy, but after a while I began to feel that I was."

"There's never just one of anything in the world," Michael said casually. He turned back to Campos. "Listen, night watchman, watcher of the night, sing me that song about the tree. I keep forgetting it."

"It's not about a tree," Campos said. "I tell you and tell you."

"All right, it's not about a tree. It has nothing to do with trees. Now sing it."

Campos began to sing very softly. The string quartet was still going on the radio, and Campos's guttural, almost rasping, voice sounded like a fifth stringed instrument, tuned to a different scale from that of the other four and playing a completely irrelevant melody that prowled around the closed circle of the quartet, hoping to be let in.

> *No hay arbol que no tenga*
> *Sombra en verano.*
> *No hay niña que no quiera*
> *Tarde o temprano. . . .*

"And repeat," Michael said eagerly. "I know that." His own voice joined Campos's, and they sang the verse again. Michael's voice was lighter than Campos's, and more distant; he sang the words clearly and on pitch, but his voice seemed very slightly reduced in scale, like a voice on a telephone. Mr. Rebeck had never heard a ghost sing before. They usually forgot music before they forgot the name of the street on which they had lived, and, once forgotten, the songs were never remembered. But Michael sat with the big Campos and sang a song that Mr. Rebeck did not know, and did not seem in the least aware that he was doing something unusual.

"You seem sad," Laura said beside him. Mr. Rebeck had not known that she was looking at him. He hastily subpoenaed a sleepy smile.

"Not sad. A little puzzled, I suppose. This has been a strange evening, and it takes me a while to get used to new things. But I'm not unhappy or anything like that."

"That's good," Laura said. She hesitated, and then said quickly, "I think I know how you feel."

Mr. Rebeck looked at her, seeing even in the dark her straight-haired, wide-mouthed plainness, and seeing also the beauty that this one night, at least, had made of it without changing it at all.

"Do you?" he asked thoughtfully. "Because I don't, myself."

"I do," Laura said. Michael called her then, and she turned from Mr. Rebeck and added her voice to the chorus of the song. The three of them sang it together, and Mr. Rebeck listened. The song rose up like smoke, rum-colored smoke.

Laura's voice was the best of the three, Mr. Rebeck thought. It was a high, sweet memory, a voice for gardens and riverbanks, and vineyards and the celebration of sea birds. She looked at him as she sang, and he closed his eyes and listened to her woman's voice, wise without being knowing. It had been a long time since he had drunk rum and heard a woman singing.

Damn it! he thought so fiercely that for a moment he thought he had spoken the words. Damn it, damn it, what is it I feel? What is it I miss? Am I sad, after all? I don't think I am. Why should I be? Michael's happy. Laura is happy—look at her. Campos is happy, or whatever emotion it is he uses at times like this. Why can I not relax and accept the moment and listen to the singing? What twists in me when they sing?

Michael's voice now, dusty around the edges, but true and sardonic, singing to enjoy himself. And Campos, laughing deeply, his voice heavier than the ghost-voices, harsh with the meaning of the song.

They never sang for me, Mr. Rebeck thought. Perhaps that is what makes me sad, that we never sang together. They came to me for comfort and conversation, they came to play chess and go for walks and simply be near some-body alive. But they sing with this man, and I have never seen them so happy. He taught them a song and now they are singing it with him. Could I have done that, I wonder?

Laura played with the melody as they sang the chorus, tossing it high like a tinsel ball, letting it wink and glitter in the light as it came down to where she waited.

Mr. Rebeck plucked a blade of grass and put it between his lips. It was sour and good to chew on.

Now is it their friendship I want, he wondered, or their dependency? I think it is very important to know. Am I sorry that they can talk to each other and to this man, am I frightened that there will be others like Campos? Am I so dull a man, even to myself, that I fear these others will take my friends from me? Am I so tired and so purposeless that I want to keep them with me forever, living off their need and their loneliness? You can't do that, Jonathan. They are minds, and you cannot make minds dependent on you. That would surely make you the devil.

> *Cuando se ven queridos,*
> *No corresponden.*

They were laughing as they finished the song. Mr. Rebeck lay on his back and applauded. "Bravo," he said. "And brava for Laura."

"Did you catch my harmony on the second chorus?" Michael asked them all. There was no answer. "Don't everybody jump at once."

"Haunting," Laura said dryly.

"Subtle," Mr. Rebeck offered, with the air of a man trying to be both helpful and honest. "Very subtle."

"Fourth-dimensional," Michael said. "But I mustn't chide you for your stupidity. You have no means of comparison, no point of reference. Campos appreciates my harmony. I can tell by his sullen silence."

"What does the song mean?" Mr. Rebeck asked Campos.

The big man shrugged. "Means women are wonderful. Never was a tree without a shadow, a house without dust in the corners, and a woman who didn't love somebody sooner or later. Means men are sons of bitches. Soon as you love them, they run. Don't trust the sons of bitches."

"Simple folk wisdom," Michael said. "Handed down

from the Mayans. Close your eyes, dear, and think of England."

"There are a lot of songs like that," Laura said. "All from the woman's point of view. Never trust men, they say. Beware of lovers. All men leave you. The faithful ones just die before they get ready to leave."

"There are just as many songs from a male standpoint," Michael answered, "only they're not sung. They're not funny and they're not beautiful. Love songs have to be one or the other, like people. So nobody ever sings them at Town Hall concerts. But every man knows a few."

"Sing one," Laura challenged him. "Sing one now."

"You have to be in an evil mood to sing one," Michael said, "and I feel rather amiable. Also, you have to sing it when you don't feel like singing, and I feel very much like singing. I'll sing it for you, if you like, but I want you to understand my handicaps."

"May I sing something with you?" Mr. Rebeck asked. "I can't really sing, but I'd like to."

All three stared at him, and he read the look in their eyes as a mixture of embarrassment and amusement. That was foolish, he thought. Why did I do that? I wish I had it back.

Michael spoke first. "Of course you can. Did you think you had to ask?" He turned to Campos. "Teach him 'El Monigote,' the one about the dummy. It takes five minutes to learn."

But Laura spoke quietly. "No. Teach us something new, something none of us knows. That's the best way to learn songs."

"I can't really sing," Mr. Rebeck said again, but Campos interrupted him.

"Know a lullaby," he said loudly. "They sing it to kids. You want to learn it?" The three nodded.

"Simple as hell," Campos said. "Like this." He sang the words deep in his throat, looking far up the road as he sang.

Dormite, niñito, que tengo que hacer,
Laver tus pañales, sentar me a comer.
Dormite, niñito, cabeza de ayote,
Si no te dormis, te come el coyote.

"I caught the coyote bit," Michael said. "What's a coyote doing in a lullaby?"

"Like the bogey man. What it means, sleep, kid, I got to wash your clothes and get something to eat, sleep, kid, little pumpkinhead, if you don't go to sleep, the coyote'll get you."

"Oh, lovely," Michael said. "They know how to raise kids in Cuba. No fooling around."

Campos ignored him. "Then it goes like this."

Arru, arruru,
Arru, arruru,
Arru, arruru,
Arruru, arruru.

Mr. Rebeck started to sing a few notes behind Michael and Laura. He had been afraid that he would not be able to sing at all, and when he heard the first notes of the new voice in the chorus he was so startled that he stopped for a moment. He had known that his voice would sound dry and rusty with disuse, but he found that it was actually painful to sing. His throat was full of sawdust and he could not swallow. His lips felt tight and crusted.

Still singing, Campos reached over and shoved the last bottle of rum into his hand. Mr. Rebeck drank from it and felt the wall of thorns in the back of his throat go down and the song step over it. He drank once more, to wash the last thorns away, handed the bottle back to Campos, and began to sing again.

Arru, arruru,
Arruru, arruru. . . .

When the chorus came to an end, he began to sing it all over again. He sang alone, his voice loud and joyous, losing the tune at once and finding scraps of it as he went along, changing the key when he couldn't hit the top notes. Laura and Michael smiled at each other, and he was sure they were laughing at him. I am making a fool of myself, he thought, but I was born to be a fool and I have had a long enough vacation from being a fool. Of course they are laughing. I would laugh myself if I weren't singing.

But he also thought, Sleep, child, sleep, little pumpkinhead—and he sang the meaningless syllables with his eyes shut because he thought he might stop if he saw them laughing at him.

Then Michael began to sing with him, softly, absently, not looking at him, not looking at anyone. They finished the song together.

Arru, arruru,
arruru, arruru.

Michael sang the last note and stopped, but Mr. Rebeck held on to the note as long as he could, until there was no breath in him and he had to let it go.

A black feather dropped into the dim light, and they heard a snort of disgust in the darkness above them. Then the raven plumped down into their midst, beating his wings wildly as if he had just fallen off the wind. He regained his balance, blinked at the four of them, and said, "What the hell is this, group therapy?"

Michael was the first to recover. He pointed at the feather in the grass. "You dropped something, I believe."

The raven looked ruefully down at the lost feather. "I'm a lousy lander," he said. "Never in my life have I made one decent landing."

"Hummingbirds land well," Michael said. "Like helicopters."

"Hummingbirds are great," the raven agreed. "You

should have seen me when I found out I wasn't ever going to be a hummingbird. I cried like a baby. Hell of a thing to tell a kid."

"What are you doing up so late?" Mr. Rebeck asked. "It must be four in the morning."

"I'm up early. You're up late. Too hot to sleep, anyway. I was flying around and I heard the glee club. Celebrating something?"

"No," Mr. Rebeck said. "We couldn't sleep either."

The raven cocked his head to look at Campos. "This one I know from somewhere."

"Campos," the big man said. "I'm a terrible guard."

"Yeah," the raven said. "I remember you. I hitched a ride on your truck once."

Campos shrugged. "Ride all you like. Ain't my truck. Belongs to the city."

"Healthy attitude," the raven said.

"He can see Michael and Laura," Mr. Rebeck told the raven. "Like me."

The raven looked from Campos to Mr. Rebeck and back. "Figures. You got the same nutty look."

"What kind of look is that?" Laura asked.

"Half here and half there," the raven answered. "Half in and half out. A nutty look. I know it when I see it."

He turned to Michael. "Latest news and weather forecast. Your old lady's in more trouble than there is in the world."

"Sandra," Michael said. He sat up quickly. "What's happened?"

Laura did not move, but Mr. Rebeck thought that she had become a little more transparent, harder to see. He tried to catch her eye, but she would not look at him.

"The cops found a piece of paper on the floor," the raven said. "Little piece of paper, folded up like a cone. Grains of poison all over it. Everybody's making a big fuss about it."

"Are her fingerprints on it?" Michael asked. He looked hungry, Mr. Rebeck thought, and somehow tired.

"No fingerprints," the raven said. "They figure she held it in a handkerchief when she used it and lost the thing before she could burn it. It was torn off a sheet of typing paper. They're trying to find the rest of the paper now."

Michael sank back slowly. "That's it, then. That's got to be it. It's over."

"Michael," Laura said softly, "drop it. Let it alone. It doesn't matter now."

Michael's voice was fierce and angry. "It matters to me. She's trying to prove I committed suicide. If they let her off, they'll come charging out here with their little shovels and dig me up. Bury me somewhere else, with all the other suicides. Would you like that? Do you want that to happen?"

"No," Laura said. "No. But I don't want her to die."

They stared at each other, ghost and ghost now, oblivious of the two men and the black bird. It was Michael who lowered his eyes first.

"I don't want her to die," he said. "I thought I did, but it doesn't matter. I don't care what happens to her, but I hope she doesn't die."

"Big discovery," the raven grunted. He cackled softly at some private joke. "Her lawyer asked for a postponement. They gave him a week. Trial's on for the fifteenth now."

"They've got her," Michael said without joy. "She must know it. The rest is just ritual. Will you let me know how it goes?"

"Don't nag me," the raven said. "I'll come around again today, after I get a look at the afternoon papers. Anything's in them, I'll let you know."

"Thank you," Michael said.

Campos was sitting cross-legged, with his head tilted far back on his neck, looking straight up into the sky.

"Lose something?" the raven asked him.

Campos lowered his head and rubbed the back of his neck. "Nobody gonna do any flying today. Rain coming."

The raven fell in with the change of subject. "How the hell do you know?"

"No birds singing," Campos said earnestly. "You hear birds singing, it's not gonna rain. Birds don't go out in the rain."

"That," said the raven, "is a large crock. I used to believe that stuff myself. No more. I woke up one morning and it was all gray, like it was going to storm any minute. But I hear the little birds singing and I think, Nah, my feathered friends wouldn't be out there singing if it was going to rain. They know what they're doing. So I went out to get breakfast, and as soon as I was out in the open it rained like hallelujah, brethren. Just sitting up there, waiting until it could get a good shot at me. And those feathered little bastards sang right through it. They sat in trees and sang. I didn't get dry for a week. Never trusted a bird from that day to this. Never going to."

"You don't like birds, do you?" Laura asked. "I've never heard you say a good word for them."

"It's not I don't like them. I just don't trust them. Every damn bird's a little bit nuts."

"You too," Campos muttered. "You too."

"Me too. Me most of all." The raven poked the lost black feather with a yellow claw. Finally he picked it up in his beak and gave it to Mr. Rebeck. "Put it somewhere," he said. Mr. Rebeck put it in his pocket.

"Tell you something," the raven said. "I was flying over the Midwest once." He stopped abruptly, closed his eyes for a moment, opened them, and began again. "I was flying over the Midwest. Iowa or Illinois, or some place like that. And I saw this big damn seagull. Right in the middle of Iowa, a seagull. And he was flying around in big, wide circles, real sweeping circles, the way a seagull flies, flapping his wings just enough to keep on the updrafts. Every time he saw water he'd go flying down toward it, yelling, 'I found it! I found it!' The poor sonofabitch was looking for the ocean. And every time he saw water, he thought that was the ocean. He didn't know anything about ponds or lakes or anything. All the water he ever saw was the ocean. He thought that was all the water there was."

"How did he get into Iowa?" Michael asked.

"Slept past his station," the raven said scornfully. "How do I know? Probably got lost in a storm. Anyway, he just kept flying around, looking for the ocean. Wasn't discouraged, wasn't afraid. He *knew* he was going to find the goddam ocean, and all the ponds and streams didn't bother him a bit. Odds are he's still flying around there. Birds are like that."

He bent his head to scratch among the soft underfeathers on his chest and belly. The stars were going out now, one by one, dropping like pennies behind the television aerials and the skylights and the washing strung between the chimneys. The sky was still dark—a sated, navy-blue woman—but the grass was jittery with the expectation of dawn.

"Did you do anything?" Mr. Rebeck finally asked. "Did you help him?"

"What could I do? What the hell can you do for a seagull in Iowa? I just flew away."

"You should have done something," Laura said. "There must have been something you could do."

"I didn't know where the ocean was, for Christ's sake. I was lost too. What else would I have been doing in Iowa?"

"You're never lost," Laura said. "Surely you could have helped him. You could have done something."

"What? What? Will you tell me what?" The raven's beak clicked like a telegraph key. "That's the goddam trouble with you goddam people. You say, 'Something should have been done. You ought to have done something,' and you figure that leaves you clean. No more responsibilities. Don't take it out on me. I'm stupid. I don't know how to help anybody. I was lost too."

He glared around at all of them, muttering to himself, the golden eyes glowing like the devil's battle decorations, aware and alone.

"All right," Michael said. His voice was very low. "You're right and I'm a hypocrite and I've been one all my life. But that isn't going to stop me from feeling sorry for seagulls."

"It wasn't supposed to," the raven said. He looked away at the pink mouth that was just beginning to open in the east. "Dawn's coming."

"We'll wait," Mr. Rebeck said sleepily. His eyes felt as heavy as ballbearings, and his neck could no longer hold his head erect. "Sing something, Laura. Sing something while we wait for dawn."

"You're half asleep," Laura said. "We'll take you home. You can watch the dawn as we go."

"No. We've sat through the night together. Let's watch the dawn together. It's important." He tried very hard not to yawn and succeeded.

"There's one of them every day," the raven said. "One's like another. You're dead on your feet."

"A singularly tactless image," Michael murmured.

"I'll sing you a song," Laura said to Mr. Rebeck. He could not see her, but her voice was close by. "Lie back, and I'll sing to you. You can watch the dawn lying down."

So Mr. Rebeck lay back and felt the grass crush under his body. He put his hand in the pocket of his bathrobe and clutched the raven's lost feather. The rum has made me sleepy, he thought. I shouldn't have drunk so much, after such a long time. Campos was saying something, but his words were like matches lit in a storm. Mr. Rebeck felt a warm redness behind his closed lids and knew that the sun was beginning to rise.

"Sing now," he said to Laura.

Her laughter was very gentle, laughter to pillow the head. "What shall I sing you? A riddle song? A lullaby? A song for lovers? A song about an early dawn and the sun rising. What will you have me sing?"

Mr. Rebeck began to tell her about the kind of song he wanted, but he fell asleep and so he never saw that particular dawn. There were others, and beautiful they were, with songs to go with them, but in later years he was always sorry for having missed that one dawn. It was the rum, he used to tell himself. You shouldn't have drunk so much. It made you sleepy.

Campos took him home.

10

"Don't let it bother you," Michael said. "If she doesn't come today, she'll come tomorrow."

"No she won't," Mr. Rebeck answered. They were sitting on the steps of the mausoleum, looking down the short path that led to Central Avenue. "Tomorrow is Sunday. She never comes on a Sunday. I don't know why, but she never does."

Michael slanted a sly glance at him. "At least you know what day it is. I used to see you looking at my grave to remember the year."

Mr. Rebeck scratched aimlessly on the step below him with a pebble. "I don't always remember what day it is. When I do, it's because a day on which Mrs. Klapper comes to visit is very different from a day on which Mrs. Klapper doesn't come. I have two kinds of days now. I only used to have one."

"I only have one," Michael said. "One long one, with subdivisions. Don't worry," he added when Mr. Rebeck said nothing. "She'll come today."

"I'm not worrying. She'll come when she feels like it. What time is it?"

Michael laughed. "Damned if I know. Time and Morgan have nothing in common these days."

"One of us ought to know what time it is."

"Well, it's not going to be me," Michael answered. The flatness of Mr. Rebeck's tone had disconcerted him somewhat. "Why do you care? What difference does it make?"

Mr. Rebeck snapped the pebble away from him. "The gates are locked at five. If she comes late she won't be able to stay very long. I hate it when she just comes, says hello, and goes."

"She doesn't have to go right away," Michael said. "Walters usually makes the rounds a couple of times an hour to see if anybody's locked in. She can stay later than five."

"I've asked her. She always has to go home and start dinner." Mr. Rebeck scowled at the hot, shiny sky. "Or she has to babysit for somebody. She loves that. The parents go to the movies, and she sits in the living room and listens to the radio. The next day she spends hours telling me how she put the child to bed and what she did when it woke up in the night and wanted its mother."

"Hasn't she any children of her own?"

"No," Mr. Rebeck said. "A lot of nephews and nieces, though. She comes from a big family." He shoved his hands into his pockets and leaned back on the steps. "She's not going to come today. It's too late."

"Don't panic," Michael said. "She's got time yet." He stood up and took a few steps on the grass. "I think I'll look around for Laura. Maybe we'll come back here later on and tell you a bedtime story."

Mr. Rebeck smiled, stretching his legs in the afternoon sun. "All right. That would be fine." The bedtime story had been a standing joke between them since the morning more than a week ago when Campos, singing and staggering, guided patiently by Michael and Laura and obscenely by the raven, had carried him home, wrapped him in his blankets, and fallen asleep himself on the steps of the mausoleum. Mr. Rebeck had found him there when

he woke in the early afternoon, and they had shared breakfast. He had not seen Campos since.

"That was a good night," he said. He liked to think
about it. "We ought to spend more nights like that."

"Stick around," Michael said grimly. "We will." He
came back to Mr. Rebeck and sat down two steps below
him. "I've begun to develop a piddling but useful concep-
tion of eternity lately. Listen to me think."

Mr. Rebeck waited, thinking, Of course I'll listen to your
thoughts. That's what I do. That's what I am, really, your
thoughts and the thoughts of others. He nodded to show
Michael that he was listening.

"I had a good time that night, too," Michael said, "but
I kept thinking, This is forever. This is forever. You will
have this good time again and again, a million times over,
until it will be like a play in which you and Laura and a
few fugitive lives sit around an imaginary fire and talk and
sing songs and love each other and sometimes throw imaginary brands at the eyes blinking beyond the circle of imaginary firelight. And then I thought—and this is where I
sounded just like a real philosopher— And even when you
admit that you know every line in the play and every song
that will be sung, even when you know that this evening
spent with friends is pleasant and joyful because you
remember it as pleasant and joyful and wouldn't change it
for the world, even when you know that anything you feel
for these good friends has no more reality than a dream
faithfully remembered every night for a thousand years—
even then it goes on. Even then it has just begun."

The air was motionless, carved, a block of warm copper
fitting neatly around the earth, molded while soft to fit
every house and every human being on the earth, and now
hardened forever so that no man could move and no air
ever came through. The earth rumbled down its alley like
a golden bowling ball, shining.

Michael went on. "People used to imagine hell as a place
where evil is done and being in hell as having evil things

done to you eternally, praise God and don't push; there's
plenty of room in the balcony for all the blessed souls.
Well, Morgan amplifies this. Hell is forever. Hell is having
anything done to you constantly, good or evil. There isn't
any good or evil after a few billion millenniums. There's
just something happening that has happened before. Think
of it—forever. For ever. We don't know what the word
means, and we die ignorant and unarmed. Don't ask me to
come to any more jolly sessions around the campfire, old
friend. I'll come, of course. Wouldn't miss it. Just don't ask
me."

He stood up again, moving down the steps and across the
grass with the loose, bucking motion of a captive balloon; a
manshaped reminiscence, a figment of his own imagination.

"I can't help you," Mr. Rebeck said. He spoke very quietly, but Michael heard him and turned.

"Why, I wasn't asking you to. I wasn't asking for help.
I'm very fond of you, but I'd never ask you to help me.
I'll never ask anyone to help me again. Say hello to Mrs.
Klapper for me."

He walked away and the sun devoured him quickly. Mr.
Rebeck sat on the steps of the mausoleum, grateful for the
shade the building offered. A cooling breeze sprang up suddenly, making itself audible by shaking the grass and hissing
richly in the trees, but it did not reach Mr. Rebeck at all.
He unbuttoned his shirt and pulled it out of his pants, but
the breeze was gone and the trees stopped moving. His skin
remained oiled with sweat and he could smell the familiar
sourness of his own body. Later, when it was dark, he
would go down to the lavatory and wash himself. He did
not like the liquid soap that you squirted out of a glass jar,
but it would have to do.

I am tired, he thought. Maybe the heat is doing it, but I
have sat through a good many summers here and never felt
like this. I am tired of being helpful. I am tired of being
comfortable. Why this should be I do not know, but my
image of myself as an understanding old man, floating in

kindness like a cherry in a sugared liqueur, is beginning to curl at the corners. I wish something would happen to me, something that would show me exactly how cruel and jealous and vengeful I can be. Then I could go back to gentleness because I chose it over brutality for its own sake, not because I didn't have the courage to be cruel. I might even like cruelty. I doubt very much that I would, but I ought to find out.

He remembered the raven, clacking his beak and saying, "I'm stupid. I don't know how to help anybody. I was lost too."

I believe myself to be good, he thought, and so I can afford to titillate myself by considering evil, like a child frightening himself with horror stories. I am not a bad man. But I am not a wise one, either, nor understanding. And yet, if I lose this rumpled and comfortable skin that I wear, how will I ever find anything to replace it? I wish I were younger and could grow skin easily.

Then Mrs. Klapper called, "Hey, Rebeck!" and he scrambled hastily up from the cellar of his mind, jumped to his feet, and started down the path to meet the woman, who waved as she came toward him. He felt his loose shirt flapping around his waist, and he stuffed it into his trousers as he walked. He buttoned it all the way up to the top and then opened the collar button.

Mrs. Klapper was wearing a blue dress that he had liked on her before, and an irrational crescent moon of a hat that she loved and defended violently. He had become fond of it himself, but that was one of the things he refused to admit to her. Now he prowled around her, hands clasped behind his back and head thrust forward, staring at the hat. She twisted her neck to follow him.

"All right, already," she said. She put one hand up to her head as if to protect the hat from any onslaught he might be contemplating. "I'm wearing it, I'm wearing it. You want I should wear a helmet like Doctor Livingstone? Leave the hat alone, Rebeck."

"It fascinates me," Mr. Rebeck said. He stood with one hand in a hip pocket and the other scratching the back of his head. "I can't take my eyes off it. Do you pin it on?"

"No, I had this jar of library paste, it seemed a shame to waste it. Rebeck, leave me the hat. The hat never hurt you." She was breathing hard and fanning herself ineffectually with her hand. "Hoo, it's hot. Ninety degrees, it says on the radio. Let's go somewhere we could sit down."

"All right," he said. He noticed that she was carrying a light raincoat over her arm. This did not surprise him too much, even in the hot weather. He knew that Mrs. Klapper regarded the weather as about as dependable as bus schedules. Had she lived during an earlier time, she would have propitiated a weather god possessed of a vindictive intelligence and a squad of little helpers that rushed to inform him whenever Mrs. Klapper decided to go somewhere.

As they walked back toward the mausoleum, Mr. Rebeck said, "I thought you weren't coming." He said it as casually as he could, not being by nature a casual man.

"The subway got tied up in a knot," Mrs. Klapper said very quickly. "There was a train in front of us and a train behind us and we were in the middle and nobody was moving and there was a big *tsimmis* with the whistle and the buzzing and the fans didn't work right in the middle. Half an hour we lost, maybe more. So excuse my being late, please."

"I waited all afternoon," Mr. Rebeck said. It was a straight statement of fact, but Mrs. Klapper took it as a mild reproach and an expression of self-pity.

"It's good for you to worry a little. That way you never get fat." She walked as if all roads were sidewalks and every one of them ran uphill. "Anyway, I hurried. Look how I'm panting, like a dog. I run any faster, I'll have a stroke. Then you'll be happy?"

"I'll dance in the streets," Mr. Rebeck said. They had reached the mausoleum, and Mrs. Klapper brushed off the top step as she always did and sat down with a large sigh of contentment. She took off one shoe and began to massage her toes, occasionally wriggling them to see if they were responding to treatment.

"Completely numb," she said, looking up at Mr. Rebeck. "My toes got no more feeling than a salted herring. Also I think I busted an arch. Call the ambulance, Rebeck. Get a stretcher, carry me out of here, what are you standing around for?" She gripped her tortured toes in one hand and crackled them like peanut shells.

Mr. Rebeck stood awkwardly in the presence of the unpretentious femininity involved even in the massaging of toes. Mrs. Klapper's foot, he noticed, was small and clean, marred only by the calluses on the ball and heel that a foot develops if its owner is in the habit of roaming around the house barefooted. An attractive foot, judged simply as a foot. He felt better when she slipped her shoe back on.

"Would you like some water?" he asked.

Mrs. Klapper nodded eagerly. "You got some? Bring it on." She frowned then. "Wait a minute. You got to go all the way back to the gate to get it, forget the whole thing. That thirsty I'm not. Forget it."

Mr. Rebeck smiled and patted her shoulder. "Fear nothing," he said. "I'll be back in a minute."

He left her, ran up the steps of the mausoleum, and emerged a moment later with a little plastic cup. Then he went around the building and walked twenty yards to where a rusty water faucet was set into the lawn near a bank of flowers. He filled the cup there and walked back to the mausoleum, where he presented the cup to Mrs. Klapper with a certain flourish. "I forgot your bouquet," he announced, "but you can take this home with you and raise your own."

Mrs. Klapper wasted no time in badinage. She emptied the cup in three uninhibited gulps, tilted it again to get the last few drops, and said, "Thank you. I didn't know how thirsty I was." Then her face clouded and she looked guiltily at the empty cup.

"Vey, Rebeck, I'm such a pig," she mourned. "I was so thirsty I didn't leave you any. Such a pig, Klapper."

"It's all right," Mr. Rebeck said. He sat down beside her. "I didn't want any."

"I tell you what," Mrs. Klapper said. "Tell me where's the water fountain and I'll get you some. Where is it, out back?" She started to get up.

"Don't bother," Mr. Rebeck told her. "Really, I'm not thirsty."

"In weather like this you're not thirsty? Don't be so noble, you'll live longer. I was so thirsty my mouth felt like a double boiler. Don't tell me you're not thirsty, just tell me where's the water fountain."

"Look," Mr. Rebeck said, unconsciously adopting something of her tone of voice, as he always did if she was with him for any length of time. "I live here. The faucet is out back. I can get a drink whenever I want one, whenever I'm thirsty. I was thirsty a few minutes before you came, so I went and got a drink. Now I'm not thirsty. Sit down and stop running back and forth."

"So who was running?" Mrs. Klapper asked, but she sat down again. She sighed. "Rebeck, you're a hard man to do a favor for. You're always one favor ahead. This is no way to keep your friends."

Mr. Rebeck grinned. He felt very relaxed and unworried. "Fortunately—" he began, but Mrs. Klapper cut him off with a sudden yelp of remembrance. "Dope! Idiot! I knew I brought you something. What a dope! Here, for you, a big gift, compliments of the Salvation Army."

Before he could speak, she had dropped her raincoat across his lap. "Here. You catch double pneumonia now, don't come blaming me. I did my best."

Mr. Rebeck blinked down at the coat on his knees. He touched the smooth gray fabric. "This is for me?"

"No, for President Eisenhower. Oh, is that a brain? Sure, for you. I'd bring it all the way out here for me? It's a raincoat, so you shouldn't get wet someday, catch a cold."

She laughed, reaching over to turn down the collar of the coat.

"It's a very nice coat," Mr. Rebeck said. He held it up off his lap to look at it. "Only I don't know—"

"Know? What's to know? Sure it's a nice coat, it keeps the rain off, keeps you dry. You think it's going to rain, you carry it with you. It doesn't rain, good you don't need it. But if it starts to rain, you just put it on, there you are. Waterproof."

Mr. Rebeck fingered the coat and did not look at her. "Yes. I know how it works." The unhappiness in his voice finally ate its way through Mrs. Klapper's gaiety. She looked at him in surprise.

"What's the matter?" She snapped her fingers suddenly. "You think maybe it's too big? It's not too big. Here." She took the coat from him. "Stand up, put it on a minute. I'll show you it's not too big."

Mr. Rebeck did not stand up. "No," he said. "It isn't that." He turned his body sideways so that he was sitting on the steps facing her. "Gertrude"—it was only the second or third time in their acquaintance that he had called her by her first name— "I thank you very much, but I can't accept this coat."

The stricken look in her eyes made his stomach contract, even though he knew it would last only about two seconds. During those two seconds Mrs. Klapper was without defenses, and Mr. Rebeck felt guilty and weak. He had never known, and would never learn, how to handle unarmed people.

Then Mrs. Klapper struck back. "You can't accept it? How come? What is it with you, Rebeck? Am I buying your soul? I'm giving you a raincoat. Something's wrong with that?"

"I don't need a raincoat," Mr. Rebeck said.

"What are you, a duck?" Her expressive mouth curved and curled like a catapult, hurling the separate words at him. "You got webbed feet, the water rolls right off your back? What is this, you don't need a raincoat? Everybody in the world needs a raincoat and all of a sudden you don't?"

"It would be a waste," Mr. Rebeck said. "In all the time I've lived here, I've never used a raincoat."

"Then you're a nut," Mrs. Klapper said promptly. "It's bad enough you live in a crazy place like this, but without a raincoat! In twenty years, you never once got caught in the rain? Never once?"

"Of course I did. But there's shelter everywhere around here—trees, mausoleums, the office buildings. I never got really wet." He searched his mind for a proof that would mean something to her. "I've never been sick."

Mrs. Klapper shook her head in disgust at his ignorance. "So you think that means you're never going to get wet, you're never going to get sick? Rebeck, believe me, when you get wet it's going to be right to the skin, when you get sick it'll be triple pneumonia, what'll you do then?" She dropped the raincoat back on his lap. "Look, just carry it around with you, it's such a big effort?" Her eyes brightened as she thought of a possible reason for his refusal of the coat. "You think I need it? I don't need it. I got a million raincoats. I got a closet full of raincoats, I could wear a different one every day. You're not stealing from me."

Mr. Rebeck shook his head. "No, Gertrude." He folded the raincoat neatly and held it out to her. When she would not accept it he put it down between them on the step.

"Thank you very much," he said, knowing that he did not dare to take the raincoat, and wanting desperately to soften the rejection. "It was a wonderful thing to do, Gertrude, but it would be a waste. I don't need it."

"A straitjacket is what you need," Mrs. Klapper answered, but she said it absently, without malice. She smoothed her dress over her knees and smiled suddenly and warmly. "So all right, don't take it. Look at me, turning into a *noodge* in my old age. We'll talk about it later."

"All right," Mr. Rebeck said. "Later" to Mrs. Klapper

could mean anything from two minutes to two years. He hoped, for the sake of his resistance, that it was the latter she meant on this occasion.

Now, without audibly shifting gears, she was off on another subject. "Listen, I was baby-sitting for my brother-in-law last night, the dentist. I told you about him. He wanted to take my sister to Lewisohn Stadium, so he calls me and he says 'Gertrude, you got a free evening, how about keeping an eye on Linda so she doesn't fall out of bed?' Well, his daughter is a doll. Six years old and an absolute doll. Sitting with her is a pleasure, not like with some children. I showed you her picture, didn't I?"

Mr. Rebeck nodded. Surprisingly enough, he had always been able to keep track of Mrs. Klapper's relatives, a thing she herself was not always able to do. More, he enjoyed hearing about them. They were the only people outside the cemetery he knew anything about, and he had decided that he liked them very much, except for the two cousins that Mrs. Klapper couldn't stand.

"So fine," Mrs. Klapper went on. "I came over about six, and my sister and brother went to the concert and I played with Linda. Such a doll, that one, it's a privilege to sit with her. She's supposed to go to bed at seven, but I let her stay up till seven-thirty, we're having such a good time. Anyway, I'm putting her to bed, tucking her in, good night, Linda, and she grabs me and says, 'Tell me a story.'"

Now she was both herself and Linda, switching from character to character, woman to child to woman, with the electric ease of a traffic light changing colors. "A story? All right, God help me, what kind of a story? And she says, 'The little red hen,' Thank God, this one at least I know. I'm the only woman in the world doesn't know 'Sleeping Beauty,' but the little red hen I know like my hand. So I start telling her about the little red hen, she lives on a farm with all the other animals, and she gets it into her head she's got to bake a loaf of bread. You know the one I mean?"

"Yes," Mr. Rebeck said. "I can't tell it very well, but I know it."

"Well, I'm going along, I'm telling the story, and suddenly this Linda, she sits up and gives me a big look like you can't trust anybody any more, and she says, 'That's not the little red hen!' Now, she's a lovely girl and all that, but this fairy tale I know, so I say, 'Sure it's the little red hen. Would I lie to you, Linda?' And she says, 'That's not the little red hen!' and I think, *Gevalt*, in a minute she's going to start crying, what'll I do? So I say, 'Okay, maybe there's *two* stories about the little red hen. You tell me the one you know.' So she doesn't cry, thank God, she starts telling me this big story about the little red hen, she's got this deal where she has to lay an egg every day or off with the head, we'll buy our egg from the A & P. A whole story she tells me, I never heard it before, I'm sitting there with my mouth open."

She spread her arms and looked helplessly at Mr. Rebeck. "Rebeck, tell me, are there maybe two stories about the little red hen, or is she making the whole thing up? I don't know. I just sat there."

Mr. Rebeck was laughing. He had begun to laugh midway through the story, accompanied her to the end, and showed no immediate signs of stopping. He laughed quietly and happily, like a man remembering a funny thing that happened a long time ago.

"I only know the story you know," he said when he finally stopped laughing. "I think Linda got it confused with some other fairy tale."

Mrs. Klapper shook her head doubtfully. "She told it like she knew it by heart. She went right straight through it, and, *boom*, she fell asleep." She shook her head again and began to laugh. "Ai, is that a Linda. Next time I come to sit for her, she says, 'Tell me a story,' I'll say, 'Okay, but decide, your way or mine?'"

When they stopped laughing, and they did not stop suddenly, but let it trail away, silence for a moment and then a snort of new laughter from one, in which the other promptly joined, but when the laughter was finally used up, then they looked almost shyly at each other and said nothing. Once Mr. Rebeck chuckled reminiscently to himself, but Mrs. Klapper did not join in again. He looked away from her and had stopped laughing when he looked back. There was still nothing to say. Mrs. Klapper smoothed her dress again with a nervous, patting motion.

"Rebeck," she began, "I was thinking—"

"Why do you always wear gloves?" Mr. Rebeck forestalled her. "I never understood it. How can you wear gloves in weather like this?"

"I bite my nails sometimes." Mrs. Klapper kept her hands firmly in her lap. "Since Morris died, I catch myself biting my nails, like a little girl. I don't know why."

"I was wondering," Mr. Rebeck said.

Mrs. Klapper looked down at her hands. She took a quick, shallow breath. "Rebeck. About the raincoat."

"Are we back to that?" Mr. Rebeck asked sadly. "I thought you said we'd talk about it later."

"So I'm a big liar. Rebeck, I'm asking you, take the raincoat. Do me a favor, take the raincoat. Why make such a big thing out of it?"

"I'm not," Mr. Rebeck said. "You are. Gertrude, let's forget the whole thing. Let's talk about something else. Maybe you could bring some cookies someday. I like cookies, and I haven't had any in years. Now that would be a favor."

He spoke lightly, hoping to make her laugh again, but the effort failed, as he knew it would. He had been afraid that something like this would happen one day, but he had avoided thinking about what he would do when the day came. Forewarned, knowing that something very good in his life was changing, quite possibly for the worse, he blamed himself for being unprepared, for having been always unprepared. He had foreseen every such change in his fortune, ignored it always, and called the refusal innocence.

"I wake up at night," Mrs. Klapper said softly. "I look out the window and it's raining and I think, Rebeck's out there and it's raining on him. What is he, a bum, a thief, he should run around in the rain without even a coat? I lie awake and worry."

"I wish you wouldn't," Mr. Rebeck said. "You don't have to worry about me. I don't."

"All right, you don't. I worry. Forgive me, I'm an old woman. So I say to myself, What's the matter, you can't give him anything to keep warm? You're bankrupt, you're burning the furniture to cook dinner? Klapper, you've got a house full of raincoats, bring him one and stop losing sleep. So I look around in the closet and I pick out a nice raincoat, and I think, This one looks good, Morris won't mind if I take it to Rebeck, it's clean—" She stopped abruptly, even before Mr. Rebeck spoke.

"Oh," he said, mildly enough. "This was your husband's coat?"

"Sure. What's wrong?" A defensive note had crept into Mrs. Klapper's voice. "Mine wouldn't fit you. Morris's coat is just right, a little big, maybe. It looks brand new. Try it on, see how good it looks." She held it out again. "Try it on."

"I don't want it," Mr. Rebeck said. He pushed it away, without force but completely without gentleness.

"Why? What is this? Something's bad about wearing Morris's raincoat? Tell me, Rebeck. Morris wore it a little, so it's no good?"

"I am not going to wear your husband's clothes," Mr. Rebeck said. "I am not going to wear anybody's clothes but my own. Most of all, I am not going to wear Morris's clothes. Not his raincoat, not his hat, not his pants, not his shoes. Nothing." He spoke faster, getting angrier as he went along. "And while we're talking about it, I am begin-ning to get tired of hearing about your husband."

"I see," Mrs. Klapper said. A calmer man might have noticed the storm warnings flying over her quiet voice. In all probability Mr. Rebeck, who was a calm man, did notice them and took pleasure in ignoring them.

"The first time you saw me," he said, "you thought I was your husband's ghost. Since then, I've had a lot of moments when I wished I was. We spend most of our time talking about Morris, we visit his mausoleum, which has everything for him except a hot plate in case he gets hun-gry, we speculate on what he might have become if he hadn't died. You tell me how wonderful he was, you tell me how much like him I look, and now you bring me his clothes to wear."

"His raincoat," Mrs. Klapper said. Her voice was a tight and humming wire. "One raincoat."

"That isn't important. I don't want to look like him, not even a little, and I don't want you ever to mistake me for him again, even for a second. I don't care how wonderful he was—in fact I hope to God that he wasn't as great a man as you think he was. He'd have been unhuman and unbearable."

On an impulse, he took her white-gloved hand in his own and gripped it tightly. "Gertrude, I'm sure he was a fine man, or you wouldn't have married him. He was prob-ably better at a great many things than I, better than most people. But he's dead"—he felt her hand buck and wrench in his, but he held it as tightly as he could—"and it is no honor to the dead to remember them as they were not, to think of them as better than they were. I don't want his clothes or his face. I don't want anything that belongs to him."

Mrs. Klapper pulled her hand free then, as though his hand were a hook from which her own had to be torn with one terrible wrench.

"What do you want?" she cried. "You want me to forget

him? You want it to be like there never was any Morris?
You want that?"

"No, I don't want that, and you know it. I want you to
stop talking about him as if he were alive and listening. I
want you to stop kidding yourself!"

"Kidding myself?" Mrs. Klapper's laugh was strident and
forced, not so much a laugh as an amplified gasp of anguish.
"*I'm* kidding myself?" She swept her arm in an arc that
took in all the cemetery they could see from where they
sat. "Look who's talking! Look who lives in a grave, like
a dead one, and tells me I shouldn't kid myself! Come out
of the grave and tell me again, Rebeck."

"That has nothing to do with what I'm saying," Mr.
Rebeck said. "Nothing at all. We're not talking about the
way I live."

"I'm talking about it!" Mrs. Klapper tapped her chest
with a forefinger. "You listen to me a minute, you've got
the *chutzpah* to tell me I'm kidding myself. What kind of
way is this for a man to live? Since when does a man, a
human being, live in a graveyard, eating a couple of sandwiches a day, running around in the night getting soaked
to his bones, hiding from people, talking to himself, going
crazy alone? You think a man lives like this? You know
who lives like this? Animals. Crazy, sad animals. What are
you, a crazy animal?"

Mr. Rebeck opened his mouth to speak, but she waved
the words back into his throat. "You think this is a good
place to hide?" she demanded, pointing at him. "You think
maybe you belong here, the dead people are saying, 'Come
on in, Rebeck, where you been, we were so worried'? You
don't belong here. You could live here a hundred years,
you wouldn't belong here. You're a human being, live like
a human being, not like a crazy animal hiding in a hole.
Don't tell me I'm kidding myself, Rebeck."

Her dark hair had become a little awry, and the foolish
crescent hat was skidding slowly over her forehead. Her
face was very pale, and her eyes seemed blacker and more

angrily alive by contrast. When she spoke again, it was in a quieter voice. The movements of her lips were less definite and less scornful.

"Maybe I do, a little. I wouldn't deny it. Maybe it wasn't always New Year's Eve, being married to Morris. That's not saying he wasn't a great man, understand that. There was nobody like Morris. But all right, so maybe I make it sound a little better than it was, who am I hurting? An old woman remembers things a little bit cockeyed, it's her privilege, she's not hurting anybody, not even herself. But a man tells himself, 'I'm a ghost, I'm a ghost, I'm only happy with dead people,' he's hurting himself, he's hurting his friends. A man should live with men, not in a graveyard where it's cold at night, he's got nothing to keep himself warm. Okay, I'm kidding myself, you're kidding yourself, only it's not the same thing. Don't tell me it's the same thing, because I know better."

"I live here," Mr. Rebeck snapped. They were standing on the steps now, shouting at each other. He could feel the cool, tickling trickles of sweat sliding down his sides under his shirt. "I like it here. This place, this dark city, is as much my home as any place on earth is ever anybody's home. I can't live anywhere else. I tried. I tried for a long time. Now I live here and I'm happy. A man should live where he fits, and if he doesn't fit anywhere he should try to squeeze himself in somewhere where he won't hurt anyone and where nobody will notice him. I've been lucky in finding a place to live, luckier than a lot of men. They're still looking."

"You think this is living? This is eating, nothing else." Mrs. Klapper grabbed at the crescent hat a moment before it fell off her forehead and shoved it to the back of her head, where it remained, tipping from side to side, like a seasick bird. "You're like all those *yentas* where I live, you sit in the sun and wait for your wings to grow. You want to live somewhere, live in a house. That's where people live."

At any other time, Mr. Rebeck would never have taken advantage of the opening she had unwittingly given him, even had he noticed it, which is doubtful. Now he drove through it, his anger tucked like a skull under his arm.

"Is it? Then tell me why you keep calling Morris's mausoleum his big house?"

In the silence they heard the sound of an engine, and they both looked up the path to see the caretakers' pickup truck turning in off Central Avenue. Even at that distance Mr. Rebeck was able to recognize it. It was olive green, for the most part, with rusty fenders and a wide paintless patch on the driver's door—Campos had once managed to get it caught in a funeral motorcade. The engine harrumphed like a Congressman, and the rim of the hood was bent up and out on one side, so that the truck wore an impersonal sneer.

Mr. Rebeck was not at first alarmed when he saw the truck, because he associated it with Campos, who loved it and drove it most of the time. But he saw Walters' blond head above the steering wheel and, as he had done so often that he no longer thought of it as running, he fled up the steps to the mausoleum door. There he paused with the iron of the doorknob under his hand and turned, expecting to see Mrs. Klapper's face wrinkled with mockery, waiting to hear her voice, that could be like the bitter shriek of knives against each other, jeering at him. He hoped, in a way, that she would, so that he would not miss her when she did not come again. For he was sure she would not return, and he feared remembering her.

But she only looked at the truck and then at him, and she said quietly, "It's too late, Rebeck. He's seen you. Come back."

And he came down the steps, taking them carefully so as not to stumble, and he stood beside her on the bottom step and waited with her for the oncoming truck.

Walters brought the truck to a hiccuping stop before them and cut the motor. He leaned out of the cab and demanded, "You people together?"

"Yes," Mr. Rebeck answered. He hoped that Walters would not recognize him. They had met twice before, and both times Mr. Rebeck had pretended to be a visitor. He tried vaguely to make his voice different.

"Well, don't you know the place closes at five? It's ten to five now."

"My," Mrs. Klapper marveled. "Look how the time flies. We just got here a minute ago, it seems like." She narrowed her eyes suspiciously and raised a finger at Walters. "You're *sure* it's ten to five?"

"I'm sure, lady," Walters answered, but he looked at his watch. "You don't get down to the gate in a hurry, they'll lock you in. And this ain't no place I'd want to spend the night."

"Well." Mrs. Klapper turned questioningly to Mr. Rebeck. "I guess maybe we better be going, huh?" Mr. Rebeck nodded.

Walters looked at his watch again. "You'll never make it in ten minutes. They'll lock you in. Hop in and I'll give you a ride down. Come on."

Mrs. Klapper glanced quickly at Mr. Rebeck, but no word passed between them. She turned back to Walters and shook her head. "Thanks a lot, but no. You just go and tell the people at the gate we'll be a little bit late, they shouldn't lock up right away."

"Come on, come on," Walters said impatiently. "It'll take you a half-hour to walk it. They ain't going to wait that long for anybody."

"So the night man will let us out," Mrs. Klapper replied calmly. "Anyway, we can't ride with you, thank you. I lost something on the way and we have to find it."

"Yeah? What'd you lose? We got a Lost and Found in the office."

Mr. Rebeck correctly interpreted Mrs. Klapper's look at him as a howl for help. He remembered having said, "Fear nothing," to her in jest, and he wondered if she remembered too. He had thrown it off very lightly.

"A ring," he said. "On the way up here, she lost a very small ring. We're going to look for it on the way back. That's why we want to walk."

Walters slapped his forehead. "Jesus Christ, you can't go looking for a ring now. It'll take you hours, a little thing like a ring. Come back tomorrow."

"It wasn't *that* small a ring," Mrs. Klapper said indignantly. "Do I look like the kind of woman would wear a little tiny Woolworth ring? We'll find it, and it won't take us so long, either. You just tell the people at the gate not to be in such a hurry, we'll be right along."

"Look, lady—" Walters began, but he did not finish. Mrs. Klapper occasionally had that effect on people, Mr. Rebeck noticed. He felt sorry for Walters.

"Thank you for offering us a ride," he said. "And don't worry. We won't take long."

"Yes, thank you very much," Mrs. Klapper said, as if she were daring Walters to make something of it. "You're a very nice young man."

"Jesus God," Walters said. It sounded almost like a prayer. He turned on the ignition, and the engine snorted with a kind of baleful humor.

"I'll leave the gate unlocked," he said to the steering wheel. "Tell the man at the gate when you leave. Would you do that for me?"

"Certainly," Mr. Rebeck said grandly. "We'd be glad to."

"And watch it with the truck," Mrs. Klapper called as Walters drove away. "Don't go running over the ring, it's very valuable." They watched the truck shudder along the path and out of sight on Central Avenue.

They had intended to laugh when it was safe, fully intended to sit down on the steps and laugh together, louder than they ever had. Neither one had spoken this intention to the other, but it had been completely understood while they were talking to Walters. But they looked warily at each other and remembered that, five minutes before, each had come very near to destroying the other for the other's Own Good. Neither was quite certain that the destruction had not actually been accomplished, and each cautiously watched the other move and did not dare to speak for fear that one might now have no tongue and the other no ears. They moved as if they were wading or picking themselves out of wreckage.

"I better go," Mrs. Klapper said at last. "He's not going to wait forever, whoever's locking the gate. I got to get home, anyway."

"I'll walk part of the way with you," Mr. Rebeck said. She did not answer, and they began to walk toward Central Avenue. Sometimes their shoulders touched.

"You think somebody'll get nervous, they only see one person leave instead of two?"

Mr. Rebeck shook his head. "No. Walters has gone home, and one of the night men has taken over. No one will notice anything."

"You sure know the routine around here. Like a bank robber."

"I have to."

Out on Central Avenue, Mr. Rebeck could feel the heat of the pavement through his thin shoes. He walked with Mrs. Klapper past the frozen fountains of the willow trees and heard, far and very faintly, the guffaw of the pickup's engine. Mrs. Klapper carried the gray raincoat over her arm.

"Rebeck," she said. She took a deep breath. "Look, I'm sorry I made such a big deal about it, about where you live and everything."

"Forget it," Mr. Rebeck said. "Let's forget it. It was nothing." He did not want her to apologize.

"Never mind forget it. What am I, God, a policeman, I can tell you, 'Live here, don't live here'? You live where you want to, it's a free country. You want to live here, it makes you happy, live here. Nobody should tell you where to live. Not me, not anybody. You live where you want to.''

"It's just that I feel comfortable here," Mr. Rebeck said. "I never felt that way anywhere else."

"I'm sure it's a very nice place," Mrs. Klapper said. "In the spring and summer, anyway. In the winter—well, what place is nice in the winter?" She looked directly at him. "Only I still worry about you getting wet. You catch a cold here, with no doctor, no drugstore, the next thing you know you're flat on your back. That's why I thought maybe it would be a good idea if I brought the raincoat."

"I couldn't have taken it," Mr. Rebeck said.

"I know, it was Morris's coat, you don't want anything that belonged to Morris. All right, don't take it. Why fight over a raincoat? God forbid anybody should think you look like Morris, it's the end of the world."

"Not anybody. You. I said it the wrong way, and I sounded too heroic about it, but I won't be Morris for you." It was growing a little cooler, he thought. Was tomorrow August? How fast the summer was going.

"If you want to give me a raincoat," he said slowly, "give me one of my own."

Mrs. Klapper stopped walking. "I don't know your *size!*" she protested happily. The look in her eyes delighted him and frightened him at the same time.

"I'm smaller than Morris," Mr. Rebeck said. "Come on, before they lock us in."

"Wonderful, you're smaller than Morris. So now I know." Mrs. Klapper began to walk again. "You think I'm a magician, I can look at you and *boom*, I know what size raincoat you take. Maybe I always carry around with me a measuring tape, it might come in handy? Rebeck, excuse me, about some things you know from nothing."

She was smiling now. It seemed a long time since he had last seen her smile. He felt that he had come to another Crossroads and passed it without even recognizing it as a Crossroads. If he turned around, he could probably see it dwindling behind him, perhaps even run back to it if he began to run now. Once it was out of sight it would be too late; he would never be able to find it.

"I'd better go back," he said. "We'll be at the gate soon."

"Wait a minute. At least let me make a guess what size you take. Stand up straight a little." She looked him over quickly and shrugged. "So I'll get you one that fits like your skin, you'll be sorry you didn't take Morris's coat. Good-by, Rebeck. Don't step on the ring."

She started down the road alone.

Then she stopped and turned back to him. He had not moved.

"Listen, I'll tell you something." She was not smiling. "Remember you asked how come I was late, and I gave you a big deal about the subway and how I had to go back to get the raincoat?" Mr. Rebeck nodded.

"Well, it wasn't like that. I was walking to get to the subway, and I met this woman, I know her from around. I said, 'Hello, how are you doing?' She said 'Fine, how come we don't see you around no more?' So I said, 'I been busy,' and she just looked at me and said, 'Busy with what—monkey business?' Rebeck, the way she said it, how she waved her finger and went like this with the eyes. 'Monkey business,' she said, 'I know how it is.' Rebeck, I went home and I lay on the bed for an hour and I said I'm not going out there. No more. What am I, crazy? So I lay like that for an hour, and then I got the raincoat and came out. So that's why I was late."

Central Avenue makes a very wide curve just before it reaches the gate. Mr. Rebeck was able to watch Mrs. Klapper down the road, through the iron gate, and onto the street. He saw her stop to let a car pass her, and then she crossed the street and he could not see her after that. There were a lot of people on the street, and it was not easy to pick out one hat among them all, even if it was shaped like a crescent moon.

11

It rained all night. Michael and Laura walked through it, watching the rain come down so hard that it bounced when it hit the ground. Toward morning the rain began to let up, and by the time they came to the wall that overlooked the city it had become a heavy mist that sat on the trees and would not be moved by sunrise. Mid-August rain is like that in New York.

"This is nice," Michael said. He stretched, which was, of course, not at all necessary, but it was one of the motions of humanity he remembered very clearly.

"Even though we've done it before?" Laura asked. She sat on the wall beside him.

"Even so. Some things bear more repetition than others. Mornings like this. Grapes. I don't think I could ever have gotten tired of grapes. I used to hoard them. All kinds—green, red, purple, black. Some men can't pass a pool hall without going in. I couldn't pass fruit stores."

"I was that way about bananas," Laura said. "But I wasn't really faithful about it. I'd eat a bunch in a day and then crawl under the sink and be quietly sick. That would cure me for two weeks or so, and then I'd be back on the banana boat. Grapes a little, but bananas most of all."

"Grapes," Michael said firmly. "But you see what I mean. I like this. I like us sitting here and talking, watching the mist burn off and the trucks in the streets. I suppose in a hundred years or a thousand years, I'll be weary unto death with it."

"It won't take that long," Laura said. "A month. Maybe a couple of months."

"All right. I know it. What are you trying to prove? Right now I like watching the morning come. Sandy and I used to do that a lot. We'd sit up all night playing cards and listening to records, and then, just before morning, we'd go out and walk until the sun came up. We'd have breakfast wherever we were and go home and sleep till three or four in the afternoon. Then we'd go through the same routine again, and we never got tired of it."

Laura looked down the hillside as she spoke. "Sometimes I wish Sandra would restrain herself from feather-footing her way into everything we talk about. If I sound petty and malicious, it's because I am."

"I was sorry as soon as I'd mentioned her," Michael said. "I know how it sounds. The most boring thing in the world is another man's girl."

"It isn't that," Laura said a little crossly. "You have a perfect right to talk about her. Every beautiful thing you can remember comes in handy after death. Only—" A plane from La Guardia Airport was thundering tinnily over the city, and she used it as an excuse to leave the sentence incomplete until it was out of sight. Then, still looking away from him, she said, "Only, I wish you'd decide whether you love her or hate her."

"I don't love her," Michael answered. "But all the pleasant things I remember seem to be tied up with her, one way or the other. Not because she was Sandra, but because the good moments were better for someone else's being there. This sounds like women's-magazine philosophy, but some things aren't any good unless they're shared. Sitting up all night would be pointless if somebody you loved wasn't sitting up with you, picking out music to play and helping you kill the bourbon. Walking by yourself in the rain is for college kids who think loneliness makes poets. You know what I mean."

"I know what you mean," Laura said.

"All right. Let it go. The point is made. You know, the raven was right about birds. They do sing just before rain. I was listening."

Michael looked sideways at her. "What's the matter, Laura? Did I say something wrong?"

"Nothing," Laura said. "Nothing's wrong. When you mentioned Sandra, I started thinking about the trial. It must be over now."

"Now? What are you talking about? It's not for a week yet."

Laura smiled for the first time. "What day is today?"

"Good God, I don't know. It's still summer, but some of the leaves are turning brown already. Is it August?"

"It's August seventeenth," Laura said. "The trial was two days ago. I know because Mr. Rebeck told me. The raven's been following it in the newspapers, the way you asked him to."

"Did I ask him? I don't even remember that. I'm losing all track of time, Laura. I thought I'd keep that a while longer."

Alarm clocks were going off in the city now. One after another, sometimes two or three together, they drove their small silver knives into the body of the great dream that sprawled naked on the housetops. Sensual, amiable, and defenseless as it was, it would still take a little while to die.

"Does it make any difference?" Laura asked. "What's time to us? What's five o'clock to the dead? We've got no pressing appointments."

"No difference. But it's part of being human, and so I hate to lose it. Didn't I tell you I hung on to things?"

"I remember," Laura said. She looked up at the overcast sky for a sign of the raven. "Anyway," she said, "we ought to know about the trial today."

"I don't care about the trial," Michael said. "It might have meant something to me if they'd tried her when I was newly dead and full of revenge. Now I don't much care. I don't even remember her as well as I used to. She's becoming a stranger who did something to a stranger. I don't wish her any harm. Let's leave it at that. Don't talk about the trial, Laura."

Behind them a tree branch shook like a wet dog and sent its load of rain splashing to the ground. Michael and Laura turned and saw a couple coming past the hothouse and toward the wall.

"Company," Michael said. "And so early."

They were very young, Laura thought. Twenty or twenty-one, no more. The boy's hair was so wet it was almost maroon in color. He wore a raincoat but no rubbers, and the bottoms of his pants legs flapped shapelessly above his equally soaked socks as he walked. The girl also wore a raincoat, but the top button was missing and her wet white blouse clung to her small pointed breasts. She wore some sort of plastic kerchief over her hair, but the rain had seeped in, and what could be seen of her hair was limp and damp. They walked slowly, with their arms around each other's waists, faces turned to each other as they talked. Sometimes, without stopping, they kissed and then stumbled because they were not looking where they were going. Then they would laugh.

"Let's get out of here," Michael said. "I don't want to eavesdrop on them. Let's go somewhere else."

"Wait a little. How wet they are, and how happy."

They heard the boy's voice then. "Sure it's crazy. Been a pretty night all around. Look at it this way. I bet you've had hundreds of guys taking you to movies and skating rinks and dances. How many guys ever took you to a graveyard before breakfast? This way you'll remember me."

"A graveyard before breakfast," the girl said. "All night out in the rain and now a graveyard. You bet I'll remember you, mister." But she was laughing as she said it, and she hugged the boy's waist tightly.

"Think of it like a park," the boy said. "Look at all the statues standing around. Look at all the trees. It's like Central Park."

The girl looked up at him and shook her head, pantomiming exasperation. "A park. Some park. Wait till my mother gets hold of me." She made her voice shrill and old. " 'Where were you, Norma, all night and not a word? What kind of a way is that to treat your mother?' And I'll say, 'It's all right, Ma, it's all right, don't panic. Harry and I had a wonderful time. We went to a movie and when we came out it was raining, and so we walked all night. And in the morning Harry took me to the most wonderful graveyard. Ma, you should have been there. What a night.' " She sneezed.

"God bless you," the boy said. "Honey, you all right? I don't want you getting sick because I'm crazy. I'll take you right home now, you don't feel good."

"No, I'm all right," the girl said. "I'll take a hot shower when I get home. Only let's not stay too long, Harry."

"A few minutes, that's all." The boy pointed toward the wall. "Come on, we'll sit down and catch our breath. Then we'll start back."

As they came on together, Michael said urgently, "Laura, let's get out of here. I don't want to watch them. Neither do you."

"Wait," Laura said. "Wait a little. I thought you were the one who spent all his time observing people."

"Not couples. Never couples. I'm not obnoxiously brave, Laura."

"I'm not brave at all," Laura said. But she remained on

the wall, watching the boy and girl approach, and Michael stayed with her.

When the couple reached the wall, the boy stooped and lifted the girl onto it. There was a good deal of puffing and giggling and flopping of wet garments involved. Once seated on the wall, the girl extended her hand daintily, and the boy took it and scrambled, panting, up the ladderlike mortar to sit beside her. He was completely out of breath and tried to conceal it by taking deep gasps of air and letting them out slowly. But the girl looked at him and began to laugh, and it was somehow different from laughing after kissing and stumbling.

"Look at you," she said. "You're all red and breathless."

"You think you're such a featherweight?" the boy said, not without rancor. "Come on, we'll do it over and you carry me this time. Let's see how you look."

"Score one for our side," Michael said to Laura. "I think I'm for him if it comes to shooting."

But the boy reached an arm out, and the girl pushed herself against his side and drew the arm about her like a cloak. She giggled once and then kissed the boy's cheek quickly when he looked sourly at her and started to speak.

"I wouldn't make fun of you if you were weak," she said, and the boy's arm tightened around her shoulders until she winced.

They happened to be sitting almost exactly where Michael and Laura had chosen to sit, in the middle of the wall where the trees on both sides did not block their view of the city. To Mr. Rebeck or Campos, the two figures would have seemed outlined in cobweb by the remembered shapes of the ghosts who sat with them; as if Michael and Laura were only sheaths for the young swords that the boy and girl were. But to anyone else passing there would have been just the two young people sitting on the wall, the girl's wet face pressed against the side of the boy's neck.

"I can see where you live from here," the boy said.

The girl lifted her head from his shoulder. "Where, Harry? Where is it?"

"Way over there, see—a block after the Coca-Cola sign. One thing I know, it's where you live."

"I see it. I even see—my God, Harry, there's a light on in the bedroom! God, my mother must be having baby elephants. She'll kill me when I get in, she'll absolutely kill me."

"I'll come up with you," the boy offered diffidently.

"She'll kill you too," the girl warned.

"I'll come up with you. Your mother doesn't scare me."

"Oh, you're so brave," the girl said. "I don't know what I'd do without you."

"Sleep your life away," the boy said. "Norma, look. The street lights are going out. Look at them."

"This is nice. You can watch the whole city waking up." The girl was tracing the boy's mouth and nose with a forefinger. "The stores'll be opening soon." She sneezed again. "Harry, if I catch a cold you better catch one too. God help you if you don't."

"Isn't that nice?" Michael said. "What's mine is yours. Love is the sweetest thing."

"The way they look at each other," Laura said. "As if one of them was going to vanish any minute, and they didn't know which one it would be."

"Young lust. Don't tell me you've never seen it before?"

"Of course I have," Laura said.

"Take off your shoes," the boy was saying.

The girl pulled away from him, frowning. "Why? What's the idea?"

"Come on, take your shoes off," the boy said. "You're catching a cold."

"I know I'm catching a cold. Is running around barefoot going to make it any better?"

"Look, your feet are wet. Take off your shoes and socks and I'll dry your feet. Then you can wear my socks until we get home. How's that for thinking?"

The girl began to laugh again. "Harry, you're crazy!

What good'll that do, wearing your socks? They're just as wet as mine."

"Oh," the boy said. "Yeah." He poked halfheartedly at his own shoes and socks. "All right, forget it. It was just an idea."

"I mean, it's an awfully nice thing to do, Harry, but there wouldn't be any point to it. I'd just get wet again."

"Yeah, I know," the boy said, still examining his feet. "I just liked the idea of you wearing something of mine."

"That's sweet," The girl touched him lightly on the back of the neck, just where the hair begins. "Harry, that's very sweet."

"Forget it. It was a stupid idea."

"Well, look," the girl said. "Look, we could trade coats. Mine might be a little tight on you, but I guess we could manage it. You want to, Harry?"

"No," the boy said. "I didn't mean it like that. Forget it, Norma."

The girl smiled slowly and vaguely, as though she were trying to remember a dream. Her finger and thumb kept gently opening and closing on the back of the boy's neck. "Harry," she said huskily. "Harry, look at me."

"That's it," Michael said. "That's the ballgame. Look into a girl's eyes, and you see everything you ever believed about yourself. And you can never see her ugly because that would mean that you also are ugly and untrue. Up the creek, up the creek. Look at the poor sucker."

"Michael, I'm jealous too," Laura said.

The boy and girl had leaned to kiss each other. Their eyes were shut so tightly that the lids were wrinkled, and it took them a moment to find each other's mouths. They kissed damply and noisily and then sat as close together as they could, hip to hip, arms around each other's shoulders. The girl was still smiling. She nipped at the boy's ear and said, "I think we better go, Harry."

The boy pushed the plastic kerchief back from her head

and plowed his fingers through the lank curls. "You've got soft hair," he said.

"Baby-fine hair. I'm the only one in my family who's got it. My mother says my grandmother had hair like that. I don't remember her. Harry, we better go."

Her voice was higher than it had been, and shaky now, for the boy's hand had dropped from her hair to her shoulder, from her shoulder to her waist, and from her waist to her hip, where it remained. There was something tentative about the arch of the fingers, as if their movement or lack of it depended entirely on the girl's reaction. Without even reaching to take the hand off her hip, she slid a little away from it, and the boy promptly let it drop.

"Harry," she said, teasing rather than scolding. "Not in a graveyard."

"Not in a graveyard," the boy said pleasantly. "Not in a living room. Not on a roof. Not in a park. Not in a movie. Not in the middle of the goddam Sahara Desert, right? Right?"

"Don't shout," the girl said. When he would have turned his head from her, she took his chin in her hand and held his hand still. "Harry, it's just that I don't want to spoil this. I don't want something bad to happen to us because one of us got—you know, grabby."

"Grabby! Holy goddam, I touch you through a goddam coat and a dress and whatever kind of suit of armor you wear, and I'm grabby. Jesus."

"Sometimes I'm afraid for us," the girl said. "I really am, Harry."

The boy wrenched his chin free from her hand. "Goddam," he said. "Holy goddam."

"Amen," said Michael.

"Harry, Harry," the girl said. "Turn around and look at me."

"Don't you do it, Harry," Michael warned.

But the boy had turned, and the girl stretched to kiss his forehead. Murmuring, "Harry, Harry, Harry," she drew his head down to her small breasts and held it there, patting his cheek and curling his hair around her fingers.

"My Harry," she whispered. "My poor, greedy Harry."

"And don't baby me, Norma." The boy's voice was somewhat muffled. "Don't baby me. You always do, and I don't like it."

The girl laughed. "Is this babying you?" She held his head even closer against herself.

"Yes," the boy said, but Michael and Laura could barely hear him. He was bent forward at a very awkward angle with his head on the girl's breast, and he kept trying to wiggle his legs and rump into a more comfortable position. He said something else, and the girl bent to listen.

"What did you say, Harry?"

"I love you." She had stopped holding his head, but he did not straighten up.

"I know it. I know you love me."

"Well, I'm telling you again," the boy said loudly. "I love you, Norma."

"And I love you." She lifted his head, kissed him on the mouth, drew her hand slowly down his cheek, and said, "Let's go, Harry. We'll get some coffee or something and take on my mother. Think you can handle her?"

"Bring her on," the boy said. He jumped from the wall, landing in a deep crouch. Turning and holding out his arms to the girl, he said, "Jump. I'll catch you."

"You sure?" The girl beckoned him closer to the wall. "You won't drop me?"

"I wouldn't drop you," the boy said. "Muscles Harry? Come on, honey. It's all right."

"Okay," the girl said. She slid cautiously off the wall, and the boy caught her and lowered her safely to the ground. He kissed the corner of her mouth and put his arm around her. As they started back toward the hothouse, Michael and Laura heard the boy say, "Nice night, honey?"

"Wonderful," the girl said. "We'll have to do it again."

When they were gone, Michael sighed and said, "Hooked.

What an all-purpose weapon the carrot of sex is, in good hands. Poor bugger."

"I think she loves him," Laura said. "She never once took her eyes off him."

"Of course not. When a cat's stalking a nice, fat bird, it isn't interested in the scenery. She knows all about eyes. 'Harry, look at me. Look at me.' Hypnotism combined with mild asphyxiation. When she dragged him down into her breast, he was still fighting. When he came up out of it, he was gone. Beaten. Sure, she loves him. But they've got two different ideas of love. He wants to dance with her on a terrace with a full moon and a thirty-six-piece orchestra; he wants to go singing through storms with her, like Gene Kelly. She knows about thirty-six piece orchestras. You have to feed them, and then there's nothing left for the children."

People were going to work in the city. Almost at the same time, they spilled out of their houses and into the empty streets, getting into cars, waiting for buses, going down into subways, marching along the gray sidewalks. In time the streets, empty a minute ago, full now, would be empty again, as the blotter of the city absorbed the men. And in time it would give some of them, most of them, back, providing that it were wrung enough and squeezed enough and torn enough between now and then.

"I sat like that with a man once," Laura said.

When Michael did not answer, she went on, "I put my arms around him, the way she did, and held him just as she did. Not quite for the same reason, but I held him the way she did and said the same things. Say something quickly, Michael, because I had forgotten this, and I'm saying it as I remember it."

"You never told me," Michael said. "I don't know what to say. Has he ever come here?"

Laura laughed. "Good God, no. That was a long time ago, when we sat together." Again she stopped and waited for some reaction from him. "Say something, Michael."

"What can I say?" He was angry now. "Stop making me your echo chamber. Talk about it, if you want to. You had a lover. Okay. So?"

"A lover," Laura said. "That was the word I used. It's a beautiful word. I was in college then. I used to sit at my desk and close my eyes and say to myself, I have a lover. Laura has a lover. I'd look at all the girls sitting near me in their spring dresses, with their mouths a little open as they listened to whatever it was they were all listening to, and I'd say to them in my mind, When this class is over, some of you will go home, and some of you will go to another class, and some of you will go other places. But I will walk out of the room and go to meet my lover. You have boy friends, dates, steadies. I have a lover. We are different."

"They were probably all thinking the same thing," Michael said. "Speaking as a teacher."

"I know that now. But they'd always had lovers, however they thought of them. This was my first. We sat under a tree one evening, and he got all choky and self-accusing, and told me he wasn't good enough for me. And I put my arms around him—no, I grabbed him around the neck, really—and pressed his face into my inconsequential bosom and went, 'There, there, I love you, don't worry, I love you.' Maybe you're right about that girl, Michael, because I grabbed him as if I'd been lying in wait for a chance to hold him like that. It felt very nice. I think he even cried a little."

In the street below them a mother screamed at her child in wordless rage and love.

"What happened then?"

"He went away in the summer. It lasted a very short time. But it seemed long then, and it still seems long when I think of it. It took the longest time to stop saying, 'Laura has a lover,' whenever I had a few free minutes."

She moved a little on the wall, as insubstantial and evanescent as poetry, and as lasting. The cars jostled and swirled in the city, bellowing.

"The funny thing is this. Before that spring and ever afterward I used to pride myself on being sensitive and understanding far beyond the range of most people. I marked out the lost and tongueless for my own, and I used to think, I understand them. I know what it is to do a pitiful evil because of knowing oneself unloved. I may be unloved myself, but boy, am I empathetic. Sometimes I even wrote about it."

Michael felt no tightness in his nonexistent throat, and no syrupy food of pity through himself, but he heard no sound except Laura speaking.

"But for that little while," she said, "I forgot all about the emotionally undernourished. I became arrogant. I was loved, I was one of the haves, and one of the secrets of being a have is not wasting your time on empathy. I gorged myself on being loved until it came out of my ears, and when it was over I didn't realize it for a time because I was living off my fat. Proving—"

She stopped and seemed to be very interested in the cheap headstones at the bottom of the hill, made so much alike and stacked so closely together that a ruler could have been laid across them to the iron gate.

"Proving?" Michael asked quietly.

"Proving nothing. Proving that everyone—meaning me—has her price. Proving that it's easier to love the downtrodden and lonely of the world if you yourself have never been loved. I've been spoiled for it. A man said, 'I love you,' to me. I made him say it a great many times. And so I feel a little above the unloved because of that, until I realize how far above me are the loved and still loving. Forget it, Michael. I'm getting all complicated. But I know what I meant."

She looked away, anywhere but at him, and Michael, looking at her, saw her more clearly than he ever had. He saw the wide mouth and the nose that was all wrong and

the eyes that went no more with the other features than the
nose and mouth and skin went with one another. He saw
the black hair falling across the lowered neck, and even
the favorite dress, gray and unbecoming, but so carefully
remembered that he could see the weave of the threads and
the one loose button in the back. Still no pity, no soupy
sorrow, but a feeling very close to tears, a feeling that could
not possibly be forced into words without breaking. But
he tried, because he was Michael Morgan and he trusted no
feeling that could not be spoken.

"I love you," he said.

It sprang from his mouth without editing, and it came
out very badly. He emphasized the *I* too much, and what
he had said sounded almost truculently protective. He knew
how clumsy it must have sounded to Laura.

"Not like that," she said a little sadly. "My mother used
to say it like that. I don't want to be defended, Michael."

"I love you," he said again, and it was better this time.
"Me. I. Morgan. Not your mother. I love you, Laura."

"I love hearing it," Laura said. "I could never get used
to the sound. Say it again. As often as you like."

He was about to say it again when he checked himself.
"Meaning that I can say the words as often as I like, but
you won't believe them."

"Michael, you don't know me. You've never even really
seen me. If we were both alive and we passed each other
one day, or you came into my bookshop to buy something,
you wouldn't look twice at me. If we were introduced at
a party, you'd shake my hand, say 'How do you do, Miss
Uh,' and forget me before you were through saying it.
You're affectionate, and you're used to being loved, and
you're lonely now. Don't practice on me. Don't say you
love me because part of being alive is loving someone. It
won't make you a living man again, and it won't make
death any easier for me."

Funny, he thought. We sit here and talk about emotion
in totally emotionless voices, like two neighbors getting

whatever little nourishment they can out of fourth-hand gossip. Can we feel things, we dead, or is that also recalled with effort? If she loves me, will I be happy? If she does not, will I be hurt? Will I even know the difference?

"I'd have known you," he said. "I'd have seen you once and known you and married you and lived with you before the party was over."

"What would you have said to me?" Laura asked. " 'Dear Miss Durand, I will love you while I live'? What do you say to me now?"

"I will love you all the days of my death, however few or many they may be. As long as I can remember love, I will love you."

" 'All the days of my death,' " Laura repeated softly. "There aren't many left, Michael. Our minds are like torn pockets. Think of all the things we've forgotten and forget every minute. Why should love be remembered any longer than any of the others?"

"Because we need it more," he said. "Because without it, there is nothing left of us. Loving each other, we last a little longer before we forget even that we lived once. Knowing ourselves loved makes us almost human for a little time."

"Such a little time," Laura said. "Is it worth it? Is it worth the effort of loving to stay awake a cigarette longer, to listen to another record? If it can't last long enough to make us wonder if it might last longer, if we know how it must end and when, what's the good of it? I'm tired of hope, and I'm tired of gallant lost causes. Shake your fist in the face of the gods and you draw back a stump. Let it go, and leave me alone."

An ice-cream truck jangled its fool's bells in the city, but only a few children came running because it was too early in the day for ice cream. Over by the housing project, a steam drill coughed and snarled, and the yell of a subway train on a tight curve came faintly through the gratings in the sidewalk. The day must be hot already, Michael thought, for most of the windows that he could see were open, and the workmen had taken off their shirts.

"Nothing's worth any effort in the end," he said to Laura, "because everyone is going to die and there is nothing in the world that will stop them from dying. Nothing lasts. A few things last longer than most people live, but they go too. Hope goes, and desire and wonder and fear and eagerness. Love lasts a few minutes longer, that's all. A minute or a month or an hour. The paper match burns down until it singes your fingers and goes out, and there you are in the dark again, rubbing your two little sticks together. But this is the last time, the last match. There won't be any more light. No more. And no more noise of things moving or of animals lying down. Only our separate, untouching selves, and soon not even that."

"Then we'll sit in the dark," Laura said. "We'll sit and wait."

"Wait for what? Nothing's coming. For God's sake, we spent our whole lives waiting, you and I. Why should anything come to us now that did not come then? There's just this, just this miserable little sketch of love to keep us from being immortal a while longer. Are you ready to be wise, Laura? I'm not. I'd rather love for a day and then be wise, even if it only means saying I love you, as I say it now."

A sparrow flew down and landed on the wall. Laura reached out to stroke its feathers, and when her hand passed through the bird she tried again. She made the useless stroking motion over and over again, until the bird flew away.

"It's whatever we can get, then," she said, "on whatever terms we can get it."

"That's all there is. That's all there ever was."

"I would have taken that once," Laura said, "when I was alive. If a man loved me I would have talked myself into loving him, and I would have loved him very deeply after a while. I can't do that now, Michael. This sounds stupid, even to me, and stupidly proud, but I won't love you simply because you need me. I want you to love me, even for the chip of time we have, but it has to be as Laura. I know it's a little late in the game for that, but I won't be loved because you see death over my shoulder when you look at me."

"Then why did you try to make that stone boy love you because he was alone?" Michael asked gently. "Why did you tell him that he had nobody but you?"

Again he saw the quick shimmer of pain that he had seen in her once or twice before and not recognized.

"That was different. I didn't want him to love me. I wanted him to talk to me and ask me to stay with him for a while. I wanted him to need me."

"All love is rhymed need," Michael said. "I need you. I needed you when I was alive. Where the hell were you then. Now I need you, and you're here, and I love you. I'm selfish about it, like poor greedy Harry. I want to give you things and watch you be pleased by them, and that's the final selfishness. I can't bargain with you, Laura. I've left all my beads and mirrors back home. All I can give you is my need. I'll take whatever you can give me and be pleased with it. I love you, Laura."

"I love you too," Laura said. "Do we sing our duet now?"

"No. Nothing changes."

She moved close to him, and the anguish in the gray eyes and wise mouth was like fishhooks across his mind. "I do love you, Michael. But I wish it could be the way I wanted to love you. I've nothing to give you, the way we are. I can only take from you, and I'll hate myself because of it."

"Don't get carried away," Michael said. "Love me as long as you have need of me. That's the way people love."

"That's not the way I wanted to love. Love to me is giving whatever you have to give to whomever you love. I can't even touch you. Michael, I wish I could touch you. I wish I could sleep with you. I wish I could please you."

Michael grinned at her. "Now you know you're not supposed to think like that. You're supposed to be pure spirit, unperturbed by the desires of the corrupt flesh. The idea is to get rid of the body so as to be free to meditate without being constantly called to the telephone. Be a flame, Laura, be a demure blue flame."

"I'll be that soon enough," Laura said. "What do we do, then, in this short forever we have? How do we love each other? How do we live together and make each other happy?"

"I don't know, exactly," Michael answered. "I think we have to stay together and not wander too far away from each other. There isn't too much we can do for ourselves or each other, Laura, except be in love because it's a little better than not being in love. Does that frighten you?"

"Can the dead be frightened? Even the loving dead?"

"They're more vulnerable. Anything is more vulnerable in love or in rut or whatever than out of it."

"What does frighten me a bit," Laura said, "is being known. We're going to know each other very well before we lose the earth, my love. I used to think how wonderful it would be if people could simply take the roofs off their minds and let other people look in, instead of trusting their souls to words. Now I'm not so sure. I don't know if you'll love me once you know me."

Michael laughed. "I'll take my chances. It's like marriage. The race there is between total knowledge of each other and death. If death comes first, it's considered a successful marriage."

He pointed suddenly into the city. "Look. Aren't they the two who were here this morning? Harry and what's-her-name?"

"Norma," Laura said. She saw the two raincoat-clad figures waiting for a traffic light to change. They had their arms around each other's waists.

"It's too far to tell," she said. "It looks like them."

They watched the couple without speaking until the light changed and the boy and the girl started across the street. They walked so slowly that the light had changed again before they reached the other side, and the cars were sniffing at their ankles.

"Luck, you silly bastards," Michael murmured. "Oh, luck."

He turned in time to catch Laura's smile and looked a little embarrassed. "See?" he said. "You were wrong. Once you feel yourself loved, you become generous, expansive, sentimental. You love everybody, even young couples, and that takes some doing."

Laura smiled and stared happily at him and said nothing.

"I wish I could touch you," he said after a moment. "I think I'd like to hold your face between my hands and look protectively down at you. You'd have very cool skin and light bones against the palms of my hands."

"I'd love it. But I would also flush, and my skin would get hot and very red. It always used to. I wouldn't mind, though, if you didn't."

"I wouldn't mind."

"Big-hearted Morgan," Laura said softly. But she smiled still and sat up straight so that Michael could look at her.

Very suddenly, he said, "Touch me. Try to touch my hand."

"It won't work, Michael." Her voice was very low. "I'll try, if you want me to. I'll break my heart trying. But it won't work. The time for touching is past."

"Try," Michael said. "Please try. Think about it. Think about loving me and wanting to touch me. Think how your hand used to feel, and how you moved it, and what it was like to touch things with it. Stretch out your hand to me, Laura. It might as well be your hand. Big symbol."

"Michael—"

"Once. One try and never again."

He held out his hand, and she reached, without hesitation, to touch it. The sun was hot on the leaves, and the city was full of the noises of cars and children; and Michael and Laura, lovers, reached to hold hands as lovers. There was a point in space where their hands, thin as breath, met and seemed to become one hand, through which the sun shone and a leaf fell. For a little while they stared hopefully at it. Then each gradually lowered his eyes to look at the other eyes with a kind of guilt, but still hoping to see something there that did not look from their own eyes. They did not lower their hands or look away from each other.

"Nothing," Michael said. "I didn't think there'd be."

"I felt something," Laura said, unable to bear the sadness in his voice. "At least I think I did. I might be imagining it—"

"Don't lie to me. Even to please me. We haven't got the time to lie."

"All right," she said. "I didn't feel a thing. It didn't work. We can't ever touch each other. Does honesty make you feel better? It's just as painful as lies to me."

"Never mind, Laura." He let his hand drop to his side. "It doesn't matter."

"It does matter," she cried out. "That's why I can't help envying Sandra, even now. Whatever she took from you, she had at least that much warmth to give you, and I have nothing. Only company and nice words."

"Laura," Michael said. "Laura, Laura. Sandra saw things a little differently. To her, holding each other, sleeping together—that was a kind of taking too. We never made love. I don't know what it was we made, but it wasn't love, and it wasn't always dead by morning."

He laughed. "I'll tell you something. Once I was very fond of a poem by Emily Dickinson or somebody. I only remember one line of it, but it goes, 'The soul selects her own society.' I used to tell it to everybody. Once I quoted it to a friend of mine, and he said, 'Maybe, but the body gets thrown into bed with the goddamnedest people.' I remember him saying that."

He looked at her for a long while, saying nothing. Once he reached as if to try again to touch her, but he drew his hand back so swiftly that she wondered if she had imagined his moving it. Another leaf fell. It would be an early autumn, she thought.

"You are my own society," Michael was saying. "I looked for you when I was alive. I was careless about it, so as not to be hurt too much by not finding you, and I got tossed into the goddamnedest beds when I got too careless, but I looked for you, Laura. For a while I mistook Sandra for you. My apologies. It was dark, and I'm nearsighted. But it was never Sandra I loved. It was never Sandra's arms I slept in."

"Damn you," Laura said. "What kept you so long on the road?"

"My horse broke down, and I had to eat him. Poor beast. Love me?"

"Yes. Very much."

"I love you. Want to go for a walk? The city can dress itself and eat and go to work without us."

"No," she said. "Let's stay here a little longer. We have the time."

The raven came from behind them, and they turned when they heard the harsh flapping of his wings. He landed between them on the wall, caught his breath, and said, "I been looking all over for you, Morgan."

"I've been here," Michael said.

"I've been up and down the damn cemetery. Rebeck said you might be here."

"It's the trial," Laura said. "The trial's over."

"It's over." The raven looked down and scratched his beak in the spaces between the bricks, where the cement bulged.

"How did it go?" Michael asked calmly. "What happened to Sandra?"

"Crazy trial," the raven muttered without looking up. "Craziest damn trial I ever heard of."

"She won," Laura said. "She won, didn't she? They let her go free."

"Darling," Michael said, "you're not supposed to think of trials as being won or lost. The idea is—"

"They let her off," the raven said hoarsely. "Not guilty."

"Good for her. I didn't want anything bad to happen to Sandra. It would have been wrong to kill her."

"Morgan, you don't get the idea." The raven could not meet his eyes. "The way they figure, if she didn't kill you, you did. Suicide. Her lawyer said you tried to frame her. So they're sending a couple of guys out here to dig you up and move you someplace else. You being a Catholic and so on."

Laura made a small high-pitched sound and was still.

"Laura," Michael said. He turned from the raven to speak to her, but after her name he said nothing.

"It was a crazy trial," the raven said. "I told Rebeck, and he thought so too."

12

"It was the paper did it," the raven said. "They found the other half of the paper."

"What paper?" Mr. Rebeck asked. The four of them were sitting on a small rise of ground from which they could look down on Michael Morgan's grave. The day had become very sunny after the fog burned off, but cool and crossed with breezes. It was the sort of day Mr. Rebeck had always loved.

"The paper the poison was in," Michael said quietly. "I remember now."

"Yeah," the raven said. "You see, they had that little part already, all rolled up like a cone, only it didn't have any fingerprints on it. So, the way the newspapers had it, her lawyer went messing around the house, trying to find the rest of the paper. Really shook the place down."

"Under my desk blotter." Michael seemed very calm. "I put it there for safekeeping. I was going to throw it away, but I must have been too drunk. When are they coming?"

"Don't know. Pretty soon now."

"I don't understand," Mr. Rebeck said. "Why was the paper so important?"

"It had a lot of numbers on it in his handwriting," the raven answered. "I didn't get all that about the numbers, but the handwriting was the big deal."

Michael was sitting cross-legged beside Laura, the way she had seen him for the first time. Frequently he turned his head to look at her, to smile. She sat quite still, eyes fixed on the long pebbly road down which the men would come. He did not speak directly to her, and she did not speak at all.

"The numbers had to do with dosage," he said. "The thing about this kind of poison is that if you take too little of it, it'll only give you an upset stomach, and if you take too much, you'll throw it up. Like an emetic. You have to know just how much to use. I looked it up in a library and wrote it down on the paper. Then, when I wanted something to keep the poison in, I tore the corner off the paper and put the rest of the paper under the blotter because I was in a hurry. And I put the poison in my own glass when Sandra and I drank together before we went to bed. I remember that now."

He raised his head suddenly. "I think I hear something. A car."

Laura looked at him then and started to say something, but it never came out. They sat without words listening for the hissing chatter of pebbles twisting under tires, for voices and the sound of an engine; waiting for a wide nose and a grinning silver mouth to come into sight where the road curved. Mr. Rebeck wanted to hold Laura's hand, or put his hand on Michael's shoulder, but he could not. He found a hole in one of his socks and worked his finger around in it, watching the tear grow bigger.

They waited, but nothing came. There was only the noise of grasshoppers.

"Nothing," Michael said at last. "I must be overeager."

"I can't imagine you killing yourself," Mr. Rebeck said almost wonderingly. "Even now I can't really picture it."

"Nor I," Michael said, "then or now. It's hard to explain,

but I never knew I was going to kill myself, not the way we think of knowing—planning it, living with it, waking up in the morning and saying, 'Two days from now I will take the poison and die.' That takes something I don't have. Even when I looked up the lethal dosage and wrote it down, it was just for the hell of it, intellectual curiosity. Something to bring up during a lull in the conversation. But I can't remember ever saying to myself, 'Look, I don't want to live any more. I'm going to kill myself as quickly as possible and get the whole thing over with.' I never said that."

He looked at Laura again. "I think that's what Laura can't forgive me. She wants her suicides to be honest with themselves, to choose a death and seek it out boldly. I couldn't do that. I wasn't brave enough or honest enough. Laura is disappointed in me. Perfectly understandable."

"It isn't that at all," Laura said. She did not turn her head. "I haven't the right to ask anybody to be honest. It isn't that. But leaving your death on your wife's doorstep, dying so that she would die—I don't know how to talk myself past that, Michael. If I could, I would."

"Yes. That was bad."

Feeling the need to touch life, Mr. Rebeck reached out tentatively and smoothed the raven's black plumage with his hand. When the bird flinched but did not draw away, he let his hand remain lightly on the dusty feathers. He could feel the raven's heart beating.

"Maybe he didn't know," he said. "It's possible. You do so many things and never know you've done them. He didn't know Sandra would be blamed for his death."

Michael shook his head. "I knew. Thank you just the same." He did not look at any of them, nor was he looking down the road. He seemed to be staring with great interest at a white cloud shaped like a horse's head.

"I knew," he said. "There isn't any real way around it. I felt that Sandy had driven me to suicide, and that it was only right that she suffer for it. Funny that I should become

such a great believer in justice. I always used to open my history courses by telling the students that if they expected to hear a series of movie scenarios, with the good guys winning in the end, they might as well all go home because not only didn't the good guys win, but there weren't any good guys."

"They have to go to college to learn that?" the raven asked. "Hell, birds know it before they know they're birds."

"People know it too," Michael said, "but it worries them a bit, and they like to avoid the whole subject. I used to tell my classes, 'There is no justice. Justice is a man-made concept, a foreign body in the universe. Tigers are neither just nor unjust when they kill goats, or men, for that matter. There is no such thing as abstract justice. There is such a thing as law. The difference should be apparent.' It's old stuff, not in the least original with Morgan, but the students were very impressed."

Laura said nothing, and Michael sighed. "What can I tell you, Laura? That I confused justice and revenge? People do that a great deal, and they always have. That's no excuse. I never admitted that I thought my wife ought to die for causing my death, but that was the idea. It seemed very fair."

"And all your anger at death," Laura said. "Was that a lie? All the struggling to stay close to life, and all the crying that Sandra had murdered you—did you know all the time?"

"No. Not until the raven came. I didn't remember anything about my death. Only that there was poison and that it had a lot to do with Sandra. That was all."

Still Laura bent her head and would not look at him, and suddenly Michael was shouting. "God damn it, how do you think I feel?" His voice tolled in Mr. Rebeck's head, and it hurt the small man to listen. There seemed to be a great pendulum swinging sluggishly inside his head.

"How do you think I feel, knowing that I was bored

enough with myself to stop myself, and vengeful enough to try to drag someone with me? Knowing nakedly, without any possible way of shading my eyes from it, that I'm a liar, and a coward, and a murderer in everything but deed? Knowing that I never loved Sandra, and tried to destroy her because she didn't love me? And I planned it. I planned the whole rickety, childish, murderous thing, and then forgot all about it because it didn't go with the picture I had of myself. God, what a man I was. How I must have hated."

"I wouldn't bang my head on the floor quite that much," the raven said. "Nothing you can do about it now. Anyway, they let her off. Happy ending. The rest doesn't matter."

Michael shook his head. "It matters. How it ends isn't important any more." His voice was quieter. "Funny to find out I didn't love Sandra. I always thought I did."

Mr. Rebeck felt the raven's compact body moving under his hand and thought, I wish this had not happened. With all my heart, I wish it were June again, late spring, before the heat came, and none of this had happened. He saw Laura gradually raise her eyes to Michael's eyes, and knew without surprise what had happened between them that morning. I suppose it is a wonderful thing, he thought, even a kind of miracle, but I cannot seem to react to it properly. I am too old for sudden beauty, beauty that is born without budding and dies without bearing. What will happen to them now?

Oh, I wish to God it were spring again, late spring, before the heat came.

Michael's voice was low as he spoke to Laura. "The chase is over. The Morgan-hunt is over. I know what I am. I am everything I feared in life, everything I hated in other people, falseness and brutality and mindless arrogance. And I have to drag them with me, wherever I am dragged, because they are part of me, skin and skeleton. I can never hide from them again."

"That's not true," Laura said. "You're kind, and gentle,

and no more evil than breakfast or sunset. Don't you think I know?"

"No. I don't think you do know, Laura, because I didn't myself until just now. I can't fall back on kindness now that nothing else is left. When I was young, I thought I was very kind. I thought that I hated meanness and brutality simply because they were evil in themselves. As I grew up I learned that I hated to see people in pain because I could imagine myself suffering in their places. I always had a very good imagination. Now I see that I made great gestures against these things because they were in me, and I knew it and didn't dare admit it."

"They're in all of us," Laura said desperately. "They're in me. Michael, listen."

Michael went on. "So I told myself that I was kind and gentle, and other people believed it, and I even believed myself, and look at this thing I've done, Laura. Look at what I've done."

This time they all heard the sound of the truck and knew that the men had come even before they saw the truck. Mr. Rebeck had expected one of the shining black hearses with long tonneaus and shaded windows that he had so often seen sliding along the roads of the cemetery. But what came to get Michael was a large, open-backed truck with a green cab that gleamed as if it had been painted that morning. There were four men, three sitting in front and one in the back, leaning against a rusty red winch that stood up like the fin of a lean fish. The truck's engine was oddly soft and muffled, even when it was very close.

"They'll see me," Mr. Rebeck said. He drew his legs under him to rise, but the raven nudged his hand and said, "Not unless you get up. Stay put." He relaxed, feeling a little ashamed of his fright, but glad that the men would not see him.

"Do something," Laura said to Mr. Rebeck, to the raven, to Michael. She kept looking from Michael to the oncoming truck and back. "Please do something."

The truck was moving very slowly now. One of the men in the cab had stuck his head out of the window and was looking at the graves as the truck passed them.

"There's nothing they can do," Michael said. "The time for doing something, like the time for touching and the time for being kind, is past. Anyway, it's not everybody who gets to see himself dug up." He essayed a frown. "Dug up. I don't like putting it that way. Exhumed. That's no good either. Disinterred. Jesus."

"Excavated," the raven said. "Mined. How about mined?"

"Mined is very good."

Mr. Rebeck heard a wordless shout from the man with his head out of the window, and the truck scraped to a halt.

"Bingo," Michael murmured. "Our side wins the treasure hunt."

The four men got out of the car and stood around the grave. They were wearing clean dungarees and heavy shoes. The driver went to the back of the truck and returned with four shovels. Mr. Rebeck had thought vaguely that there would be picks, but it was summer and the ground was soft. They would have no trouble with the earth.

One of the men lifted his shovel, held it high a moment, shifting his grip, and then struck it into the earth at the foot of the grave. He put his foot on the shovel to drive it in deeper. When he wrenched it free, tossing the dirt to one side with a quick flip, there was a dark brown gash in the middle of the grasses.

"Oh, God," Laura said softly. She turned suddenly to Mr. Rebeck, her imploring shadowiness very close to him. "Do something," she said. "You must do something."

She is beautiful, after all, Mr. Rebeck thought, and I never noticed. But why does she turn to me? Why to me? I can't do anything.

Michael said it for him. "There's nothing, Laura. What do you want him to do? Would you have him go charging down the hill, yelling, 'Unhand that specter! If you take him away, I won't have anybody to talk to'? There's nothing to be done. What's the good of yelling?"

Nothing at all, Mr. Rebeck thought. But there must be yelling. There ought to be a good deal of yelling and fist-shaking and cursing, for how will we know we are alive if there is no noise?

Laura, Laura, for your sake I might be a little brave and go running down at those men, cursing them very loudly and telling them to leave Michael alone. That doesn't take too much bravery. But when I ran out of curses, when they saw how small I am, they would look at each other and laugh and go on digging. They might even dig me up. I am not brave enough for that, and no one can convince me that I am.

The first man nodded at another, and this man also plunged his shovel into the ground until only a thin flake of blade showed. They dug together, one at the foot of the grave and one at the side, while the two other men leaned on their shovels and talked to each other. The broad-leafed ivy on Michael's grave was ripped from its tentative hold on the earth and shoveled casually to one side, where it lay like a worn bedspread. For a moment the grave was outlined, a dark brown oblong in the grass, black-wounded where the shovels had struck.

"The ivy didn't even have time to take," Michael said. "It looked very thick and protective, but the poor damn thing probably hadn't even taken root. Poor old hothouse ivy. I wish they'd get it over with. How long does a thing like this usually take?"

"I don't know," Mr. Rebeck said. "I never saw it before."

The raven's head was small and surprisingly hard under Mr. Rebeck's fingers. He had read once that birds' bones were as light and fragile as the glass balls on Christmas trees.

The bird said, "I've seen a couple. Half an hour. Maybe less, maybe more. Depends how much trouble they have getting the coffin into the truck. That's what they have the winch for."

"Half an hour," Michael said. "Thank you. Could you manage to love me for half an hour more, Laura?"

The men were working very fast. They were beginning to stoop as they dug on the grave and threw the dirt over their shoulders. Already two straggly wings of earth spread away from the grave.

"Is that all you want?" Laura asked quietly. "Half an hour of my love?"

"It's all I'm going to get, so it's all I want. I believe in rationalizing before the fact. But I need that half-hour very badly, Laura."

"All right, Michael. Half an hour."

"Give or take a little. Maybe they'll have trouble with the winch. How fast they dig."

As he spoke, the two men stopped digging and the hitherto idle pair took over. They dug eagerly, barely allowing themselves time to spill the dirt away before their blades were in the ground again. One had taken his shirt off and could be seen to bare his upper teeth in an abstracted grin at every lunge and twist of his shovel. The two relieved men dabbed at their foreheads and necks and drank sparingly from a nearby faucet.

"I wonder what happens when they're finished," Michael said. "Probably nothing until they drive out of the cemetery. Then what?" He glanced inquiringly at Mr. Rebeck.

"I've never seen anything like this before," Mr. Rebeck repeated. "I don't know what happens."

"That's true. I don't imagine you would. Well, it doesn't matter. They can't make me any more dead or any less. That was a mistake of mine. I would like to know where they're taking me, though."

"Mount Merrill," the raven said. "A little place way down at the butt end of the Bronx. They get all the Yorkchester rejects. Your old lady made the arrangements."

"Pleasant name. Alliterative." Michael did not appear to

have noticed the raven's last remark. "You know, if you stop to think of it, this—mining operation shouldn't affect me very much. It isn't as if I'm actually leaving anyone I haven't left already. Except Laura. Always excepting Laura."

He turned quickly to Mr. Rebeck. "I didn't mean that the way it sounded, Jonathan." He had never called Mr. Rebeck that before. "We've been friends here. We would have been friends if we'd known each other when I was alive. We might have grown old playing pinochle, and the children would have been forcibly encouraged to call you Uncle Jonathan. But, as man and ghost, we had only a little time left to be friends. You know that. It was like the red second of light that remains after you have switched off a lamp. That short."

Very suddenly, Michael's tombstone began to fall. Mr. Rebeck heard one of the standing men shout a warning and saw the two diggers scramble out of the grave as the stone moved above them. Like the ivy, it had not had time to settle into the ground, and now it toppled slowly forward, crumpling the little earth that still held it up, making no sound at all. It swayed for a moment before it fell and vanished into the shallow hole that the men had dug. The four watching on the hillside heard the flat sound it made on the earth, and Mr. Rebeck thought he detected a slight hollowness under the sound. The shovels could not have much farther to go.

Laura said, "Ah," as if the stone had fallen on her. The men stood around the grave, looking at one another.

"What a sound," Michael marveled. "Like a suitcase slamming shut. Very symbolic. Even the stone cries out. Well, it should give us a little more time. I'm grateful for it."

They watched as the shirtless man waved the others back and jumped into the grave. He rubbed his hands against his thighs and bent down to the stone. Mr. Rebeck could see only the man's broad brown back from where he sat, but he could hear the whistling grunts of effort that burst past the man's teeth as he struggled with the headstone, and see the prison stripes of dirt and sweat forming on his sides. There was a moment when he almost had it lifted; when he stood nearly erect, with his shoulders curved and neck thrust forward, and his arms hanging straight down, a bowstring to his sweating back, and the stone in his hands, clear of the ground. His elbows were scraped and very dirty.

Then they heard the stone fall again, and saw the man straighten up slowly, rubbing his back and opening his mouth in pain. The man who had driven the truck grinned at him, a grin full of triumph and sympathy, and leaped down into the grave to join him. He stood opposite the shirtless man and said clearly, "You got to squat." So they both squatted on their haunches until only their heads showed out of the grave, and together they gripped the stone and lifted it as they rose. They dropped it on the grass and climbed out of the grave, breathing hard and laughing in deep gasps. The other two men took up shovels and began to dig once more.

"That's it," Michael said. "That's the true last of Morgan. The body in the coffin that they're trying so hard to reach doesn't matter at all. All bodies are alike. But when the stone with my name on it went over, old Morgan went too. Everybody should have a stone with his name on it. Also the dates of his birth and death. I haven't got one. Pat down the earth and let the grass grow back. Morgan is finished."

"They always take the stone with them," the raven said. "They'll put it up again in Mount Merrill."

Michael did not answer. He was watching the men. Mr. Rebeck watched them too, feeling more and more nervous. Now he did not wish for spring. He only wished himself away from the hillside and the grave that was being opened as eagerly as an unexpected present.

"It isn't fair." Laura's voice was sad and childlike. "It isn't fair."

"What's fair?" Michael asked gently. "Nobody's doing this to me. I did it myself. I must have wanted it once. Hush, Laura. Don't cry."

"I'm not crying. I'm a ghost."

"Don't argue with me. I know when you're crying. I love you. I know everything about you."

The grave had grown very deep. The smallest of the men stood in it up to his shoulders as he added his shovel loads to the great pile of dirt at the foot of the grave. When he bent over to dig he could not be seen at all.

Michael said, "Maybe this is the right way. We've loved each other for half a night and half a day and been warmed a little. What more could there have been for late lovers like us? Even if we had only the half-hour I asked you for, we'd have loved longer than people do in whole lifetimes. People love for scattered minutes: five minutes here, a minute with this girl, two minutes in a subway with another girl. We know how to love. We practiced in our minds, thinking, This is how I will love if anyone ever asks me. And now we've had a morning of love. How much more is there, ever, for the living or the dead?"

"Much more," Laura said fiercely. "You don't believe a word of what you've said. You haven't even been listening to yourself. Don't try to comfort me. I don't want comfort, Michael. I don't want a tiny, perfect love. I want you. I want you for as long as I can have you, and I know the difference between a half-hour and a lifetime."

"Laura—" Michael began. But she had turned swiftly to Mr. Rebeck, her beautiful, utterly plain face commanding his eyes.

"Is that unghostlike?" she demanded of him. "I don't feel very much like a ghost. I feel greedy and human. Am I wrong not to resign myself and make the best of things, accepting the beauty in loss? Am I wrong to want more than I have? Tell me. I want to know."

How did I ever think that she had the voice of a sad child? Mr. Rebeck wondered. The voice I hear is the voice of a proud and anguished woman. What is a woman doing in this place? What can I tell her? Why should she listen to me? I wouldn't, if I had any choice.

"No," he said. "Who am I to tell you not to want anything? But I know what Michael meant. There is a kind of love that can only be spoiled by consummation."

That wasn't what you meant, was it? No. No, I didn't think so. If you didn't take the things you want to say so seriously you might get a few of them right. Feel the raven laughing under your hand.

He decided to tell them about the girl. If he could remember. He would have to speak carefully.

"Once I went somewhere with a girl, when I was a long time younger. It was in the evening. I don't remember where we went, but I know that other people were there too. And somehow we were alone, this girl and I, in a very big room with a high roof and no chairs. We could hear the other people in the next room."

You sound like an old man telling the only dirty story he knows. Put in the cello quickly, because the story is really about the cello and not about you.

"There was a cello leaning against the wall. It looked old, and one of the strings was missing. But we went over to it, and we touched it and picked out tunes on the three strings. Once in a while we would look at each other and smile, and once our hands touched when we were both playing with the cello at the same time. We stayed there for a long while, telling each other jokes in an Irish brogue, and plucking the strings of the cello. Then some of the other people began to come into the room, and we went outside on a terrace."

Just then the shovels found the coffin. There was a short sound of metal on wood, and then another. All the men shouted in triumph, and the shirtless man, who was not digging, waved his shovel over his head. The other shovels rasped up and down the coffin, clearing away the few remaining clods, and the driver slapped the shirtless man on the back and went to the truck.

"Not much time left," Michael said.

"Some," the raven answered. "They still got to get the chains onto it and fill in the dirt after they're through."

"I wouldn't know what to do with much more time. All the time they were lifting up that headstone, I kept thinking, 'Here's a gift of five minutes, maybe more, surely time enough to say something important to Laura or explain myself to myself.' But nothing came out. Not a word. I love you, my Laura, but I never said anything important in my life, and I am not about to start now."

I must finish the story, Mr. Rebeck thought. I am not as honest as Michael; I must believe that whatever I am saying is important and should not be left incomplete. Finish the story, then, but do not blame them if they do not listen to you. They know what is important and what is not.

"In the moment that the girl and I stood in the room, playing with the cello and making jokes, we loved each other as much as we ever could have. When we went out into the garden it was not the same thing. And after a while we went away from each other, because both of us knew that it could never be as good again as it had been in the room with the cello. We had spent all our love in those few minutes, and what came after that was only remembering and trying to make it the way it was before."

The driver had backed the truck to the edge of the grave, and a chain was rattling down the winch, sounding very much like silverware in the sink. The shirtless man reached into the back of the truck and drew out two coils of rope. He tossed one of them to another man, and they both climbed back into the grave, letting themselves down very carefully, because it was a long way down and it would be easy to fall and get hurt.

Laura was moving more and more restlessly now on the small hill. Her eyes were huge; they hurried back and forth in her face like trapped and panicky squirrels in a cage too small for them. They moved from Michael to Mr. Rebeck's carved silence, to the raven's pirate-treasure eyes and sharp yellow beak, to the men in the grave, bending to tie their ropes around the coffin, and back to Michael. Always back to Michael. She sat as close to him as she could.

"They work so fast," she said. "Why are they in such a hurry? I can't stand watching them."

"Don't watch them, then," Michael said. "Watch me. What are you doing with your eyes away from me?"

"Michael, there must be something we can do. There must be something."

"No. There's no way, Laura. There's nothing but looking at each other and hoping that we remember each other's faces after we have forgotten our own."

The two men moved in the grave, and now and then the third man shouted their progress to the driver. Laura sat close to Michael and watched them. Whenever their heads and shoulders rose out of the grave, she knew that they must be standing on the coffin.

"We'll forget," she said bitterly. "As soon as you're gone, I'll forget you and die. And you'll forget me."

"What can I tell you? That my love for you is so great it will burn the black gates between us to ashes? That we'll meet again and know each other in that Great Ellis Island in the sky? That I'll come to thee by moonlight, though hell should bar the way? You know better than that, Laura. I love you, more, I think, than I know, but our kind of love isn't a sword. It's a light. Not a fire. A small light, just bright enough to read love letters by and keep the animals at a growling distance. In time it will go out. All lights go out. So do all fires, if it's any comfort. Love me, and look at me, and remember me, as I'll remember you. There's nothing more. Sit close and shut up."

The winch motor rumbled like a giant's belly, and the bright chain dipped leisurely into the grave. The shirtless man seized it in both hands with a kind of fierce affection, and he and the other man became very busy attaching it to the ropes that ran around the coffin. This took a few minutes, during which Michael and Laura looked at each other and not at the grave, and the winch idled, mumbling obsolete curses to itself.

Then the watcher between the grave and the green truck yelled something to the two men, and they came scratching out of the deep hole. The third man gave his hand to each of them and pulled them over the edge, one after the other. They did not stop to laugh or breathe deeply, but staggered a good ten feet from the grave before they finally sat down on the grass and waved to the driver in the cab of the truck. They were covered with sweat and streaked with the dark dirt of the grave.

The chain went taut and trembling. For a moment, nothing moved. There was only the noise of the winch; there was no other sound. Even the grasshoppers were silent.

Laura started to make a sound that might have turned out a whimper, but she broke it off so quickly that no more than half of it came out.

The raven crunched a silent grasshopper in his beak, and that was definitely a sound.

At that moment the hungry whine of the winch rose to a wintry howl of triumph. The whole truck shuddered under the sound. The chain rattled like a loose fiddle string, and the coffin began to rise slowly out of the grave, banging against the sides of the hole and sending soft showers of dirt sliding down into the grave. The men beside the truck bit their fingers and waited.

Laura made the "Ah" sound again, and Michael said, "Hush, Laura, hush, darling." The coffin rose clumsily, the front higher than the rear, and the whole thing canted over on one side. But it cleared the grave, and the winch howled louder than ever. A great clod of earth fell from the coffin and splashed into darkness at the bottom of the grave.

"Like pulling a tooth," Michael said. "It's exactly like pulling a tooth."

When the coffin was well above the grave, the driver

shut off the motor. The coffin swung high and black, and the sun glinted off its silver handles and small silver name plate. The chain creaked a little, and the ropes fretted against the corners of the coffin.

Michael rose to his feet with a strange grace and stood with his hands at his sides and his head tilted to see the hanging coffin. The motor started again, and the winch deposited the coffin by its side in the back of the truck. One of the men went over to unhitch the chain and shove the coffin farther back in the truck. And Michael nodded, and nodded again.

Then he turned back to Laura and said quietly, "I think I'd better go now."

He gave her no time to reply. Trying to avoid her eyes, he went over to Mr. Rebeck and said, "Good-by, Jonathan. I'll miss you very much. Take care of yourself and talk to Campos when you get lonesome. The living are wonderful company at times."

Mr. Rebeck had barely time to begin a puzzled "Good-by," when Laura burst between them and stood facing Michael, crying out, "No! It isn't time yet, you don't have to go! No, Michael!"

"I might as well, Laura. They're going. It'll be easier if I go when they do."

"But it isn't time," she said desperately. "Stay, Michael, please. They aren't ready to go."

Mr. Rebeck said hesitantly, "They have to fill in the grave. That will take a little time."

"Don't," Michael said to both of them. "Don't do that. I have to go. It's better if I go now."

"God damn you," Laura cried, and her voice was ugly with sorrow. "Will you for once stop being so brave? Will you please get your gallant chin out of the air, and lose your dignity, your goddam new-found dignity? Will you do me the honor, my dearest love, of breaking down just a little? Do that for me, Michael. I want to remember you the way I am, immature and uncivilized, without pride, and crying."

Michael stood close to her and said, "This isn't bravery or dignity. I was never brave or dignified, not once. This is cowardice again. This is the easy way out. I have no courage, and my sadness is not graceful. I can't say good-by, and I want to go before I have to say it."

"Stay with me," Laura said again. "As long as there's a minute left, stay with me. You don't have to go until they pass the gate. Stay with me until then."

"I can't, my Laura. Forgive me. I can't stay."

Deeply embarrassed, feeling like an eavesdropper even though they paid no attention to him, Mr. Rebeck stroked the raven's rough feathers and watched the men spilling the dirt back into the grave. Three of them worked at the same time, lifting the earth, tossing it, packing it down. They worked lazily, talking to one another, as if they had sweated away the taloned need and eagerness that had attended on the removal of the coffin. Nevertheless, even as he watched them, they finished filling up the hole in the ground. The surface dipped a little, because there wasn't quite enough earth to fill it up completely. The coffin had taken up a lot of space. One of the men was patting down the dirt with his shovel; the other two crouched to lift the headstone and put it in the back of the truck, next to the coffin. The driver stuck his head out of the window and watched the men work.

"I can't bear to sit and lose you and not be able to do anything about it," Michael said. "I haven't the courage. I'd wait with you if I dared, Laura, and say wise and warming things to you, and all the time I'd be thinking, *Five minutes, four minutes, up a hill, down a hill, through the willows, now the road curves, now the bleak gate stands open, what can I say to her, what can I say? There must be something I can tell her, something that makes our losing each other good and meaningful, something that will make some sense out of this sad, stupid thing.* And then I'd think *Two minutes, one minute, the gate is open,*

and I'd say, 'I love you, Laura,' over and over, until I was
gone."

"That's meaningful. What has more meaning than that?
Stay with me, Michael."

"I can't," Michael said. "I haven't changed. Dying and
loving haven't made me brave and gallant. I'm still Morgan,
dead Morgan. Let me go, let me be done with it."

The men threw their shovels into the truck and climbed
in themselves, three in the front and one in the back, as
they had come. The engine made the truck shiver and the
shovels clank against each other, and the man in the back
braced his feet against the coffin. Then the truck drove
away, and the last they saw of it as it rounded the curve
was the lean red winch with the brown spots where the
paint had flaked off, and the lone man sitting in the back.

"I'm going now," Michael said.

"I love you," Laura said hopelessly. "I'd love you if you
were afraid of everything in the world."

"I am. Except of being alone. I love you, Laura."

Again he said good-by to Mr. Rebeck, and then he turned
and walked down the hill toward the patch of dark earth
with the torn ivy strewn all around it. He was a lightly
sketched figure, with no color of his own, but he was the
color of the grass and the loose earth of the grave, and the
color of the pebbles on the road. The sun shone through
him, and he was that color too. He did not turn, and he
did not look back. But he stopped twice and stood still
with his shoulders hunched before he walked on.

"He wants to turn back," Laura said. "If I called him
again, he would come back."

"Call him, then," Mr. Rebeck said with his head down.

"No. Because he might not turn, after all, and I don't
think I could stand that."

She moved up and down, not a ribbon any more but a
veil; and not beautiful any more, if she ever had been. She
watched Michael pass by the empty grave, over which the
grass would grow soon, and, watching, said, "Oh, God,

God, what will I do?" Mr. Rebeck remembered the same voice singing to him long ago, before somebody's sun rose, and he knew that this too was singing. The raven was silent, not looking at anything in particular.

And then suddenly Laura stood still, so still that Mr. Rebeck was sure that she had seen Michael vanish in front of her eyes; and, even as he was trying to say something to lessen her grief, she began to turn. Before she faced him, he knew what she was going to ask him to do, and the fear sprang up in him from where it had been sleeping and capered with savage joy.

She came to him and knelt by him, and she said, "If you moved me. If you dug up my coffin and buried me in Mount Merrill, I could be with Michael. We could be together."

"Laura," he said. "Laura, my dear, you know that if it were at all possible—"

"It is possible." Her voice was trembling as if she were about to laugh with delight. "You can do it at night, so that no one will see you. And if you leave my headstone the way it is, nobody will know I'm not buried there. You can do it. I know you can."

He ran his suddenly wet hand along his jaw, thinking absurdly, I must shave, I look terrible with a stubble. Like a tramp.

"I'm not strong enough. I haven't even got a shovel. And if I had, I wouldn't be strong enough to lift the coffin. You saw how they did it. It takes four men. And you have to have a truck. What would I do for a truck?"

"Get Campos," Laura said eagerly. "Campos is as good as four men, and he's got a truck. He'll help you. Please. I know you can do it. Help me now."

Under his hand the raven cackled in soft amusement and muttered, "Ho-*ho*. Screwed like a light bulb. So long, friend."

"No," he said. How hot it was. "Don't ask me, Laura. I'd have to leave the cemetery."

Laura misunderstood at first. She blurted, "You'll be with Campos. He can drive you out and back, and no one will know."

"It isn't that," he said, and then Laura did understand.

"I've never left the cemetery. Never in nineteen years. I just never have."

"It would only be this once," Laura said, but the hope was gone from her voice. "You could come right back."

"I can't," Mr. Rebeck answered. He thought, It has happened, it has happened as I knew it would, and I am no more able to cope with it than I was that long time ago, when I was so anxious to be kind.

It shocked him to see Laura on her knees to him. His head jerked back and forth, as if he were being slapped. He extended a hand to her, knowing that it was a wasted gesture, but wanting her to get up. He could not bear to see her kneel.

"Laura," he said, having always loved her name. "Please get up, Laura. I'd help you if I could, if I possibly could. But I can't pass the gate. I've tried. Laura, listen to me"— for her dark head was still bowed. "I have tried. I cannot pass the gate. No more than you can. I'm as helpless as you are. There is nothing I can do."

She said not a word, and he thought he might die right there, with her kneeling before him. He thought it would be a very good time for it.

"I can't help you," he said. "A man could help. But I'm like Michael, and like you. Nothing that hurts a man can hurt me, but there is nothing a man does that I can do. I can't walk through the gate and take you to Michael, Laura. It's like walking into the wind. You take the same step again and again, and little by little the wind blows you away from the place you wanted to go. Don't ask me any more, Laura."

He did not see her rise from her knees, because his face was in his hands. His fingers gripped and rubbed at his skin as though he were trying to find out whose face he had put on by mistake. The raven scratched for insects.

"It isn't working," Laura said very softly. "The animals outside are rapidly becoming the animals inside. I'm sorry, Jonathan."

There was no hatred in her eyes when he looked at her. He would have welcomed hatred. There was nothing in her eyes, really, except himself and, perhaps, a little pity.

"I'm sorry," she said again, and then she turned from him and ran down the hillside, past the hollow of the empty grave, and out onto the pebbled road. She moved like a ribbon, like a veil, like a feather, like a kite, like whatever gets caught by the wind and blown far away from the place where it belongs, and is lost, and then in time whistled back to its rightful place again.

The sun was so bright that Mr. Rebeck could barely see her. Now he saw blackness between the trees and knew it for her hair, now a moment of gray that was her dress. Most of the time he could not see her at all, but he heard her voice calling, "Michael! Michael, wait for me! Michael! Oh, Michael, wait!"

And just before she reached the bend in the road and he lost sight of her altogether, he heard her say, "Michael," again, and he knew somehow that Michael had waited.

He felt a little better, and much sadder.

"He wanted to turn back," he explained to the raven, "but he was afraid to, so he walked slowly and hoped that she would follow him. Now they will walk to the gate together, or at least as far as they can. I think that's better than his going alone."

"Ducky," said the raven. "Jesus, I don't like the taste of crickets. I don't know why I eat them. They're supposed to be good for you."

Mr. Rebeck tried to stroke the bird again, but the raven sidled away from him.

"I was right," he said. "Wasn't I? I couldn't possibly have helped her. You know I couldn't."

"I know nothing," the raven said. "Don't come sniffling around me, friend. I don't make decisions. I'm a bird."

"That's right," Mr. Rebeck said. He got slowly to his feet and stretched a little, because he was cramped from sitting in one place so long.

13

"What shall I do?" he asked, still hoping that the raven would answer him. "What shall I do? What shall I do?" He stood in the grass with his hands in his pockets and his legs close together, as if it were windy, and he said, "What shall I do?" without remembering that Laura had said it. His legs ached, and his back felt stiff when he moved.

He ought to walk down to the gate, he knew, if he were ever to believe again in his fiction of being useful to the dead. Laura would be there, and in need of someone. It was clearly his place to go to her and be consoling, affectionate, and gently wise. He had seen more of life than she, and known more of death; so, naturally, the word that would make her wise too must come from him. It was fitting. Anyway, there was no one else now.

But he did not want to go alone. He asked the raven to come with him, even part of the way, but the bird said no, and flew away. Mr. Rebeck watched him as long as he could, because he thought the raven flew beautifully. He felt listless and lonely when the raven was gone. A little while ago he had been sitting with three friends; now there was only himself on the hillside, and the transition was too sudden for him. He wondered if very old men felt that way. Perhaps children did, children who had fallen asleep in a room full of light, and pleasant smells, and the sounds of silver and glass, and wakened much later, alone in a strange bed in the middle of the night, in a room that might have been friendly and familiar once, but was no more.

Even without the raven along for company, he would go and find Laura. Someone should be with her now. He took a few slow steps down the hill and then stopped, bracing his legs against the slope. Below him, the grave was a brown bald spot on the earth. He wondered how long it would be before the grass covered it again.

"She will be by the gate," he said, "and there will be a few marks on the ground where the truck has passed." It was easy enough to imagine her, a frantic whisper in front of the mockingly open gate, crying out to the black iron to let her through. He did not like to think about it. It made him feel as if he had no legs.

"I cannot help her." He said it very loudly, looking around him. As far as he could see, there was no one. He waited for a moment, as if he were hoping that someone would challenge him; then he turned and walked back up the small hill to the scrawny dirt road that ran from it. Once he looked back and saw the deep scars in the earth that the heavy truck had made. They would fill with water when it rained again, and in time, weeds would grow out of them.

But he could not slam his mind against Laura. The moment he relaxed, the moment he ran out of things to think about the goodness of the day, she returned and stood like a torch in the middle of his mind. He drove her away by admiring the beauty of some flowers, but she returned again, more beautiful, with her black hair and gray dress and dead-of-winter eyes, saying, "It's not working. I'm sorry, Jonathan."

"There was nothing I could do," he said to her. "I was

the wrong man to ask for help. Would you rather I had promised to help you, and then disappointed you? At least I was man enough to face my own weakness. It is not everyone who is honest enough to do that."

Laura said nothing. Instead she retreated quietly to the back of his mind, where she remained, glimmering in shadow. He told her again that she was wasting her time, and hurting him into the bargain, but she did not answer.

Even the trains were silent. There was an elevated train running past one side of the cemetery, and a subway on the other side, so that he thought of the trains as his fences against the city. He liked the noises they made. At night, in the slippery moments before he fell asleep, their deep clattering and cat-shrieks made him feel less alone. He knew their schedules by heart, and he knew that it had been too long a time since he had heard a train go by.

Laura has stopped the trains, he thought, or at least she had made them run without noise, so that I might be free to concentrate on feeling guilty. He knew, of course, that this was not true. Undoubtedly the trains were running as they always had. He was simply not hearing them.

The road widened and became pavement, and he walked on, saying to himself, I can understand her point of view very easily. She cannot imagine a living man not being able to walk in and out of the cemetery as he chooses. She has seen men do it every day. They are undoubtedly doing it now, as she kneels by the gate. In and out they walk, so confident of themselves that they do not break their strides in the least as they pass through the gate. Even Campos— and Campos is very much like me. She does not see why it should be such a hard thing for me to do. Well, neither do I, really, except that this place is not merely the place where I live, the place where I sleep. It is my skin, and a man only walks out of the skin of his body with a great deal of difficulty, and much pain afterward. I am afraid of pain, and pain is cold and aging and being useless. I should have made Laura understand that.

He was coming to a more well-to-do section of the cemetery. Then, farther on, the mausoleums began to thin out. The last one was an old favorite, a large cylindrical building, based on three concentric marble circles which formed steps leading up to a small glass door with a cross on top. The whole thing reminded Mr. Rebeck of the head and shoulders of a knight. The cupola would be the helmet, he thought, the door the mouth-opening, and the three steps the whatever-it-was that protected the throat. A bas-relief band ran all around the mausoleum, exactly where the knight's forehead would be. It was carved deeply with a pattern of crossed swords tangled in vine leaves. That might be the knight's lucky piece, if they had such things, or a favor from a rich lady. Perhaps the knight had merely stood still for a moment, or fallen asleep, and the world had risen around him, like a pile of dead leaves. It could have happened. It was one of the things about the world that frightened him. You closed your eyes for a little while, and when you opened them again you were up to your shoulders in earth and dead leaves. You had to be awake all the time, and moving.

"The animals outside are rapidly becoming the animals inside," Laura said in his mind.

"No, they aren't," he answered irritably. "Fear has stopped at the gate of this place. If I left, it would be on me again, but it cannot follow me here. I am safe here, and nothing can harm me."

"If there is nothing you fear," Laura said from a great distance, "then you are not a man."

"Did I ever claim to be?" he demanded, feeling that he had scored an important point against her. "Manhood is not something you put on and take off and put on again. It is not a reward for courage. There is no prize of manhood waiting for me if I am brave enough to leave the cemetery. I am neither man nor ghost. For your sake I wish I were the one, for my sake I wish I were the other. As it is, I can help neither of us. Try not to blame me. It is not altogether my fault."

A patrol car honked behind him, and he stepped quickly aside to let it pass. They still made him nervous, and he still tried to turn his face away from the driver, but he no longer thought to run and hide when he saw one of the black cars with the oak-leaf insignia on the sides. He walked along the road, occasionally reaching out a hand to stroke the green, sharp fur of the small pine trees that grew in this area. Only a few of them had been there when he had first come to live in the cemetery.

"Anyway," he said, although the Laura in his mind had said nothing, "it isn't only the idea of leaving the cemetery. Suppose I were not able to come back? Suppose I could never live here again?"

Wanting to be fair, he added, "Of course, I don't see why I couldn't. If I were strong enough to pass the gate once, I ought to be able to do it a second time. But suppose, for the sake of argument, that I could never return. What would I do then? How could I live?"

He found himself pleading with the quiet woman whom he could not see. "I couldn't live out there, Laura. It's been too long a time, too long a time of sleeping on marble and playing chess with ghosts. How can I talk to people, I who have told jokes to the dead, and sung songs with them? How can I ever get used to eating in restaurants, having been fed by a raven? What will I do with myself? How will I earn money? Where will I live? I have no place to go if I cannot come back here. Who will teach me to sleep in a bed again, and to cross streets? In God's name, Laura, how can I live in the world without dying?"

Laura did not answer. He passed the roofless ring of pillars that Michael had seen when he first walked through the cemetery looking for someone to talk to. A revolving sprinkler in the center darkened the bases of the white columns as it watered the grass they surrounded. He stood between the pillars for a few minutes, letting the bright water splash against his hands and wrists.

"I am too old," he tried to explain to her. "I am older than I thought. Not my body. My body doesn't care what I do. But my mind is old and does not accept change easily, and challenge sends it scurrying for cover. You and Michael are very dear to me. You know that." He said that part quite loudly. "But you must believe me when I tell you that there is no way I can help you without certainly hurting myself. And I am very much afraid of hurting myself. At least I am being honest with you."

When Laura still did not answer, but only shone dimly in the arched corridors of his mind, like a dagger at the bottom of a well, he became angry, feeling that his honesty had been rejected. Then he thought of Michael's suicide and Laura's unsureness of the reasons for her own death, and, because he thought he was put-upon and knew he was suffering, he said a cruel thing.

"It isn't as if I were the only one who did not fit into the world. Think of yourselves before you send me on my errand of mercy. Of the three of us, who hid in the earth like frightened foxes, and who lived? You may have looked more at ease in the world than I, and been more able to keep up the pretense of living with your neighbors, but who lived, who lived?"

Even as he was saying the words he hated and disowned them, but he said it all, straight through until he was sure he was finished, and then he shivered and felt wretched. There was a thin, liquid bitterness in the back of his throat.

"All right, I'm sorry," he said to Laura. She stood so quietly in his mind. "You know I'm sorry. Either forgive me and be at least a little tolerant, or else hate me and leave me alone. Right now, I don't much care which."

For a while he thought that Laura had left him, for he could find no trace of her inside his head. He sighed, telling himself that the inevitable is a great blessing to a man weary of making choices. In time he would undoubtedly forgive himself, absorbing his loss the way a fish's wounded mouth gradually absorbs a broken fishhook. Given a little time, he would not only forget Laura, he would come to believe that she had never been real, that he himself had made her up out of a head full of unicorns and sad virgins. And perhaps he had.

It might be, he thought, that Michael and Laura and every other ghost with whom he had talked and passed time had never existed except as he was lonesome and wanted company. Perhaps the dead were dead and there were no ghosts except his own memories of lost chances, friends never spoken to, letters never written, never answered, women never accosted on the street or smiled at in subways. Or perhaps, to be blunt about it, he might well be a good deal madder than he thought. He had always considered himself a little mad.

But they had needed him a little, he thought, and perhaps that meant that they were real. Dreams never needed you to remind them that they existed—it was always the other way around. Perhaps they were real after all, Michael and Laura and all the others; for they had come to him, calling him by his name, asking him for the small kindnesses he had never been able to give away before. And he had given them all away, eagerly, almost frantically, and now there were none left. He could feel the difference in himself, as though he were beginning to cave in. There had never been very much to give, really, and now there was nothing, nothing except the little that he had always planned to save for himself so that he might be warm when he was old.

"I will not do it," he said, knowing that Laura was listening, even though he could not see her. "Not even for you. I will not help you because it is too much effort for too little return. I do not love you"—this to Michael as well, and whoever else might be listening to him—"and I am sorry if I led you to believe that I loved you. The fault was mine. I only love myself, and that affair is dying of time and knowledge, as all love dies. Soon it will be over, and I shall have some sort of peace, with nobody asking me to do things for them."

He thought of Mrs. Klapper and wondered if she would come today. If she did, he would tell her the same thing and get it over with. He should never have accepted anything from her—concern, companionship, or the story about Linda. If she came, he would give her back the raincoat and tell her to stop bothering him. He hoped she would listen.

Stopping to get his bearings, he discovered that he was approaching the Wilder mausoleum, but from a different direction from his usual one. The road was beginning to rise before it sloped down into the shallow valley in which his mausoleum was located. At the top of the hill, scrolled and white, white as soap, there stood up the castle whose foundation was the chest and belly of Morris Klapper. The building seemed bigger every time Mr. Rebeck saw it. It was the only thing he had ever seen that did.

I will sit on the steps for a while, he decided, because I am tired. I will open my shirt and roll up my sleeves and get some sun. When the sun goes down I will go down the hill to my own place and wait until the raven comes to find me.

When he reached the steps of the Klapper mausoleum he stood still, looking up at the white roof. He had read or heard somewhere that the earliest gravestones were just that—stones piled thickly on top of a hasty grave to keep the wolves from digging up the body. If that were the case, he thought, then Morris Klapper was quite safe. The animals inside—whatever Laura meant by that—could not touch him. God himself would break a few fingernails getting at Morris Klapper.

He sat down on the steps, which were not nearly so comfortable as the ones he was used to, and raised his face to the sun. With his eyes closed, he felt the warmth soaking into his skin. He liked sitting in the sun. It made him feel like a father, lying on a park bench with a newspaper over his belly, almost asleep, watching his child play in the dirt. But the daydream seemed a little ragged around the edges today. He could not feel at ease on the wooden bench, no matter how often he shifted his position, and the boy vanished whenever he took his eyes off him.

"Very well," he said aloud. "I have a bit of a guilty conscience. This is perfectly natural, and nothing to be ashamed of. It will pass. This too shall pass away and become a nought."

Behind him a voice said, "I wish I'd said that."

Mr. Rebeck turned quickly and saw nothing. There was nothing at all between him and the door of the mausoleum.

"Hello," he said nervously. "Is somebody there?"

"What?" said the voice.

"Is anyone there?" Mr. Rebeck asked again, feeling a little silly about it now.

"Oh," said the voice. "I'm here. For quite a while."

The voice was faint, but clear and very dry. It made Mr. Rebeck think of thin shoes walking in sand.

"Are you Morris Klapper?" he asked.

"I don't know," the voice answered slowly. "I hadn't thought—" Then, with sureness, "Yes. Yes, I must be. I am Morris Klapper."

"My name is Jonathan Rebeck." He wished that he could see Morris Klapper, to find out if he really did look like him.

"What are you doing here? I don't know you, do I?"

"No," Mr. Rebeck said. "I live here."

"Here? In the cemetery?"

Mr. Rebeck nodded. The voice said nothing, but he was sure that he sensed disapproval.

"You have a beautiful house," he said, unconsciously adopting Mrs. Klapper's term. "I was just admiring it."

"What, this place?" He thought he heard a dusty sigh. "You don't know. All I wanted was a nice small stone, with my name on it and perhaps a few words of recommendation. Look what I got. A synagogue. A courthouse."

"Well, your wife wanted you to have an expensive tomb," Mr. Rebeck said.

"Oh yes," Morris Klapper said. "The place has 'Gertrude Klapper' scrawled all over it. It's a monument to her, not me."

"She didn't mean it that way," Mr. Rebeck said angrily. "You're a fool if you think that. She loves you."

"Love is not an excuse for bad taste."

Mr. Rebeck felt that he was being peered at closely, and it made him tense. He had never felt ill at ease with the dead until now, when he spoke with Morris Klapper and could not see him.

"Why are you so interested?" the voice asked. "You don't know my wife."

"I met her when she came to see you. She comes here a lot."

"Ah," Morris Klapper said. "Yes, of course. You did say you lived here. I forgot."

"I've lived here for a long time. Almost twenty years."

"How interesting," Morris Klapper said without interest. "May I ask why?"

"Because I didn't fit into the world, and because everyone else did." He was tired of talking about it. Talk rusted everything in time.

"I see," Morris Klapper said. "So, not belonging in one world, you had no choice but to adopt the other. By default, you might say."

The impersonal scholar-voice was beginning to irritate Mr. Rebeck. "No," he said sharply. "Maybe it was that way at first, but then I found out that this was my place, and that there was room for me here among my own people. I like this world. I feel right here. Even if I could go back to the country I came from, knowing that there would be a place for me, I would not go."

"Bravo," Morris Klapper said. "A speech to move the short-circuited hearts of the dead. Wrong, but even more beautiful because it is wrong. I am glad that I am not too long dead to appreciate a little misdirected beauty. This is not a world. There is only one world, and this is its junk-yard. The dead did not make this junkyard, nor have they any interest in turning it into a world. There is nothing here with which to make a world."

"There is love," Mr. Rebeck objected. "I have seen it myself. There is humor, and contention, and friendship. All these I have seen."

"They are here only because you brought them with you. Do you think you have left the world, do you think one escapes that easily? You carry the world with you, wherever you go, like a turtle. You yourself are soft, naked, shapeless tissue, but you carry the hard shell of the world to protect your back and belly. All men carry the world on their backs, wherever they go."

"I don't want the world on my back," Mr. Rebeck said. "I never asked for it. Can I run out from under it? Is there a way out?"

"Death. Not the appearance of death, nor sleeping in the same bed with death. Nothing but the genuine article."

Mr. Rebeck sat on the steps and stared at the barred iron door. There was an inscription above the door, but he could not read it from that distance. My sight is not so good any more, he thought, and then, God, what a great hollow tooth this building is.

Laying his words down carefully, he said, "Sometimes I have thought that I might be a ghost myself. Could that be? Could I have lived here and died and not known it? I think about it a lot."

Again he felt Morris Klapper's dead eyes on him, but the ghost did not speak. Mr. Rebeck bit at a ragged fingernail. It gritted against his teeth and tasted bitter. Far away a car horn yapped. He hoped it would not come this way.

"We are all ghosts," Morris Klapper said at last. "We are conceived in a moment of death and born out of ghost wombs, and we play in the streets with other little ghosts, chanting ghost-rhymes and scratching to become real. We are told that life is full of goals and that, although it is sadly necessary to fight, you can at least choose your war. But we learn that for ghosts there can only be one battle: to become real. A few of us make it, thus encouraging other ghosts to believe that it can be done."

"What is it like?" Mr. Rebeck asked. "To be real, I mean."

Morris Klapper's laugh was like the faint sound of an hourglass being turned over. "Good God, I don't know. I never made it."

"Oh," Mr. Rebeck said. Then he said, "Your wife loved you. Isn't that one way of becoming real?"

"Will you get love off your mind?" Morris Klapper demanded. "Love guarantees nothing. Anyway, Gertrude never loved me. She loved the man she wanted me to be. It was like having a stranger in the house. We were quite happy together, all three of us, but it was not the sort of love that makes a ghost real. I think the only way to become real is to be real to yourself and to someone else. Love has nothing to do with it."

For no particular reason, Mr. Rebeck thought of Mrs. Klapper's crescent hat roosting, thin and foolish, in her hair.

"I have two friends," he said. "They want me to leave the cemetery. Not for my own sake, but because they want me to do them a favor. It isn't a fair thing to ask."

"Nothing is free," Morris Klapper answered. "If you have friends, you have to pay for them sooner or later, like anything else. Nor will the cemetery protect you from this kind of debt. One friend, and the iron around this junkyard is a ring of butter; one debt between friends, and the things you love and fear walk in through the gate, whistling. It is a great mistake to have friends if you like living in cemeteries. You should never have done it, Mr.— what did you say your name was? I am old."

"Rebeck," Mr. Rebeck said. "Do you think I ought to go back, then? Do you think I ought to leave the cemetery?"

"I don't care. It doesn't matter a damn to me. I'm dead,

and what you do or do not do does not interest me. You could catch fire as we talk here, and burn to the ground like a hayrick, and I wouldn't care. Except that I haven't seen fire in a very long while, and I don't remember what it looks like."

He was silent. Mr. Rebeck looked at the iron door, but he felt that the ghost was very close to him. When Morris Klapper spoke again, however, his voice was fainter, and Mr. Rebeck had to strain to hear him.

"But I tell you that you are a living man and that you have deceived yourself. For a man there is no choice between worlds. There never was."

Then Mr. Rebeck rose to his feet and cried out, "I am afraid! It is not starving I fear, or talking to people, or even being alone. But I cannot bear to be useless and ineffectual. There must be some meaning to me, if not to my life; there must surely be some purpose that has my name written on it. If this is not so, if I am deceiving myself about this too, then why should I want to become real? What reason have I to live anywhere?"

"Oh, so now you want reasons," Morris Klapper said. Again Mr. Rebeck heard the distant laugh in the air. "I have no reasons for you. Die, if you choose. Die, and you and I will sit together and talk about friendship."

Mr. Rebeck stood on the steps and thought desperately about Mrs. Klapper's hat. His mind was filled with blue-black feathers held together by hope and a shiny-headed pin. Laura was there too, somewhere, waiting. He felt sudden pain in both his thighs, and looked down to see that his hands were clutching him like frightened children. His thin fingers arched and clung, and the muscles between his thumbs and forefingers tightened into little ridges and hollows. He could not make them let go, for he knew that there would be more pain when they did.

"What is it like to be dead?" he asked. He had never asked that question before.

Morris Klapper's answer followed as closely as blood follows a knife. "Like nothing at all. It is like nothing at all."

For the moment more that he stood on the steps, shaking a bit, hands chewing into his thighs, he thought he saw Morris Klapper. It was only a fragment of an image he saw; gray, and vague as someone else's remembered sorrow, and he might easily have imagined it. But it seemed to him that he saw Morris Klapper, and it seemed that Morris Klapper did look something like him, as one man looks like another.

Then, behind him, he heard Mrs. Klapper's strident, city-colored yell. "Hey, Rebeck!"

He stood without turning, and she called again, "Rebeck! Hoo, *Rebeck!*" There was anxiety in her voice, and he knew that she thought she might have made a mistake and called a greeting to a man who looked very much like him but was actually somebody quite different. His hands fell away from himself, and he felt the quick pain as the blood rushed back to his thighs.

She called again, and this time Mr. Rebeck turned and walked down the road to meet her. He went partly because her voice was high and clear and made him think at once of the cry of a street peddler, the yelp of an outraged policeman, an auto horn, and the triumphant bugle of the cavalry riding to the rescue. But mostly he went to meet her because she was so glad to see that it was really he she had been calling that her voice skidded off the scale and came out as a kind of joyous squeak.

Much later, a long time later, when he was thinking once again of the afternoon he decided to leave the cemetery, he concluded that it was the squeaky "Hey, Rebeck," that did it.

14

Oh, that was a moment, when Campos stood up straight, black over the black grave, with the coffin on his shoulders. It cast a shadow in the truck headlights, and Mr. Rebeck could not see Campos's face at all. But he saw the big hands gripping, the hands whose backs were badlands of tight muscles and thick blue veins, with the knuckles like skulls under the moon; and the naked back, where the muscles bunched like fists; and the ribs, so tight against the skin that they made Campos look tiger-striped; and, most of all, the thick legs, spread wide apart to support the man and his long burden. Campos himself cast no shadow, for the earth was very dark.

In that moment without morning, Mr. Rebeck found himself wondering, Is the world holding up Campos now, giving him a place to stand, or is it really Campos who weighs down the world and keeps it from blowing away?

The coffin was heavy up front, and it teetered forward a little, but Campos bent quickly and shifted his hands, and it was all right. Then Campos began to walk to the truck. He took slow, even steps, carrying the coffin high on his shoulder. His legs and back were straight, but his shoulders were perceptibly bowed, and his neck was twisted so that his mouth was close to the coffin, as if he were speaking love to the woman whose body he carried so tenderly. When he reached the truck, he turned and bent his knees until the coffin rested on the lowered tailgates. Then he fell away from it, touching his hand to the ground for support, and straightened up again.

"Okay," he said to the two people who sat near the truck and watched him. With a casual hand he pushed the coffin farther into the back of the truck and reached for his shirt, which hung on the tailgate where he had left it.

Mr. Rebeck heard Mrs. Klapper sigh with exaggerated relief beside him. Before he could say anything, he said to Campos, "Are we going now?"

Campos nodded. He held his shirt without putting it on. He was breathing deeply, cautiously touching a raw spot on his neck where the coffin had rubbed away the skin.

"Okay," he said again. He walked to the front of the truck and stood by the door. In the dim light there his body gleamed gold with sweat, and brown with sweat, and black. He put on his shirt, leaving it unbuttoned.

"Shouldn't we fill in the grave before we go?" Mr. Rebeck asked.

Campos looked over at the empty grave with the piles of dirt scattered around it and shrugged. "Fill it in when I get back. Come on."

Mr. Rebeck rose from the stone he sat on and offered a hand to Mrs. Klapper. Grasping it, she pulled herself to her feet, brushing her dress with her free hand. She was not wearing the crescent hat, after all.

"Well," she said. "So now everything's all right? Nobody's left anything behind?"

"Everything's fine," Mr. Rebeck said. They started walking to the truck. Campos had started the engine.

"Now what?" Mrs. Klapper asked.

"Now we have to take the coffin to Mount Merrill," Mr. Rebeck said. "It's not far."

Mrs. Klapper blinked at him. "And you bury it all over again? *Vey,* what people. Like a dog with a bone."

"It's a favor for a friend. I told you about it."

"I know you told me. It's a favor for a friend. All right, who can refuse a friend? So fine, we sit here all night and watch your friend dig up a grave, and now we got to go with him so we can watch him bury it again. Rebeck, you got some friends I wouldn't even want for enemies."

"I couldn't refuse him," Mr. Rebeck said lamely. "He's a very good friend."

"All right, to you he's a very good friend. Me, I don't like him. He scares me."

The last few words were whispered because they had reached the cab of the truck. Mr. Rebeck pulled the door open and stepped back to let Mrs. Klapper get in first. She gave him a sour look, wagging her head slightly, and he realized that she was a little afraid of sitting next to Campos. However, there was nothing for it; Campos was looking at them, waiting impatiently for them to get in, and they would have enough trouble fitting three people into the cab without worrying about the order. So Mrs. Klapper got in and gingerly seated herself next to Campos. Mr. Rebeck climbed in after her. There was barely room enough for him, even when Mrs. Klapper moved closer against Campos's hard, sweating body. But he sat down next to her and closed the door carefully.

The engine hiccuped fiercely, and the truck jolted off. Mr. Rebeck leaned his elbow on the window and felt the door handle pressing against his leg. It was three in the morning by Mrs. Klapper's tiny wrist watch, and very dark. Mr. Rebeck found it hard to breathe, and even the beating of his heart was painful. He turned his head away from Mrs. Klapper, not wanting her to see how frightened he was.

When he had told Mr. Klapper that he had decided to

leave the cemetery, she had literally whooped with delight. After that, she sat down on a rock and began to cry. She stopped abruptly when he told her that he would have to wait until night to leave. And when he told her about Campos and the coffin she got to her feet, holding her purse in both hands, and said that he was a crazy grave-robber, and that it would undoubtedly be better if he stayed in the cemetery where the psychiatrists couldn't get at him. He had gone mad from being alone, just as she had warned him.

But she stayed, snapping her fingers for an explanation she could accept with dignity, whether she believed it or not. The one he finally chose, about doing a last favor for Campos, was not as solid as she would have preferred, but it would do. She accepted it, saying that friendship was a fine thing, and adding that she would wait with him, because he would certainly get lost if he went into the city alone at night.

There was still Campos to be approached, but he would not come on duty until midnight. So they strayed around the cemetery, trying hard to look like an average middle-aged couple, and secretly believing that anyone could look at them and tell that they were very unusual people who were about to do a very unusual thing. From five o'clock on they stayed out of Walters' way as he drove around the cemetery looking for stragglers. Mr. Rebeck was afraid that Mrs. Klapper would become bored very quickly, but he realized after a while that she was having a wonderful time playing cops-and-robbers because she knew that it was the last time they would ever do anything like this. It was then that his heartbeats began to hurt, even though the time of leaving was hours away.

Together they sat on the mausoleum steps as the sun went down and ate the little food that he had left over from the previous day. They were oddly shy with each other because they had never eaten together before, but they smiled at each other often and sometimes talked with their mouths full. When the meal was over he brought her a glass of water from the faucet behind the building.

Then he excused himself for a moment and went into the mausoleum, closing the door behind him. The room was dark and stuffy with the sun down, but he had long since ceased to need his eyes here. He knew where everything was: his clothes more or less in one corner; his few books in another, covered with paper bags and waxed paper; his blankets and cushions and raincoat in a third. The raincoat was folded carefully; it was too new to lie crumpled. A tennis ball lay on top of the blankets. The raven had found it in the cemetery, years ago, and had brought it to him. He never used it for anything, but he always kept it where he could see it, even though it had turned greenish-black with age.

It was a very narrow room, he realized, although it had always seemed wide enough for his needs. His mind must look like that to an outsider: many old things cluttered in a narrow space; neat, but without any real order. But, like the room, his mind had always suited him, and he knew that both would continue to do so if he stayed, because there was nothing to compare them with except the barer minds and narrower houses of the dead.

"I must take some things with me," he said aloud. "How can I go to the city again with nothing of my own?" He stooped and picked up an armful of clothes, thinking vaguely that he might sort them out and take the best ones with him. But he had picked up much too many to sort properly, and he held them too close to his chest.

"I must certainly have something of my own," he said hoarsely, and then the door creaked hesitantly and the room brightened a little. Mrs. Klapper stood in the doorway.

"I heard you talking," she said. She saw him standing with his arms full of clothes, and came farther into the room. "Rebeck, what is this? You expecting a moving van?"

"I'm just taking some of my things with me," he said,

knowing how ridiculous he must look to her. "I didn't want to leave the place all littered up."

"What's the matter, you can't leave your stuff here one more day? Who's going to steal it? Look, don't load yourself down now, you won't be able to help your friend. We'll come back first thing tomorrow with a couple of big shopping bags and get everything in."

"No," he said quickly. "No. I have to take it now. I won't be coming back."

"All right, so I'll come by myself and get it. Rebeck, don't worry about it, it'll be fine." Gently she took the bundle of clothes from his unresisting arms and held them herself. She smiled at him, and he managed to smile back.

"Rebeck," she said, "you know, if you changed your mind all of a sudden, if you don't want to go, it's all right. You can tell me. It doesn't matter."

With those words she had locked him outside the gate. Until then, he might have stayed.

"Leave them, then," he said, and walked out of the door of the mausoleum for the last time. She followed him a moment later. They held hands as they walked and did not say anything.

Midnight and Campos came together. It was as if he had ridden the midnight to work the way other people took buses, and tied it outside the black gate to wait for him until he was ready to go home. Mrs. Klapper almost ran the first time she saw the big man, and Campos seemed equally wary of her. She stayed outside the office while he and Mr. Rebeck talked together. The radio was playing all the time.

And inside, shouting sometimes to be heard over the radio, Mr. Rebeck pleaded for Laura and Michael and, because of them, for himself. He never remembered anything he had said to Campos that midnight, as a man has no memory of the words he speaks in his sleep and thinks them the words of a mad stranger when they are repeated to him.

Asking a favor of Campos, Mr. Rebeck thought, was like praying to a jade god with blind onyx eyes. Campos sprawled in his chair with his eyes almost closed and his dark face without expression. Mr. Rebeck left long pauses in his proposition, like blanks in a questionnaire, but Campos never said anything, and he had to go on. He must have talked for fifteen or twenty minutes, with the radio going and Campos hulking in his chair like a blind god.

When he finished speaking, Campos did not move. He stared at Mr. Rebeck with his eyes closing and closing until the last flicker of black had disappeared. Quite still, quite still, Campos; as calm as a window face to face with tragedy.

Then, still blind, he reached out a big hand and turned the radio off.

In the silence Mr. Rebeck heard the breaths of two men, himself and Campos.

Campos opened his eyes and got up. He walked out of the office, leaving the light on. Mr. Rebeck followed him. Mrs. Klapper went with Mr. Rebeck. They had to hurry to keep up with Campos.

Now, squeezed between Mrs. Klapper and the door, with the window open and the hot wind of their passage blowing on his face, Mr. Rebeck looked at his hands. There were new scabs of dried blood on his knuckles, and a scrape on the back of his right hand still bled sluggishly. He had tried to help Campos dig at first, until he scraped his hand and the big man turned on him and told him to go somewhere and sit down. He was rather proud of his bleeding hand as he looked at it. He hoped that Laura could see it.

Mrs. Klapper craned her neck to see what he was looking at. "You put some Mercurochrome on that, first thing," she said. She touched his hand lightly and leaned back.

This thing we have done is illegal, he thought. I ought to tell Campos. Maybe he doesn't know. It is only fair to tell Campos. We will be at the gate very soon.

"Campos," he said. "If the police find out what we have done, they may arrest us."

"Rebeck, don't talk like that," Mrs. Klapper said worriedly. "The devil can hear you."

Campos did not even turn his head. "They won't find out."

"If they do," Mr. Rebeck pressed, "it will certainly cost you your job. I just wanted to tell you."

"Work somewhere else. Street's full of jobs."

"Rebeck, *sha!*" Mrs. Klapper said. "What kind of talk is this, policemen and losing jobs? Don't worry so much."

"I just wanted to tell Campos," he said to her. He leaned on the window and watched the tombstones go by like sailing ships.

The truck swung wide around a curve, jouncing as one back wheel slipped into a water-filled rut and out again. Mr. Rebeck knew the road well. There were long ridges of earth and dry grass on each side, and few graves. There would be one more curve before the gate.

If he turned around, he knew, he would be able to see Laura. He was sure of it. She would be sitting on her own coffin, looking forward as he was looking back to find her, and she would not be gray in that moment, but the color of morning. Her dress would be the color of morning, too, and of Queen Anne's lace. Her eyes would be as bright as the eyes of a living woman, and her black hair would fall down to her shoulders. It would be nice to turn and see her, to raise his hand to such beauty.

But if he turned she would speak to him, wanting to thank him for what he was doing for her, and he did not think he ought to be thanked.

In his mind, he said to her, "I am taking you to Michael, as you asked, Laura. But it is not life I am taking you to, and you must understand that. I am taking you to the few minutes or hours of happiness that you earned simply by never having them. Though you close your hands on them, they will pass from you like wild birds, and you will not even remember having had them. It might have been a better thing to leave you where you were. The one delusion you never had in your life was the one about the permanence of happiness. This is what I am giving you. Not life. Not even love. Only this. I am sorry that I cannot give you more. In time I may be sorry that I gave you anything at all. Do not thank me for it. Be happy, if you can, but do not thank me."

He looked past Mrs. Klapper to where Campos sat at the wheel, humming very softly to himself. The big man drove well, without seeming to pay much attention either to the road or to the truck itself. But there was a strange expression on his heavy face as he gripped the wheel and hummed his tune. Mr. Rebeck would not have called it love. The truck might have.

On a sudden impulse Mr. Rebeck leaned forward and said, "Campos, Laura sang well, didn't she?"

Campos turned slightly to regard him out of dark, calm eyes. He drove with one hand, buttoning his shirt with the other, taking the road without looking at it.

"Pretty good," he said, and turned his head away.

"Thank you, Campos," said Mr. Rebeck.

Mrs. Klapper sighed and wriggled a little, trying to make herself more comfortable between the two men. "Rebeck, who is this Laura? Don't tell me if I shouldn't know."

Is she jealous? he wondered in halting delight. When was a woman ever jealous over me? How late I shall have to begin so many things.

"A woman I knew once," he said. "I'd almost forgotten her."

Then round the last curve, and the hill sloping away before them, and at the bottom of the hill the black gate.

It was wide open. Campos had left it so. To the left, the one light of the caretaker's office still shone; beyond was a deeper, gray-patched darkness that Mr. Rebeck knew must be the street. The gate moved a little in the night air. He could hear it squeak softly, like a bat.

The iron squeaks and murmurs in the ground and the iron snakes slide through the green leaves. The world is crouched to drop on me out of the first green tree. Why am I doing this, what was it I said I would do? Help me now, Laura. Michael, stay with me a little. Somebody stay with me. A man should not go into the world alone.

Halfway down the hill, the light from the caretaker's office blinked blue and went out. The gate disappeared. Mr. Rebeck was not surprised; the bulb had burned all through that night. The only light now came from the truck's headlights, and from the moon, which was pretty but not really useful.

Campos said, *"Mierda,"* as if he were trying to spit out his tongue. He tapped the brake lightly with his foot as a grudging concession to the darkness. The truck slowed a bit, but not much.

"Rebeck," Mrs. Klapper said softly, "you sure?"

He looked at her as she sat next to him, glad she had asked but wanting to tell her that with every escape she offered him she forced him deeper into the world. Did she know that? Probably, he thought. It made no difference.

"No," he said. "I'm not at all sure."

Mrs. Klapper gripped his hand tightly. Her own hand was small and soft, but surprisingly strong. Campos sat behind the wheel and hummed to himself, now and then singing a line or a few words of the song. Mr. Rebeck had never heard it before.

Because the truck's headlights did not reach very far, they did not see the gate again until it was almost upon them. Mr. Rebeck actually rose to his feet, and only knew it when his head bumped on the roof of the cab. Mrs. Klapper held his hand but did not pull at him. Campos did not even bother to look. He hurled the little truck at the gate as if it were a rock to be thrown at a dark window.

It might have been easier if the gate had been the way Mr. Rebeck had dreamed it by night and imagined it by day: the spikes atop it tipped with drying blood, and the

iron snakes hissing a silent warning of silent death, poised
to strike at the head and heels of any man who came too
close. These could be faced, for he had two friends with
him, and a man can draw strength from his friends when
the iron snakes are all around him.

But the gate was only a gate, after all, and the spikes
were very rusty. The truck brushed against it as it passed
through, because Campos took his hand off the wheel for
a moment to wipe his nose. And then a new road was
under their wheels and the gate was behind them, and Mr.
Rebeck became slowly aware that he was standing with his
head touching the roof of the cab, that Mrs. Klapper was
still holding his hand, and that Campos had never stopped
his deep, monotonous humming. He sat down, but he did
not look back.

"I made it," he said to Mrs. Klapper. "I made it."

"I was holding my breath all the time," Mrs. Klapper
said. Her voice sounded very tired.

Mr. Rebeck looked out of the window. He was fascinated
by the houses and the cars parked along the curbs.

"Where are we?" he asked.

"This is all Yorkchester," Mrs. Klapper told him. She
pointed past him. "Over there my doctor lives. A wonderful man, only with a bad breath on him like his mouth is
a thousand years old. You'd think, he's a doctor, a doctor
could do something, but no. A fine man. He plays the
violin. Rebeck, I was so worried, I thought I'd go crazy."

"It's all right," Mr. Rebeck said. He was leaning back in
his seat with his eyes closed.

"I didn't know what to do. I thought, My God, I made
him do this, I dragged him all the way down here, look
how frightened he is. I thought, If anything happens to him
it's your fault, you stupid woman. Rebeck, you're sure you
feel okay? You don't look so good."

"I'm fine," Mr. Rebeck said. They were driving under
the elevated railroad that ran past the cemetery. The truck
bounced on the cobblestones, coming so close to the El

pillars that he could have touched them. They were a reddish-gray in the headlights stippled with soft lumps of paint that were crusted on the outside and semi-liquid underneath. It was dark, four-o'clock dark, but some of the stores along the way had left their neon signs on, and their windows seemed very bright in the empty streets.

"You know," he said, "I always thought that there should be a graciousness to life. It was very important to me. Sometimes I would say to myself, 'When the world learns how to be gracious, then I will go back. Not before.' I thought I would know, you see."

An empty taxicab pulled abreast of them as they stopped for a traffic light (Campos was capricious about traffic lights; sometimes he stopped for them), and the driver and Mr. Rebeck stared at each other with real curiosity until the light changed and the cab vanished between the pillars like a deer among trees. Campos turned left and drove up a long paved street choked with two-family houses. There was a light on in one of them, and a middle-aged woman standing at a window. Her eyes were tired but amused as she watched the little truck rattle by.

"And now I've left the cemetery," Mr. Rebeck went on, "with no guarantee that the world has improved at all. In fact, I am sure it hasn't, not in any way that means anything. But it doesn't bother me, for some reason. Not right now, anyway. Maybe tomorrow, or a little later. Right now all that makes me sad is a feeling that I have wasted almost twenty years of my life. It would not be waste if I had learned something, if I were a better man because of those years. But I am as I was, only older, and that makes it waste. And waste to me is a terrible thing, a crime."

He was sure as he spoke that Mrs. Klapper would agree with him, but he was also sure that she would shrug and say, All right, so you wasted. So what? What can you do about it? At least, you didn't get sick and die there, thank God. What else counts? He needed her reassurance.

Instead she said slowly, "Everybody wastes time. A little

here, a little there. You wake up in the morning, it's all bright and shiny, you get out of bed and say to yourself, Today is the day! Today I'm going to be a great man. Then you look out the window, you see a pretty girl on the sidewalk—*zoom*, into the pants, into the shirt, downstairs, 'Hello, did you drop this?' And you say to yourself, All right, so tomorrow I'll be a great man. Who ever got anywhere by rushing? Tomorrow positively, Thursday for sure. . . . Tell me, Rebeck, that's not wasting time?"

Mr. Rebeck only looked at her. Her forehead was in shadow, but he could see her eyes.

"So let's say you marry this girl. All right, you can still be a great man. Look at all the great men who had wives. Go ahead, be a great man, don't let me stop you. Only first you should stop by the grocer and pick up something for the dog. Also for the baby, soft, because he's getting his teeth. To do this, you have to have a job five days a week, you can be a great man on week ends."

The streets were very empty. The few cars that passed were all taxicabs. Once a cat galloped across the street in front of them and hid behind the fender of a parked car, watching them until they were safely past.

"Rebeck, this is not a waste? This is the big waste. Five minutes here, an hour there, maybe a week somewhere else. You count it all up, you got your twenty years, and maybe more. At least you got yours over with in one lump. Now you got them out of the way, you can go be a great man."

"Only I'm not a great man, Gertrude," Mr. Rebeck said quietly. "I could never be. It isn't in me."

"So who's breaking your arm, be great? Did I say it like an order? Don't be great, you don't feel like it. Just don't do anything you don't want to, that's all I'm saying. You shouldn't have to do something you don't like."

She looked at him thoughtfully, nibbling at her gloved forefinger as she always did. "Rebeck, what are you going to do, now you're out of the cemetery? You got any idea?"

"I don't know," Mr. Rebeck said. "Pharmacy is the only trade I ever learned. I suppose I could go back to it."

"Pharmacy is good," Mrs. Klapper agreed. "A druggist makes a very nice living. Only it's changed a lot in twenty years; they have a lot of new things now. Miracle drugs."

"I could study. It would be funny, going back to school at my age."

"What's funny? Lots of people do it, people older than you." Mrs. Klapper frowned. "I'm trying to think of all the new drugs they got now you'd have to know about. Penicillin. You know about penicillin?"

"Yes," Mr. Rebeck said. "I read about it in the newspapers."

"Good, so at least you know penicillin. They also got a lot of things that sound alike. I mean, they end the same way. Let me think a minute—"

"The sulfa drugs?" Mr. Rebeck suggested. "The myacins?"

Mrs. Klapper stared at him. "Rebeck, you know all this, what are you bothering me for? What are you *hocking* me you got to go back to school? You're out of the cemetery five minutes, already you're a druggist again."

Mr. Rebeck laughed. "No. I just read about those drugs. I don't know how they work. I'd have to study."

"All right, so study. Sometimes you worry me, Rebeck."

When they stopped for another traffic light, Mr. Rebeck saw a group of boys standing on a streetcorner. They wore sport shirts and heavy cowboy boots. All of them had pale faces, and they leaned against a wall and one another, looking idly at the truck. They looked weakly vicious, and lonely.

"Hoods," Mrs. Klapper said, following Mr. Rebeck's glance. "This I'm sorry you had to see. Bums, all of them. What good could they be doing, up so late? *Nudnicks.*"

Mr. Rebeck grinned at her as the truck jerked forward again. "And what are you doing up so late, a respectable Bronx woman like you?"

"My fault? My fault? I said, Hey, let's go over to Mount

Merrill and drop off a corpse? This was my idea? I got nothing to do with this, Rebeck. If a cop stops us, you kidnaped me. You and the big one over there."

She yawned and stretched, looking past Mr. Rebeck at the unlighted apartment houses and the moon going down behind them. Her forearm rested gently on Mr. Rebeck's shoulder as she looked out of the window.

There weren't any trolleys any more, he remembered. The raven had told him. The flimsy-looking cars were gone, all of them, and the tracks they had run on were paved over. Now and then, looking carefully, he could catch a wink of silver out of the hidden heart of the street, and then he would know that a trolley track still ran there, wrapped in ragged tar and asphalt.

He looked back once, through the glass slit behind him, because he wanted to see Laura once more. But the back of the truck was empty, except for the smugly stark coffin and the few tools that rattled beside it. There was nothing of Laura herself, neither dark hair nor autumn voice, neither gray eyes nor remembrance of soft laughter. Only a coffin in the back, and a pick, and a shovel, and a crowbar. Of Laura, who had sung to him and loved Michael, nothing.

And yet he knew she was there. As surely as he knew that he would never be able to see ghosts again.

Well, I made the choice myself, he thought. I knew what I was doing. Sooner or later I would have had to choose. No man can speak with both the living and the dead forever.

Then he heard Campos humming in a kind of metallic harmony with the snarling engine, and he thought, Campos can. Campos will always be at ease in both worlds, because he belongs to neither. He loves no one—no, forget that. Morris Klapper was right; love has nothing to do with it. Campos simply does not care about either world, and it is caring about things that grinds down our souls and makes us do stupid things. He will always be able to see ghosts and people, because neither of them can touch him, to please him or to hurt him. I thought I was like that.

For a little time he thought of Laura, and envied Campos the life that he himself had left. Then he forgot envy as he watched the houses pass by in silence. The houses amazed him. There was an unreality about them, a cleanness of glass and new bricks that made it impossible to imagine people living in them, eating and making love and flushing toilets. Yet obviously people did. He saw ashcans in front of most of the buildings, and baby carriages; these are the two sure signs of human occupancy anywhere. He wondered if Mrs. Klapper lived in a place like these.

"Gertrude," he said, nudging her elbow, "is this still Yorkchester we're in?"

Mrs. Klapper blinked and sat up straight. She had been half asleep, he realized.

"No," she said, trying to get her bearings by the street names. "Where we are, I'm not sure, but it's already way out of Yorkchester."

"I hope Mount Merrill isn't far," Mr. Rebeck said. "We haven't got too much time."

"Hey, you," Mrs. Klapper said to Campos, familiarity having whittled away her fear of him. "You. Sitting Bull. How long to Mount Merrill?"

For answer Campos turned the truck so sharply to the left that Mrs. Klapper was thrown against Mr. Rebeck, jarring the breath out of him. The big man drove the truck up a steep, pebbly hill, flanked on both sides by a few small private houses. When the hill leveled off he let the truck coast a little and then brought it to a stop in front of a gold-painted iron gate. There was no watchman behind the gate, and no light in the wooden caretaker's shack.

"This is it?" Mrs. Klapper asked, sounding mildly chagrined. "This little thing is Mount Merrill?"

"Back entrance." Campos grunted. Leaving the motor on, he got out of the cab and walked forward to investigate the lock on the gate.

"Hoo-*hoo*," Mrs. Klapper said. "Back entrance. We come in with the groceries, huh?"

"It's easier this way," Mr. Rebeck explained. "They always have someone on duty at the main entrance, Campos says."

Campos flicked the padlock casually with his forefinger and went around to the back of the truck. He returned a moment later, carrying a crowbar, which he fitted into the hasp of the lock. Without preamble, he placed both hands on the crowbar and pushed down. He actually rose on his toes and threw his whole weight on the bar. The long muscles of his wrists and forearms swelled briefly, and then the lock flew apart with a sound like that of a spoon being dropped into a glass. Campos opened the gate wide and came back toward the truck.

"My God!" Mrs. Klapper said in the whisper she ordinarily reserved for hurricanes and quadruplets. "Rebeck, my God, didn't he ever go to school? What are we doing here?"

"There was no other way to get in." Mr. Rebeck was a little worried himself. Having broken his own lock, he would have broken a good many more to bring Laura to Michael, but he was beginning to think that it had not been wise to bring Mrs. Klapper. If they were arrested, would she be also? He had never considered that possibility.

Mrs. Klapper was considering it. "For that kind of thing," she muttered as Campos climbed back into the cab, "for that kind of thing they put you in jail and eat the key for breakfast."

"It can't be that bad," Mr. Rebeck said, sure that it was.

"No? Rebeck, I don't think they even let you get mail. They probably read you the newspaper once a month."

And so they drove through the Mount Merrill Cemetery, staring ahead in the cottony dark for a place to bury Laura Durand. In time they found one, a rather arid patch of land with a few small graves around it, and none close by. It would have been good, Mr. Rebeck thought, to bury her close to Michael's grave, but it would have been merely a nice gesture, and the dead do not appreciate the importance of gestures to the living.

Campos marked out the lines of the grave with the edge of his spade and began to dig. Mr. Rebeck and Mrs. Klapper sat in the cab, Mr. Rebeck's offer of help having been silently refused. For a long time neither of them said anything. They watched Campos standing ankle deep, calf deep, knee deep in the earth, hurling the dirt over his shoulder with an odd, blind twist of his body. Dawn was not near yet, but the dark had softened as the stars went out, so that Campos was no longer the black shape that waits where man thinks his destiny should be standing; he was just Campos, no one's friend, digging a grave for Laura for his own reasons, or for no reason at all.

Presently Mrs. Klapper looked at Mr. Rebeck and said thoughtfully, "You know, Rebeck, this whole thing is crazy. Everything. Look, it's after four in the morning, the sun's going to come up soon. Everybody's going to wake up. I'm an old woman, I should be waking up too. So instead I'm sitting in a graveyard in a truck, at four in the morning, watching King Kong tearing up the grass, and waiting for the police to come along. Rebeck, for you maybe this is not crazy, God alone knows. For me, believe me, this is crazy."

"I know," Mr. Rebeck said, wanting to tell her about Laura and Michael, and knowing that it was the one thing he could never tell her. "But it really is a last favor to a friend. Someday I'll tell you about it, if I can."

Mrs. Klapper shrugged. "Tell me, don't tell me. I believe you. It's too late not to believe you. Anyway, Rebeck, when you are my age you find out it doesn't make any difference if you don't believe something somebody said to you. Who cares? It leaves you with nothing. A woman my age has no choice. Believe. Who knows, maybe it'll come out right."

She pushed her thick hair back from her forehead and

scavenged frantically in her purse, trying to hold back a
sneeze until she found a handkerchief. Watching her at the
especially unbecoming moment, Mr. Rebeck felt his heart
grow warm for her. Wanting his features to show at least
something of this, he contorted them into an awkward
smile.

"You're not old," he said quietly.

Mrs. Klapper smiled then, rubbing the back of her neck,
her eyes half closed.

"I know it," she said happily. "You think I could say I
was if I was?"

Then Campos was finished digging the grave, and the
rest was all three of them lowering the coffin into the hole
and Mr. Rebeck helping Campos fill the grave with earth
and stamp it smooth. Watching them hopping and prancing
under the blue dark, big scarecrow, little scarecrow, Mrs.
Klapper burst out laughing. "Like the kids in the candy
store," she said.

No matter how flat they tried to make it, how flush with
the ground, it looked like a grave where no grave should
be. They could only hope that no Mount Merrill official
would pass that way until the ground had settled. The winter would freeze it and frost the turned-up brown earth to
the color of the earth around it, and in spring the ferny
wild grass would grow on Laura's grave, hiding it and
warming it.

"Anyway, it's got no headstone to give it away," Mr.
Rebeck said. He paused and added, "Isn't it strange? Laura
will be buried here and no one in the world will know it
except us. Everybody will see her headstone in the Yorkchester Cemetery and think she is buried there. And for
them it will be as if she were."

"People don't know," Campos said surprisingly. He
leaned on his spade, sweating again, but breathing easily.
"The stone's all they want. Put up a stone, tell them their
mother's buried under it. That's all they want. They go to

the stone and say, Sorry, Ma, I'm a bastard. Makes no difference."

They walked slowly to the truck, but Mr. Rebeck kept turning to look back at the grave. He did not really expect to see Laura spring lightly from the ground, lovely and immortal, and run among the stones until she found the man who loved her, but he would have liked to see them together. There are no happy endings, he knew, because nothing ends; and if there were any being dispensed, a great many worthier people would be in line for them long before Michael and Laura and himself. But the happiness of the unworthy and the happiness of the so-so is as fragile and self-centered and dear as the happiness of the righteous and the worthy; and the happiness of the living is no less short and desperate and forgotten than the joys of the dead.

Campos drove them back to the gate, which he closed carefully and pointlessly behind them, and then drove the truck down the steep hill. A young couple sat on the porch of one of the houses, talking softly, very close to each other, but not touching. They looked up as the truck passed the house, and then looked away.

"That's the best way in the world to catch cold," Mrs. Klapper said. "Dopes." But she was smiling sleepily.

At the bottom of the hill Campos stopped the truck. Mr. Rebeck and he looked at each other.

"Well?" the big man asked. "You coming back?"

Mr. Rebeck sat quite still. Mrs. Klapper drew her hand from his and waited.

Meeting Campos's passionless eyes, he thought, This man is pure, and as beautifully sterile as all cemeteries. I am neither pure nor sterile. I am infected with life and will die of it in time. Sainthood is not for me, nor wisdom, nor purity. Only pharmacy, and such love as I have not buried and lost. This is a very little out of all a man might have, but it is all a man ever gets. I will sell coltsfoot candy, if there is any left in the world.

So he shook his head and said, "No, Campos."

Campos nodded and started the engine again. Mrs. Klapper climbed out of the truck, but Mr. Rebeck remained behind for a moment.

"Good-by," he said. He held out his hand.

Campos looked at the thin, brown hand without much interest. Finally he took it briefly in his own, which was rough-skinned and dry.

"See you," he said, and drove away.

The man and the woman watched the truck with much greater intentness than it deserved until it turned a corner and was gone. Then Mrs. Klapper stretched elaborately, still without looking at Mr. Rebeck, and said, "So?"

"So?" he mimicked her. "So what?"

"So where to now? It's almost dawn, Rebeck. You got a place to go?"

The man looked at the strange houses, and at the street lights, which were going out like stars. He put his arm around the woman's shoulders.

"It's not dawn yet," he said, smiling at her. "This is what they call false dawn."

"All right, dawn, false dawn. I'm not going to fight with you. Come on home with me, have at least a cup of coffee. It'll wake you up."

"I'm up," Mr. Rebeck said. "I've been up all night."

"Rebeck, you're a trial and a trouble to an old woman. So you're coming or not?"

"I'm coming, Gertrude."

They walked along the street together, slowly, because they were both very tired. Mrs. Klapper's heels clicked on the sidewalk. They were the only people on the street, as far as they could see.

"There's a subway around here," Mrs. Klapper said. "Gets you right home." She looked up at him—a pleasurable feeling, he thought. "Rebeck, you like sour cream with cottage cheese?"

"I don't remember," he said. "I haven't had any in a long time."

"Wonderful in hot weather. With blueberries, if I still have some. I probably ate them all up. Walk slower, Rebeck, where are you rushing to? Maybe we can see the sun come up. Which way is the east?"

Mr. Rebeck pointed to where the sky was the color of the bricks in the new houses. He saw a bird flying. It was the only bird in the sky, just as they were the only people walking on the street. It was far away, flying in wide, unhurried circles, contemplating the world on which its shadow fell with the arrogance that all flying things have. He thought it might be the raven, and wished that he had had a chance to say good-by, although he knew that it would have meant nothing to the raven. But men must always say good-by to things.

Aloud he said, "I wonder what happened to the seagull."